The Mafia Love Code

Book 1 of the Underworld Love Guide Series

Brit Leigh

All rights reserved. Text Copyright © 2025 Brit Leigh

No part of this publication may be reproduced, transmitted, or stored in an information retrieval system in any form or by any means, graphic, electronic, or mechanical, including photocopying, taping, and recording, without prior written permission from the author.

PUBLISHER'S NOTE

This is a work of fiction. Names, characters, places, and incidents either are the product of the author's imagination and experiences or are used fictitiously, and any resemblance to actual persons, living or dead, events, or locales is entirely coincidental.

The Mafia Love Code

Chapter 1

Violetta

The melancholy sound of beeping machines almost sends me to sleep, but I fight the urge and take a sip of my canned espresso. Night shifts in the ER are no joke, but it was the first job I was offered out of nursing school, so I took it. I took it because I'm determined to earn my freedom from the man who keeps me as his ward. Enzo DeLuca is a man my father worked for. He was Enzo's second in command of the DeLuca mafia until my father betrayed Enzo to the rival mafia family, the Ronkas. Instead of killing me or selling me into sex slavery, Enzo took pity on me, mainly because his son, Nico, advocated for me to be his father's ward. Nico DeLuca is determined to make me his wife, and maybe there was a time I wanted that. However, I want my freedom more. Whatever plans Nico and his father have for me are purely for their gain only.

    I don't want their plans. I want my plans. I want to be free from the violent world the mafia is shrouded in. I want to help people, maybe even become a doctor or a midwife. I'm not even sure I want to get married. I've been controlled by men my entire life. First, my father kept me on a tight leash as he was clearly grooming me to become a mafia wife. I'm not sure if my father meant for me to be Nico's wife or Anthony Ronka's wife, but I was meant to be someone's mafia wife. My father was apparently playing both Enzo DeLuca and Marco Ronka for years. Eventually, it caught up to him and got him killed. I was fourteen, and I was terrified for my life because I was certain I would be killed by either Enzo or Marco. I wasn't killed and instead made Enzo's ward where he then controlled my life. If I marry Nico, then I know I'd be giving him control over my life. I want to be in control of my own damn life.

    Part of me hates that Nico stepped in for me because I hate that he cares about me, but I hate even more that I still care about him. It's been five years since I saw him. The minute I turned eighteen, I enrolled in nursing school. Surprisingly, Nico and his father backed me. They paid for my entire education and even let me move out of the house and into an apartment. Of course, I'm suspicious as to why they let me go so easily. I'm sure their little spies keep tabs on me and report back to them. That's the shittiest part of this whole thing. Even if I have my freedom, I will always be looking over my shoulder wondering when the man I shouldn't have feelings for will come crashing into my life. I'm not sure I want to date because if Nico comes back into my life and finds me with another man, that man is dead on the spot. Nico is jealous and possessive. There's also the fact that he still holds my heart slightly captive. I'm not sure there is another man that could pull my attention like Nico does.

Pushing thoughts of my past and the man that haunts me, I focus on checking on the patients who are waiting for results or for the doctor to do their rounds. Most of them are asleep. It's a quiet night in the ER which is rare especially for a city hospital. However, I work in a hospital that is in a nice part of the city. Most of the people that come through the doors are wealthy or famous, and can pay for every test under the sun. Still, most nights there is some flutter of activity. Then on occasion we get the rare quiet shift. On the nights it's quiet no one will dare speak their thoughts out loud as we all know the minute someone says it's quiet the shit storm is about to roll through the ER doors.

After all my patients are checked I head back to the nurses station. I decide to take my hour break because I need to eat and get some more caffeine. I thought I would be able to handle the night shift because I stayed up late studying while I was in school. I also worked a part time job at a coffee shop to earn some money that was mine. However, I sorely underestimated what night shift would be like. I wave to my fellow nurses who are manning the ER with me as I head toward the cafe that is inside the hospital. Thankfully, they are open twenty-four hours because the hospital cafe closes at eight. After eight, the only place to get something to eat and drink is at the little coffee stand, which is conveniently a short walk from the ER.

THE MAFIA LOVE CODE

I stand in line at the cafe waiting for my turn totally oblivious to everything around me because right now caffeine is all that matters. Seriously, I've been doing night shift for a little over a year and I'm still not adjusted. It's like my body refuses to comply with being awake at night. It's starting to irritate me.

"What's a pretty girl like you doing in scrubs?" A suave voice says behind me. I turn on my heels to face the second most handsome man I've ever seen. He's on the taller side, dark olive tone skin, short slicked back black hair, and warm brown eyes. Correction, there is apparently someone who can draw my attention from Nico, and somehow it's not a bad thing.

"I'm sorry, do I know you?" I ask, realizing the man looks slightly familiar as I am no longer struck by his tempting features. Looking him over properly I take in his navy blue suit. He's got money. The question is, is he mob rich or just another rich playboy?

"You may have seen me in pictures, but we've never met in person." He answers.

"I'm not in that life anymore." I firmly state realizing he's mob rich and I need to stay away. Thankfully, it's my turn in line. I give the barista my order eager to get back to the break room that is for staff only. However, when I go to pay the handsome mob man offers his black credit card to the barista as he comes to my side.

"Please, allow me to pay for your order, and..." he pauses looking at the barista's name tag. "Molly, could you please add a large black coffee and a lemon blueberry scone."

"Sure, can I have a name for the order?" Molly, the barista with her ginger hair pulled back in a tight ponytail, says with a smile stretching the freckles that speckle her face. How the hell is she this chipper while I'm over dragging like a slug?

"Anthony." The handsome mob man answers, and my world stops.

What are the chances that he's Anthony Ronka? Here I was expecting Nico to be the one to ruin my, what I like to call, fake freedom. I never thought Anthony fucking Ronka would be the one to shatter my blissful bubble. The fact that he's here means he wants something, and he wants something from me. My mind can't help but race with questions, but there is one that sticks out the most. What the hell did my father promise him and is here to collect?

Chapter 2

Anthony

Violetta Calla stands next to me as we wait for our order. She's on edge as she nervously plays with the black stethoscope around her neck. Her ceil blue scrubs hide her coca cola shape figure as well as her nice sized breasts. I've been watching Violetta from afar for years. Her father said she was to be my wife, and I want her to be my wife. I wanted to claim her when her father died, but the DeLuca's claimed her first. War isn't something I wanted to start. Besides, she was only fourteen at the time and I was already eighteen. I figured it was best to let her be with them until I could reclaim her as mine.

Violetta going off on her own was a good thing. However, it was clear she was on a mission to separate herself from the underworld the mafia resides in. Nico gave her that space so I decided to respect it as well. I've been waiting for the right chance to approach her since she's been out on her own for five years. I figured she was ready for me to approach her.

"You can relax, Violetta . I'm not here to hurt you. I just want to talk." I inform her in an attempt to ease her anxiety.

"Fine, we get our food and go find a seat. You have ten minutes to convince me to keep speaking with you." She firmly demands as she stops fidgeting and straightens her demeanor.

"Agree to your terms." There's no reason to fight her. I simply want her to hear me out. It's not like I plan to force her to marry me, but I'm not sure I'm thrilled about her marrying Nico either.

Our order is called, and Violetta quickly walks over to grab her drink and food. Her ponytail bounces behind her. Violetta has beautiful wavy hazelnut brown hair that goes to her mid back, but she keeps it pulled back for work which I understand given her occupation. I follow suit in grabbing my part of our order and follow her to a secluded corner of the seating area for people to eat their purchased goods. We are sitting across from one another. I gaze into Violetta's hazel eyes. She's so fucking beautiful and she doesn't even know it.

"Okay, ten minutes. Go." Violetta directs, glancing at the watch on her right wrist as she sips her mocha. The dark circles under her eyes indicate she's over her shift. She usually is on the last day of her rotation.

"Look, I know I'm crashing your life, but you know you don't have true freedom. I don't know what Nico has planned for you, but I can tell you what I'd offer you if you decided to be my wife instead." I propose, trying to gain her curiosity.

"You mafia, alpha males never let women have freedom. I'm not stupid. I know Nico is watching me. I'm sure he's manipulated me from afar in ways I don't even know." She answers, taking a bite out of her breakfast sandwich.

"He got you this job." I inform her.

"Of course he did. Why am I not surprised? So what do you want, Anthony? You want me to come with you. Trust you? I don't know you. I'm not even sure I can say I know Nico anymore either. My goal is to live separate from the mafia." She firmly states.

"I know that asking you to trust me is a lot. It's not fair that your father promised you to two different men. You don't have a say, but I will give you a say. Can you tell me that Nico will offer you the same. To be his equal at his side?"

"I don't know because I haven't seen him in five years. I haven't spoken to him in years. Yes, my father has promised me to you and Nico without my knowledge or thoughts. You are here to collect just as Nico will eventually come to collect. The fact that you are here means Nico is planning to crash my solo party soon. You wanted to beat him to plead your case to me." Violetta surmises. She is not stupid that's for sure. She's observant as hell. I'm honestly impressed right now that she pieced all that together so quickly.

"You would be correct. We both want to claim you, but ultimately you would have to choose. Unfortunately, if you don't pick, Nico will force you back with him and I won't be able to help you then." I inform her.

"Why are you even fighting with Nico over me? I bet that's what my dad wanted. I'm sure he planned to be alive when he finally would have you two fighting over me so he could strike. Much like I imagine the other underworld families are on to as well. I want to escape the underworld and not be dragged back into it." She keeps her stance. I figured she would

"You're right, maybe we shouldn't be fighting over you. You know you can't escape the underworld. Not the way you truly want. Look, I'm trying to offer you a level of freedom to have your own life. Something you aren't sure you can say about Nico." I try to reason with her. "Think about it, that's all I'm asking you to do, and to take this." I take the burner phone in my inside suit pocket, and slide it to her.

"I'm not taking that." Violetta firmly states staring me down.

"Why not?" I challenge. I was expecting some resistance from her.

"Because I don't want to. I don't know you, Anthony." She counters as she folds her arms and her breast to fully make me aware that she is going to stand her ground.

"I don't accept bratty excuses, Little Violet. If you don't take the phone you will have no way to contact me if you decide I'm the path you want to take over Nico. I could be an escape if need be. It's wise to take the phone just in case." I swiftly retort.

"Fine," she concludes as she takes the phone and quickly sticks it in her scrub shirt pocket. Violetta glares at me as I see the questions swirl behind her defensive glare. "Be honest, you stalked me as a way to get to know me." She firmly accuses as her eyes harden at me in disapproval.

I chuckle. "Sorry, Little Violet, I had to make sure you were safe. I wasn't sure if the DeLuca's were watching you properly or not. Mario had many enemies, Little Violet. You need protection even when you don't realize it. Just think about what I had to say and where you want to end up because at the end of the day you know you are going back to the underworld."

I don't want to push her too hard. I know I'm a stranger to her. I know I'm giving her something tough to think about. I also just broke her very blissful bubble. There's also the fact that she is at work, and I totally crashed her break. Leaving her is harder than I expected. I wanted to reach out and hold her hand or touch her in some way. There's a connection between us or maybe I just want her to want me. I want someone to accept me.

I'm Don of my family now but that only happened after I killed my father and made it look like natural causes. My mother was out of my life early on. My dad says she ran off with some soldier that worked the streets for my father. Do I believe him? Not one bit. I wouldn't be surprised if she is dead and he killed her. Even when my mom was around she wanted nothing to do with me. She never wanted to be a mom, but she needed to give my father an heir and she got lucky that I was a boy on the first try. My sister, Sofia, was an accident.

I've never had much acceptance from the people close to me. My soldiers and everyone who works for me accepts me, but they have to because they don't want to end up dead. In my personal life, Lorenzo is my best friend and second in command then I have Sofia, but she is eight years younger than me. I'm her guardian and she adores me like I do her. Other than that I have no one. Perhaps that's why I stalked Violetta in the first place. I wanted to feel connected to her. I can only hope she will give me a chance.

Chapter 3

Nico

Sitting at my desk in my large office in the back of the casino, looking over the books as I drink a very expensive bottle of Merlot while puffing on an expensive Italian cigar. It's about four am. I'll be leaving soon to go rest in the penthouse suite of the hotel that the casino is located in. That's where I've been living since Violetta went off to do her own thing. I didn't like the idea of her breaking free on her own, but I needed to let her spread her wings or my little dove would be a sad little caged bird. So, I let my little dove spread her wings and fly, knowing one day I'd have her as my wife.

Violetta has had five years to spread her wings. I have to bring her home soon because my father is not going to hand me Don unless I'm married. I know the only reason he is putting the stipulation on me becoming Don is because the bastard doesn't want to give up his power that Don provides. My father is a greedy man, and he is starting to get a little too drunk on his power. He's starting to become a problem.

My thoughts are interrupted by a knock on my door. "Boss, one of the men assigned to keep an eye on Dove has reported to me something you need to know," Jullian, my head of security and best friend, informs me through the door.

"Come in." I reply before Jullian opens the door and strides into my office, making sure to close the door behind him.

"One of the men assigned to Dove at the hospital said she got a visit from Anthony fucking Ronka." Jullian informs me his voice is laced with displeasure.

"What!" I rage as my fist slams onto the desk in front of me, rattling the wine glass and bottle, which are set very close to some paper documents that happen to be a bit important.

"I know. It's not something you want to hear. I was informed they didn't talk for long, but it appeared he gave her a phone. Probably a burner." Jullian continues to deliver bad news, but he's not the one I'm angry at.

"Why the fuck is Anthony making a move on my dove?" I demand, tossing the wine glass against a nearby wall.

"I don't know. We've always suspected that Mario might have also promised Violetta to Anthony. He was playing both Dons. Not to mention Anthony is now the head of the Ronka family mafia. He doesn't have to abide by any rules or agreements his father set in place while he was in charge. You need to push your father to give you Don."

"I know, Jullian." I seethe. "The asshole won't hand me Don until I'm married."

"I think it's time you rush that wedding with Violetta or seriously think about pushing your father out in other ways ." Jullian suggests, giving me a look I know means he's deadly serious.

"I know. I didn't think Anthony Ronka would make a move on my dove. That definitely is a problem because I can't have Violetta taken from me. She means far too much to me. It's not even about marriage at this point. It's about the fact that she is someone I need in my life. I don't like the idea of Anthony tempting her away from me." I confess.

"I know, Boss. Think about what you want your next move to be and let me know. I'm on your side, and I will only follow your orders. Just do me a favor and don't go to war over Violetta. I know she's important to you and that you love her. However, war over a woman is fucking stupid. I won't participate in some tragic Shakespeare shit." Jullian responds.

"Thank you, I will." I say as Jullian leaves my office.

"I'm not that blinded by love, and I will plot my next moves. I'll update you when I can. Keep me informed about Violetta. I want to know every move she makes, every patient she treats, any person who says a word to her, I want to know every damn thing." I direct, scrubbing my hand down my face in frustration.

"You got it, Boss." Jullian responds before leaving me in my office to stew over my current predicament.

I've always known it was possible that Mario had promised Violetta to Anthony. He was playing both families. The Ronkas and DeLucas have been enemies for decades now. I'm not really sure why our families hate each other at this point other than territory. Anthony is freshly appointed Don of his family. He has an advantage right now with being Don while I'm still stuck in my father's shadow. I don't want to be enemies just because our families have been for years, but I swear if he steals my dove from me, I will wage war.

Chapter 4

Violetta

I'm thrilled when my shift ends at seven am. I waste no time going to my locker, grabbing my things and hightailing it out the door. I take the bus to my little one-bedroom apartment in an average part of town. I try to avoid the wealthy part of the city and the not so wealthy part of the city. I find the average parts of the city are where I prefer to hideout. I have a cozy standard one-bedroom apartment with a bedroom, kitchen, full bath, and a living room. There's also a small dining area that I have set up with a small table and one chair.

My little apartment is my safe place. My mind is spinning, so I desperately need my safe space. I need to come down from the adrenaline pumping in my veins from tonight's shift. Once I enter my apartment, I lock my door and drop my backpack by the front door before I kick my black sneakers off. I make my way to my bedroom and grab my cotton cream nightgown and a pair of fresh panties before I head to my bathroom. I pop on my shower, lay my clothes and fresh towels out, and then undress. I make sure I take out the phone in my pocket that Anthony gave me. I stare at it in frustration before opening the bathroom door and chuck the burner phone on to the soft carpet of the hallway. I recluse to the bathroom, shutting the door, determined to not be intimidated by a stupid phone.

After I strip from my scrubs and undergarments, I toss them in the dirty clothes hamper before stepping into the warm shower. I let the warm water pebble over my skin as I try to sort my thoughts. I don't have work to distract me now. I shouldn't be surprised that my father would foolishly promise me to two very powerful men, determined to make me theirs. All I want is out of this life and I'm being sucked back in. I knew I wasn't truly free, but I wasn't hoping to earn it somehow.

Now I'm faced with two fucking men who want me as their wife. It was bad enough when I thought it was just Nico. Now I have Anthony, who is swooping in like some superhero to save me from the control freak that Nico can be. However, I don't know Anthony. Although, can I say I know Nico anymore, either? Five years I've spent trying to not let thoughts of Nico consume me. I was so in love with him at one point, and maybe a part of me still is. Now there's Anthony, who definitely makes my heart flutter and heats my core. I can't pretend Nico doesn't set my lady parts on fire, either. For a brief moment, I picture what it would be like to have them both at the same time. It would be hot to be owned by two very powerful men who would make my head spin until my body was jelly.

Pushing the sexy, tempting thoughts away, I focus on getting showered. I am desperate for some sleep and I have three glorious days off. I plan to hide away in my apartment and figure things out, but before that I need to eat some breakfast or dinner, technically, for me. Then I need some rest. I can't think anything over well if I'm dead tired. I'm coming off four days of twelve hour shifts. I'm spent.

After I finish my shower, I dry off and get dressed in the clothes I plan to sleep in. In the hallway, I pick up the stupid phone and put it in the drawer of my bedside table before taking my sleep meds. I have anxiety, and I need help sleeping. How can I not have anxiety with two crazy ass mob men stalking me? With my meds now working in my system, I head to make myself a tasty bacon, egg, and cheese sandwich on an everything bagel from the local bakery I enjoy. Like a good Italian woman, my father made sure I knew how to cook. My Nonna taught me how to cook. I would often spend my weekends with her when she was alive. She made sure I learned Italian, that I could cook, bake, sow, and even taught me to crochet. I can literally make pasta from scratch and homemade gravy to go with it. Well, other people call it pasta sauce, but growing up in a heavily influenced Italian home, I call it gravy.

Those were simpler days. My Nonna was able to keep my father inline. She was a pigheaded Italian woman and you did not mess with her or she would beat your ass with a wooden spoon. When she did pass, my father went off on his own insane path that got him killed. He almost got me killed or worse, sold into sex trafficking. I am glad Nico saved me. I owe him that and perhaps that's why I feel some sense of loyalty to him. However, just because I owe him doesn't mean I want to be his wife even if there is a part of me that still loves him. Still, I'm presented with a conundrum. One I will worry about later on.

    I enjoy my breakfast and then curl my ass into my double bed and bury myself under my blankets. For the next eight hours or so I'm going to get some much needed sleep. The rest of the world and the two mob men stalking me will still be a problem. However, it's a problem to figure out later on. I close my eyes and let my mind drift into what I hope is a peaceful sleep.

Chapter 5

Nico

I'm running on four hours of sleep, but I don't care. I'm going to Violetta's apartment. I hate where she lives, but of course she would pick some cheap, basic ass apartment complex to live in. Violetta has always been a stubborn dove. She would defy her father at every turn. Her mom died when she was young in some mafia involved violence, well, that's what Mario claims. My theory is that Mario killed his wife because after Violetta was born, her mom started fooling around with one of the men under Mario. I don't know all the details, and to ask my father about it now, I doubt I would get the truth.

My father used to tell me everything. I was in on all his plans and secrets. That was until two years ago when my father started to become paranoid that everyone was trying to kill him, even me, which at the time I thought was crazy. Now, I'm actually considering it because things have only gotten worse with time. I think he's losing his mind from years of doing terrible deeds. My father has done some serious fucked up things that I never agreed with. My father likes his power which is why he put the obstacle of marriage in the way to hold on to his power longer. Once I'm married, he has to hand me Don. If he doesn't it will make him look bad. At that point I could kill him and not one person would question it because it would be my right since he refused me Don even though I complied with his terms.

That's why I need Violetta to get her stubborn, bratty ass home now. If she runs off with Anthony or anything crazy like that, I'm fucked. I need to be married and I need to be married now. I can force my father out if I'm married. I need a legit wedding that won't take forever to plan, but is a step above eloping at the courthouse. Desperate times call for desperate measures. At least that's what I tell myself before I have my driver take me to my dove's temporary residence.

I get out right at the entrance to the apartment building. I punch in the code and make my way to her apartment. I've come here when she is at work or out doing something. My dove has always been a creature of habit. I think it's her way of trying to organize the chaos that surrounds her. It's almost two in the afternoon which is about when she wakes up. Sometimes she sleeps in until three. She hates night shifts, but she is willing to fucking torture herself to prove she can be Miss Independent.

At first I thought her need to move out was natural. I too wanted my space when I turned eighteen. It was cute, and I supported it. Violetta is determined to break free from the mafia underworld, and I knew trying to stop her would make her go behind my back. So, I let her spread her wings and falsely believe she was free. Violetta has to know deep down she will never break free from the underworld. Her family's blood is deeply rooted in the city's Italian mafia along with mine and Anthony's families.

Originally, the three three families were united until greed divided them causing the three families to be at odds for years. The Callas decided that they would choose a side but they never truly chose as they played both families. DeLuca and Ronka have been the two prominent families as the Callas began to fade into the background. Mario wasn't the first in his family to play the two dominating sides. The Callas have been trying to take main control of the city and be the reigning mafia head. Except, they have mostly all gotten themselves killed for betrayals and poor choices. It's almost as if the whole fucking family is cursed to yern for power only to eliminate their family bloodline in pursuit of said power. Violetta is one of a handful of Calla family members left.

Before I know it, I'm standing in front of her door. Number three on floor three. I knock gently not wanting to sound threatening. I know she is paranoid. She's been that way since her father was killed. Violetta was aware of her situation when her father was labeled a traitor. She knew her life could easily be on the line depending on how vengeful my father wanted to be. Her life was always going to be protected. I would never let my father hurt her. Thankfully, my father did not see her as a threat. My father also knew I would keep Violetta in line, so to speak. I love her and I know she loves me even if she thinks her love for me has died. I know it has not. Violetta will do whatever she can to convince herself she doesn't want to be a part of the underworld, but it's in her blood and one day she will learn to embrace it. Until that day comes, it's going to be a fight to get her to realize that.

After my knocks are ignored, I reach for my wallet and open it to retrieve the key I keep in it. I open up her door and then lock it once I'm in. I make my way to her bedroom to find her passed out asleep. I shake my head at her buried under the massive comforter. I can see the top of her head peeking out. I move toward the bed and lean over her before I gently shake her awake. My dove groans her displeasure.

"Come on, Little Dove, time to wake up." I say, shaking her a bit harder to get her to come to. Those damn sleeping pills make her groggy as shit. I know she took them because she takes them most nights. I've watched from afar long enough to know her habits. I hate that she takes them. Her body stiffens under my hands.

"Please tell me this is some taunting dream or nightmare?" She mumbles as she slowly pulls the blankets away, peeking at me before she groans.

"Sorry, Little Dove, you're awake." I smugly answer her.

"Barely." She complains as she sits up. "You could have at least brought coffee and a chocolate croissant."

I chuckle at her. "We can pick that up on the way back home."

"Nico, I'm not going back to your family's residence. I don't want to be your wife." Violetta firmly states as she crosses her arms against her chest, making her perfectly peachy breasts more prominent.

"Little Dove, we can do this the hard way or the easy way. I know you don't like being ambushed, but Anthony left me no choice. I need us to get engaged and married in a month. My father is slowly losing it and he won't hand me Don until I'm married. I wish I could give you more time, but I can't. The family business is at stake, and I will not let my father be the downfall of our family." I declare, ripping the blanket off her.

"Sounds like a you problem, Nico." She replies, getting out of the bed on the opposite side from me. I briefly close my eyes. I really should have had a plan instead of going on impulse and showing up here.

"Little Dove, please don't push me right now." I say trying to hide my irritation.

"Nico, you can't just show up here five years later and expect me to just jump at your commands. We aren't a couple and never have been. You aren't the boss of me." She counters coming around the bed to face me. Her hair is disheveled from sleeping under a pile of blankets. I quickly grab her, pulling her to me. The movement is sudden, causing her to gasp in shock before I move my arms around her to secure her to my body. She won't get away that easily especially after all that damn back talk.

"I let you have your freedom, do your own thing for a bit, but now I need you to come back and help me keep my family business alive and thriving before my father destroys it. You owe me, Little Dove. I saved your life when I didn't have to. The traitor's daughter, well, let's just say you wouldn't be a nurse. In fact, you'd probably be getting ready to take some early customers if you get my drift. So, stop being a little brat, get your ass dressed so we can get going. Don't make me pull my gun on you." I threaten no longer in the mood for her games. I don't like reminding her that I'm her savior because I didn't do it to have an advantage over her. I did it because I love her, but I'm not playing her brat games right now. Not when there is too much at stake.

"So, that's what I am to you, huh? An investment that you are now coming to collect? You act like you are so noble saving me, but you did it for your own selfish reasons." Violetta angrily counters as her nose scrunches.

"Please don't twist it like that," I close my eyes to gain my composure. I didn't think I'd get so frustrated with her. I inhale a big breath and let out as I open my eyes. "You know you are more to me than a prized possession. I respected the space you needed, Little Dove. I let you live in a pretend world where you could simply be a nurse and have a regular life. It was temporary, you had to have known that." I try to reason.

"Still, it doesn't mean you can break into my apartment and demand I come with you. What is it with you mafia men and your demands? Although, you seem a bit more demanding than Anthony." She taunts. She's playing dirty to bait me into be an asshole

"Nice try, Little Dove, but you aren't going to turn tables on me. I already know Anthony talked to you. It's not a secret, and I won't let you use him to bait me into an angry fit. I think you'll find I'm a bit more controlled in the anger department these days." I swiftly counter. I quickly became known as Hot Head Nic. I have an Italian temper that would rival the Roman gods. I knew I couldn't stay hot headed when I became Don. So, I lowered my pride and hired some fancy therapist to help me with anger management.

"Aren't you a little jealous?" She taunts.

"No, because you are coming with me now. Anthony wont get his hands on you unless I say so, and who knows maybe I'll just let him have his own fun with you. So, don't fucking test me, Little Dove. Now, be my very good girl and get dressed. While you're at it gather some shit you want to take, and let's get moving. I'll be sitting in the living room waiting. You have fifteen minutes, so make it count. Anything you don't grab, I will have men come back later and clean out your apartment." I command releasing her from my hold. My dove says nothing, simply glares at me before stomps to her dresser

I make my way out to her living room and plop on the lump ass sofa. I look around the apartment that I've been in many times, but honestly never observed. Mismatched furniture is throughout the entire apartment. I know she bought everything secondhand. Why? I don't know because she sure had access to money to make this place nicer or even have a nicer apartment. However, Violetta is determined to make her own way in the world and while I admire that, I know she can't escape this life. She has no idea how many enemies her father has made or the amount of people he owes money to that would surely take advantage of Violetta if they ever got their hands on her. I've been protecting her for years from afar from her father's enemies. I've always tried to shield her from the more negative, intense, and gory side of the family business, but maybe I shouldn't have because Violetta now has a false sense of security that I created in trying to protect her. Perhaps it's time to take the blinders off so that Violetta can appreciate what I have done for her. Besides, she has no idea what I have planned for her. Something that will allow her to use that nursing degree of hers and allow her to help people. I just need her stubborn ass to hear me out first.

Chapter 6

Violetta

My heart beats hard as paranoia begins to fuel my adrenaline. The first thing I do is grab the burner phone from my side dresser. Then I grab a pair of my skinny jeans with a red rose colored t-shirt before I grab a cotton black bra and pantie set. I dash to the bathroom and make sure I lock the door. My hands fumble with the phone. It's a black flip phone that brings me back to being a teenager for a moment before the panic of my reality takes back over. I flip the phone open and text Anthony.

911! Nico just showed up in my apartment while I was sleeping. He's forcing me to leave with him. What should I do? I hit send and set the phone on the counter and begin changing my clothes while I wait for Anthony to text me. Why am I texting Anthony? I have no fucking clue, but I feel like a stray dog who just got caught by animal control. As I finish dressing, the phone lightly vibrates. I snatch the phone up desperate for a way out.

Of course he fucking did He's impulsive when it comes to you it would seem. Try to keep this phone out of his hands so we can stay in touch. I'll do my best to help you if I can.

Well, fucking great! That's not helpful.

Uh, that does not help me! I will do my best to keep this phone, but I make no promises. Oh, and this doesn't mean I trust you, I'm desperate. That's all this is. Desperate to escape a fate we both know I can't out run. I hit send before turning the phone off and tuck it in my front pocket.

I quickly brush my teeth before running a brush and some detangler through my wild hair. After that, I head back to my room and grab my on call backpack that I have ready. I toss all my scrubs and whatever else is in there out and replace everything with regular clothes and daily things I need. I do end up placing a pair of scrubs and my stethoscope in the bag. I can't help it and I need it as a reminder that just because Nice is taking me back to his family home doesn't mean my fight is over.

Reluctantly, I pull out the burner phone and toss it in a secret compartment in the backpack before I swing the backpack over my shoulders. I walk out of my room and down the small hallway before I find Nico sitting on my couch. Shit, he's handsome. His medium olive tone skin perfectly comment his warm chocolate hair that is a bit on the shaggy side. Nico makes it work because his hair is just the right length to make his shaggy hair sexy. His hazel eyes narrow in on me. His light facial hair indicates he hasn't shaved in a bit, or maybe that's how he keeps his facial hair now.

"Ready Little Dove?" He questions as he rises from his seat.

"It's not like I have a choice. So, sure, but I better get coffee and a damn chocolate croissant." I grumble back as I moved toward the door.

I hear Nico chuckle behind me before he strides past me, using his damn taller length against me. I'm a short Italian woman who barely reaches five two. I'm used to most people being taller than me, but both Nico and Anthony are closer to six foot so they tower over little me. Begrudgingly I follow Nico downstairs into the black SUV. Nico opens the door for me before he takes my backpack. I slide into the back seat and make sure I move in so Nico can sit back here with me. Sure enough he climbs in and places my backpack on the floor between us. Nico shuts the door.

"Where to Mr. DeLuca?" The driver asks. looking in the rearview mirror at Nico.

"How about Belisimos? I know you just woke up, Little Dove, but I want real food. I promise tomorrow you will have your mocha and chocolate croissant." Nico answers looking at me.

"You got it, Sir." The driver replies with a nod before he rolls the black divider up.

"You look like you need a break. I've never seen such dark circles under those blazing honey brown eyes." Nico comments.

"Cut the small talk bullshit, Nico. I don't want to go to some early dinner at our favorite spot. Let's not pretend

I have a say in a damn thing that happens next. So, whatever romantic bullshit you are trying to pull, I'm not in the mood. You better plan on getting that food to go." I state, folding my arms under my breast as I look out the tinted windows.

"Violetta Amelia Calla, I'm not in the mood for your defiance right now. We can get the food to go, I don't fucking care. I'm trying to be nice the best way I know how, but you are making it difficult." Nico states, clenching his fists in his lap. That's my que to back off. Nico has never hit me. No matter how pissed I've made him, he's never hit me. Even with all his anger issues, not once has he gone to strike me.

"You're on edge and tense. What, Madam Connie doesn't have good whores anymore?" I question, looking at Nico. Am I still pushing a bit? Yeah, but I can't help myself.

Madam Connie owns the legal burlesque club where the mafia runs their illegal brothel in the basement of the burlesque club. It's like a speakeasy, you need the password to enter Candy Land. Madam Connie helps manage the girls who work in the brothel as well as her club. Nico and many of the men who work for the DeLuca family get serviced at both establishments. It's also sometimes a place business is conducted depending on who they are entertaining. I know more about the mafia world than I will ever care to admit.

Nico snorts. "You think I would stick my dick in one of those whores? I have standards. Besides, now that you are home I'm sure you will be very good at keeping me entertained in our bed."

I feel my cheeks heat at his comment. "I don't have experience like them so I doubt I'll be able to keep you entertained." I snip back, trying to deny the fact that being close to Nico is dangerous. I missed him. He's a comfort to me when he shouldn't be. Even after all these years, he makes me feel safe when he should be a threat.

"Oh, Little Dove, I can train you to be what I want when it comes to my pleasure. You have no idea what I have planned for you. I wouldn't have that attitude when we visit Madam Connie. I already have her recruited to help give you some pointers or one of her trusted ladies to help. Don't worry, I won't fuck you until our wedding night." Nico informs. My core heats at his words. Fuck, I hate that he does this to me. I want away from him, but is running to Anthony wise? What if I don't want to run to Anthony, but instead have him join Nico and I? Here I am wanting my own life away from the mafia yet I'm entertaining being owned by two men. What the hell is wrong with me?

"You have everything planned out. Good for you. I guess just let me know what the plan is because I clearly get a say in nothing." I spit at him before I go back to looking out the window. I hold the tears that threaten to spill in my frustration.

Fear fills me. The fate I thought I could escape has come knocking on my door in the form of the man my heart still yearns for yet now my heart is tempted by a new man. A new man who might offer me exactly what I want. I don't know Anthony, but I want to. He piques my interest, but I have to be cautious with both Anthony and Nico. There is one thing I have to remember. This is all a game and I'm a pawn being moved between two kings who both want me to be their queen. I can't trust either of them. I have to view everything as a potential trap because I'm now surrounded by enemies. There's one thing I won't forget and neither will Nico and Anthony; and that's that our three families are supposed to hate one another. The question is how many lives will the hate claim? Well, that's to be determined I suppose. The illusion of freedom has been shattered, and I'm sorely once again reminded of my very harsh reality. I'm back in a world where men rule and women do as they are told or pay the price. A world painted in blood and hate. A world that is nothing more than my gilded prison.

Chapter 7

Anthony

I sorely underestimated how quickly Nico would react to me visiting Violetta. He's desperate to marry her, but why now? I think it has something with him getting Don from his father. It makes the most sense. It's not ideal that my violet is back with Nico. At least, she had the good sense to text me on the burner phone. She might not trust me, but she did reach out to me in desperation. So, I'll take it.

Nico acted impulsively, which means he must be feeling desperate. I might be able to use that to my advantage. The hard part is going to be getting Violette away from him. I know he is going to keep her under lock and key. The strange thing is, I don't necessarily want to take her from Nico. However, I'm not sure there is a world where we can share her. Our family feud is complicated to say the least.

The feud between the three families has been going on for decades since greed got in the way. The three Italian families have been fighting for control over the Italian parts of the city for far too long. The Russian,

Japanese, Mexican, and Irish mobs or whatever they choose to be called each have parts of the city as well. The Italian's clearly have more territory, however, the divide in our own territory has always been in issue. One I fear that might lead to our demise if we aren't careful. I already know the Russian's are eager to gain the Italian territory. Even if the territory the Russians desire is technically the DeLuca's responsibility, it still doesn't bode well for my family. I need to find a way to meet with Nico. Maybe enemies isn't the way to go anymore. Perhaps unity is better. There could be a hell of a lot of power potential if the three Italian families were united instead of divided.

 Nico won't let Violetta go, and neither will I. So that's obstacle number one, I suppose. Nico is a hot head. That Italian temper is strong in him, and Violetta has the stubborn nature of a typical Italian woman not wanting to be told what to do by men. Violetta's need to escape the mafia life has always been a problem. Part of me always wondered why Nico let her believe she could have freedom. I thought it was a little cruel of him to give her that false hope because there is only one way to truly escape the underworld, and that is death.

 So, I have two people I have to deal with on different levels. Nico will mostly take forever to see reason and Violetta, well, who knows with her. Either way, I have my work cut out for me in more ways than one. There's a knock on my office door. I'm in my private townhouse at the moment. There's only one person who has a key besides my sister. I head over to my door and open it to find Lorenzo, my friend and trusted second in command.

"I take it you know Nico snatched Violetta this afternoon?" Lorenzo questions as I let him in.

"Yes, thankfully Violetta was smart and texted me on the burner phone. Impulsive asshole." I reply before I start pacing.

"You knew neither of them would make this easy. You need Nico if the Italians plan to keep their reigning rule as top dog in the city." Lorenzo reminds me, heading over to my wet bar.

"I know. Nico is never going to give me Violetta. He will wage a civil war to keep her, but I don't want to give her up. I know they have a history I can't compete with, but she was mine before I knew she was also his. I shouldn't have to sacrifice everything. I have given up a lot to become Don. I thought the one thing I had nailed down was having a wife, but Mario had to be a greedy dick. The hope was that Violetta would come to me naturally because it would make life easier. However, it's harder with her being in Nico's clutches now." I vent my frustrations.

"Why don't you two just share her?" Lorenzo suggests, helping himself to some brandy. "She was promised to both of you so toss her back and forth if it means avoiding a civil war. I know you don't want to give her up, but you might have to. It might come down to what's more important to you. Your family legacy or a girl you only know through stalking her. It's harsh, I know, but that's what it might come to." Lorenzo explains.

"Sharing. That's something I guess." I ponder out loud. I never thought about sharing my violet with Nico. I might have to, but do I want to? It's not the worst idea because it is a compromise for both Nico and I, but Violetta might not see it that way as she is determined to be her own free spirit that might get her killed in the underworld where women are to be displayed as prizes.

"With how stubborn Violetta is, she might need two men to put her ass in line and she has the perfect two lined up." Lorenzo adds, taking a sip from his glass before he pours me one as well. "Either way, you have to figure out what matters the most to you. I know you want Violetta, but is she worth the hassle? You have so many other women who would jump at the chance to be your wife" He says bringing me the glass he poured. I nod my head in thanks as I take it before taking a sip contemplating the complexity of the situation.

"I know I do, but I don't want those women. I want Violetta. I know that sounds foolish, but I can't help it. What I need is to talk to her and Nico. Nico might not even be aware of the danger the Italian mafia is to losing its rule. He's so consumed with becoming Don that I don't know if he realizes there is war about to blow up his front door. A civil war between the two of us fighting over Violetta is not something we need right now. Not when we have enemies waiting to strike at any sign of weakness." I say, setting the glass on my desk.

"Sounds like you need to have a meeting with Nico. I would meet with Nico first before you have Violetta join your discussion. That's if you decide to even include her." Lorenzo questions going back over to the wet bar to put things away while he finishes his drink.

"See if you can reach out to Nico's second in command. Maybe we could use him to help get to Nico in a civil manner. I don't want to ambush him because that might come off as a threat which I don't want when I'm there to talk about peace." I suggest, trying to figure out the best to approach this whole fucked up situation.

"I'll see what I can manage. For now, I suggest you get some rest, Boss. At least you know Violetta is safe from our enemies."

"True, she is at least safe with Nico. It's better than her being vulnerable on her own. Still, let's keep eyes on Violetta the best we can and maybe in the meantime she will text me. I also think of other ways to meet with Nico in case his second in command turns out to be a bust."

"You got it, Boss. Don't forget you have dinner with your sister and her fiance tonight."

I groan. "Don't remind me. I hate that little leach she got knocked up by. I don't trust him at all."

"Don't worry I have eyes on the leach. He is certainly not to be trusted. He's not been properly vetted."

"You know we can't properly vet him." I remind Lorenzo.

I would love to properly vet the leach my sister started dating around the time I killed my father. I knew that killing him would mean I was responsible for Sofia. She is eighteen going on nineteen with no direction in her life. She started dating some Irish boy named Connor Conely. It didn't take long before she got pregnant. My sister swears she's on the pill and that they used a condom, yet she still got pregnant. According to the doctors it's rare but does happen, however this is the underworld and nothing happens without reason. Rare is often a term for suspicion. I can't doubt my sister is pregnant because I've seen the sonogram pictures. The conception of the child is what I question. I can't rule out that Connor is a potential spy the Irish planted.

"I know, but maybe just a little." Lorenzo suggests.

"No. Tempting, but no. I need to get ready for this bullshit family dinner. Keep me posted on everything." I direct.

Lorenzo bids his goodbye and leaves me in my office. I sigh in frustration. There is too much at risk right now. I'm tense. Too tense. I need a good fuck, but it's hard when all I want is the one woman I can't have. The one woman who is in the hands of my enemy. By all rights, Violetta is my enemy because she is a Calla. It seems it's falling upon Violetta, Nico, and me to carry on our family legacies. The question now is, can we unite to save our asses or are we doomed to be knocked down from the top tier?

Chapter 8

Violetta

Against my better judgment I let Nico take me out to dinner instead of getting the food to go. I realized that would mean going home sooner with Nico, and I prevented that for as long as I could. However, now we are home, well, Nico's home. Nico has four homes. One, a condo in the best part of the city. It's his private place and that is where he has taken me thankfully. The Second home is also in the city, but it's the DeLuca home where his parents reside. Nico is an only child which is partly why I think he liked having me around when we were kids. I'm an only child as well, so I guess in some way we bonded over having no siblings. The third, is the DeLuca's family manor in the country. It's beautiful. The fourth is the DeLuca family villa somewhere in the mediterranean. It's the only home I've never been to before and I never dared to ask why.

Nico takes my backpack and begins making his way to his bedroom. I know the layout of this condo well. Part of me thinks Nico intends this to be our place. When he bought it he made sure I liked it. He has brought me here every chance he gets. He's even called this a great starter condo for a family.

"Uh, I'm not sleeping in your bed, Nico!" I yell after him before I move my ass to follow him to continue

"Little Dove, the fact that you think you would sleep anywhere else that isn't my bed is ridiculous. You should certainly know better." Nico scolds as I storm in the bedroom after him. A smug grin crosses his features before he opens a zipper of my backpack.

"What are you doing?" I question, trying to snatch my backpack back from him, but he holds it up where I can't get it. Damn Italian short genes that I get from my beloved Nonna.

"I didn't think you'd hand it over willingly, so I figured I'd search for it myself." Nico answers as he turns his back to me to riffle through the bag.

"Nico!" I screech as I see my clothes and various items being tossed on the floor. After a few moments Nico drops the backpack before turning back around with a trumpet grin as he wiggles the burn phone. "How the hell did you know?" I ask as my lower jaw drops a bit. I knew Nico had spies on me but to this level is a bit creepy. Then again, apparently Anthony has been stalking from afar himself, so why am I surprised by anything at this point?

"I know everything, Little Dove. Every fucking move you have made since you went out on your own to spread your wings." Nico answers.

"You've been controlling my life even though I was supposed to be out on my own?" I accuse, pointing my finger at him while popping out my hip.

Nico chuckles. "Of course I have and of course I did. You are mine, Little Dove. I have to protect you from the enemies that knock on our door. You are a target. Do you not understand that? You think the daughter of Mario Calla could just disappear from the criminal underworld and live a regular life? Wake up, Violetta! You don't think the Russians or the Mexicans might not be interested in you. Your father promised you to me and Anthony. What makes you think he didn't promise you to other less unsavory leaders of the underworld. You think I'm the monster, maybe I am, but I'm the monster keeping you safe."

"You really think he promised me to other underworld leaders?" I ask in a panic tone as my right hand goes to my chest. Nico has a point I never even considered.

"I don't know, but it's possible. I wasn't even sure about Anthony until he showed up at the hospital. Your father was backstabbing a lot of people. Just because Mario is dead doesn't mean that his enemies won't come for you out revenge. I don't control you to be an asshole, Little Dove, I do it to keep you safe because you aren't even aware of the real nightmare the underworld is." Nico states, taking the burner phone inside his inner suit pocket.

"Why do you bother keeping me safe? You don't have to. My father clearly didn't promise me to just you, so why fight for me when it would be easier to let my father's enemies hunt me down?" I question, looking right into Nico's dangerous eyes.

"You haven't figured why yet? All these years, Little Dove, and you truly haven't figured out why?" Nico questions bridging the gap between us. His one arm snakes around my waist pulling me to him as his other hand grabs my chin forcing me to look at him.

"Because you love me." I answer breathlessly. Shit he takes my breath away.

"Exactly, Little Dove." Nico replies before his lips capture mine in a brutally, passionate kiss that heats the fire in my core. "Tell me you love me too, Little Dove." Nico demands breaking our kiss.

"It's not that simple, Nico. I do love you, but I hate feeling like I'm just a pawn." I reply, leaning my forehead against his chest.

"You are not a pawn, and you never have been. You are my friend who I fell in love with long before your father promised you to me." Nico says, holding me close to him. It's too soon for such strong emotions, but how can I ignore how I feel when I'm in his arms. Even with Anthony tugging at the back of mind, Nico currently pulls my focus.

"It feels like forever ago since we were just kids sneaking cannolis behind the adults back." I reply, looking back up at Nico. We both chuckle at the memory.

"That is forever ago it seems. You should unwind with a nice bath while I make sure Jullian is having success procuring you some things. Get rest, Little Dove, we have a packed agenda for the next couple of weeks." Nico says, pulling away from me, and I hate that I feel cold without him.

"What about my job?" I question, attempting to hide my irritation because I did work hard for a degree that I would like to continue to use.

"They will be informed that you have taken a new position at the Angel Clinic." Nico informs me.

"The Angel Clinic?" I ask in confusion.

"In time, Little Dove. Relax, rest, and I'll join you later in bed." Nico pecks my on the lips before he strides out the bedroom.

I'm not sure what I'm supposed to make of anything right now, so I head to take a bath because right now that's an order I wouldn't mind following. I hate how Nico bypasses my stubborn nature. I don't know what it is or why he has such power over me. Perhaps it's our bond that we forged long ago that has my heart captivated making me bend to his will. Attempting to clear my mind, I take advantage of the soaking tub and fill it with some natural epsom salts that are lavender scented. I haven't enjoyed a nice bath in awhile. I need to figure out my plan. Being back with Nico is proving difficult already. His charm is hard to resist. What's even harder to resist is his sincerity. I want to doubt Nico's love and intentions, but my heart is secretly leaping for joy.

Anthony pops into my mind. I lost the damn burner phone. That didn't take long, however, I'm not surprised. I should be thrilled I have two handsome men fighting over me, but I'm not because either way I have no control. Yes, Anthony offers the illusion of control, yet I'm not sure I buy that. Anthony is a powerful man there is no way he would just let his wife do whatever she wants. He said within reason, but what is within reason when it comes to the rules of the underworld?

Then let's not forget the perfectly terrifying thought that Nico brought up, and that's what if my father promised me to other leaders of the underworld. My father was a greedy, foolish man. My nonna always said so. It's bad enough he was stupid enough to promise me to Nico and Anthony, but the man is insane if he promised me to other leaders. If he did promise to other leaders, why haven't they come to collect me? Why is Anthony waiting until now to make his move? There are far too many questions and I'm not sure I can trust any of the answers I'm given. I'm surrounded by snakes, traitors, and corruption. How the hell am I supposed to sort out the truth from the lies? I want to trust Nico, but I don't trust his hidden intentions. I don't trust Anthony's hidden intentions either. I don't trust anyone right now. I'm not even sure I trust myself right now because my life has officially been flipped upside down, again.

Chapter 9

Nico

I'm in my study nursing some vodka on the rocks while I flip the burner phone in my hand contemplating what to do with it. The truth is, I know I need to talk with Anthony. There's a lot at stake right now and I'm not talking about me getting passed Don by my father. There's enemies lurking waiting to take down the top dogs. Unfortunately, Mario's greed and poor choices continue to affect us. He gave the other underground families the key to wedging themselves in our operations. The Russians and Irish have always primarily been gun and other illegal weapons. They fight over weapon territory and distribution. While everyone else chose other things to pursue.

    The Mexicans obviously have their drugs that they use as their main operations. Although, there are rumors they are into more unsavory things than just drugs. The Italians stick to illegal gambling, brothels, and those types of scenes. Of course, there are other underworld families like the Japanese that prefer to keep to themselves and do their own thing. They fight more among themselves than they do with the other influential families.

Mario wanted to be the top dog, the top family, the top everything. His goal was to be the only ruler of the Italian mafia and maybe take out some other underworld families and take over their territory in the process. Mario made dirty deals with many people. I'm still not entirely sure of the damage Mario's deals have. He was into so many things. He was far too ambitious for his own good.

While Mario's damage is still slightly unknown, I do know that his lingering threats aren't the only thing I have to worry about. The Italians are looking weak with new changes in leadership. It's almost as if everyone is waiting for us to take each other out so they can swoop in like the vultures they are. My father will cause a civil war for some foolish reason. He's greedy like Mario was. They often bonded over their greed, yet it also caused a divide between them. My father and Mario were best friends much like how Violetta and I started off before things became more of a romantic interest between us. I don't know what happened between them to cause Mario to go to the Ronkas and betray my father. Anthony isn't his father and I'm definitely not mine. We have to be better than our fathers.

Without hesitation I flip the phone open and call the only number in the damn phone. The line trills for a few seconds before I hear Anthony's frantic voice on the other end. "Violetta, are you okay?"

"I assure you, she is as happy as clam in her bubble bath." I reply.

"Nico," Anthony's voice turns stern and cold. "I should have known you'd get the fucking burner from her." He pauses, trying to gain his composure. "Well, you called me, so what do you want?"

"A truce, so the two of us can discuss becoming allies instead of enemies. I think we have enough of those, don't you?" I suggest.

"I do agree, we have enough enemies circling us like eager vultures. I didn't think you would be level headed enough to agree to a truce so easily. I thought I was going to have to use Violetta to ambush you. I do assume you want something or need something like maybe your father out of the picture." Anthony makes his own suggestion.

I chuckle. "Something to discuss in person. Do you have any demands for our meeting?" I inquire.

"I do. I want Violetta there." Anthony makes his demand.

"Fair, I agree with that term. Let's meet at my burlesque club and after I say we have fun in the brothel showing Violetta a taste of the sexual world. She's a virgin, and she thinks she knows sex because she's a nurse, but she has no clue of what real sexual experiences are. What do you say we have fun with the stubborn woman who we both have a vested interest in." I suggest taking a sip of drink.

"You make it sound like she belongs to both of us." Anthony comments.

"She was promised to both of us, so technically she does belong to both of us. Even if we aren't exactly fans of one another, Anthony, I think we both can agree it's better that we share her in some way and stop whatever other men she might have been promised to from touching what rightfully belongs to us. Just remember one thing, Anthony, I was the first man in her life and I will marry her. However, I can't deny that you do have some right to Violetta."

"I will acknowledge that you have a relationship with Violetta that I do not. I want to know more about why you need to marry her, but we can discuss that at our meeting. I think it's time we suck up our pride and put our differences aside so we can survive the impending turf war we both know is coming. What time tomorrow?"

"Eight. I'll tell the guards to let you in and see that you go to my private table." I reply.

"Good, I'll see you and Violetta then." Anthony replies before he disconnects the call.

I sip my vodka before I chuck the phone hard against the nearest wall and watch it break apart into chunks. Cheapass burner. I don't know how Violetta is going to feel about being shared. Shit, I'm not entirely sure how I feel about it. I just went off an impulse that felt right. It does make sense to at least talk with Anthony. Even better if we can come to some compromise that we all can agree to. It's better the Italian families be united than divided because our enemies are circling like vultures just waiting for the moment to feast.

Chapter 10

Violetta

After my bath, I change into the silky black nightgown that has been laid out for me. There's no panties or thong so I guess that means Nico wants easy access to his goods. Although, he did say that he wouldn't have sex with me until our wedding, however, that doesn't mean he can't touch me in sexual ways. Not that I would be mad about the sex part with either Anthony or Nico. Both of them, though, that appeals to me, but there is no way that will ever happen. They hate each other.

It's only eight o'clock. I'm not tired. Usually I would clean my apartment, do my food shopping to have it delivered to me because it's what's easiest for me, and probably doing laundry. Adult things that I currently find myself no longer needing to worry about as my warden will make sure I'm taken care of. Nico is definitely my warden, but he's more. I hate that he's more, but I can't help my heart from wanting him. I love him even if I try to deny it, which is why I find it so strange that I'm equally drawn to Anthony.

THE MAFIA LOVE CODE

Anthony is surely a distant memory now. Nico has the burner phone, so I have no way of contacting Anthony. Nico will plan my every move and those moves involve us getting married. Nico is on a mission to make me his wife and I doubt that involves Anthony. I can't pretend there isn't a part of me that is thrilled about marrying Nico. There was a time it was all I wanted, but then I opened my eyes when my father was killed. I don't care that he was killed. My father was a man with big ambitions, but was absolutely terrible at executing plans. My father's plans only made sense to him. I surely never understood it and neither did my mother or Nonna when they were alive. It would seem I'm left to clean up my father's messes and make good on his promise to Nico and even Anthony if possible. I rather them than some of the other leaders of the underworld. I'm still a woman and this is very much a man's world.

I decide to climb into Nico's ridiculous comfortable four poster bed with carved bars in between the posters so they connect. The sheets are soft and the bed itself feels like a cloud. I don't even want to know how much this mattress cost, let alone the rest of everything in this place. Money is never a problem when it comes to the mafia. I'm used to the luxury the mafia life can provide. Part of being on my own was about experiencing things like a regular person would, well the closest I could get to it from the hidden puppet master pulling strings with my life.

Grabbing the TV remote on the one bedside table, I turn the TV on and find some trashy reality TV to binge. I love reality TV because it's the only thing that is entertaining when you live in a fucking TV or movie mafia script to enjoy regular entertainment. I get why mundane people would be fascinated with shows and movies about mafias, gangs, violence, and the whole illegal underground. It's a world that doesn't exist in reality to many people because they live among civilized society. However, when you know the harsh reality of the underworld and live in it, those movies and shows are hard to get into.

Around one in the morning Nico comes striding into what I assume is now our bedroom. "Still awake, Little Dove?" Nico questions as he begins to strip out of his clothes.

"Of course I'm still awake. You decided to give me a job that required night shift." I counter, trying to not enjoy the sight of his toned body.

Nico chuckles. "I wasn't going to make it easy on you. However, I do admire you for going to college and obtaining your nursing degree. I'm proud that you achieved a goal you set for yourself." Damn him for being sincere.

Nico has always been able to see me and appreciate the things I do. My father would have thought me becoming a nurse was a waste of time. Women shouldn't have careers or that's what he thought because my father is from an old time where having women under his thumb is power. Nico could have used his power of being my warden over me, but he didn't.

"Thank you for letting me do it and giving me the means to do so. I guess I should give you some credit there. You could have told me no like my dad would have, but you didn't." I reply as Nico is left in black boxers. I have to stop myself from licking my lips.

"I do want you to have a life that you enjoy, Little Dove. I hate that you feel hindered by my control because my control is meant to help you live the best, safe life that you can. I know you think you know this world, but I promise there are parts that you do not. This underworld we live in is dangerous, and you only know half of the dangers." Nico replies approaching the bed.

I sigh, letting my guard down. I can't hold a damn defense to this man. I wonder if I would cave this easily with Anthony. I should not be thinking about him, but it's a little hard not to. However, I need to focus on Nico because he is the man I'm presently with. "Maybe we can find a way to make things work between us." I say with a hopeful smile as Nico climbs into bed next to me. Maybe I shouldn't push so hard against him.

"We will find our balance, Little Dove, but you have to be willing." Nico confidently states before he pulls me into his arms. I snuggle into his arms and lay my head on his shoulders. Shit, he really is a comfort I can't resist. Nico is my warden, but he has always made me feel safe.

"I'll try to keep an open mind. That's the best I can give you for right now." I offer.

"I'll take it. You'll find I'm a patient man, Little Dove, especially when it comes to you. You should get some rest, you have a big day tomorrow." Nico informs me

"Oh, and what exactly is my big day tomorrow?" I inquire.

"You need to go shopping for some real clothes. Not those rags you have in your apartment. Time to stop dressing like a peasant. I also have you booked at one of the top day spa places in the city. I have you booked for hair, nails, massage, wax, and a facial. You will also need to go shopping for beauty products. You're a fucking mafia princess who is about to become a mafia queen, time to act the part, Little Dove." Nice advises.

I know he's not wrong. Being a mafia princess is role that requires a level of sophistication. Nico forgets I was groomed to be a mafia wife because that's the only purpose my father gave me. It's why I was determined to have a meaningful career as a nurse.

"Is that all for tomorrow's schedule?" I inquire, trying to not let Nico's little scolding that I need to now play my part bother me. I would ask who the fuck he thought he was, but I already know Nico looks at himself as my protector and owner. My very own personal warden, and I secretly like being his prisoner.

"First, we will go out to dinner to get some pizza, garlic knots, and cannoli cake before we head to a surprise." Nico informs me.

"I hate surprises, you know that." I remind him, stuffing my irritation down and trying to enjoy my cuddles.

"I know, but this one is one I believe you will enjoy. Trust me, even if it's just for this one thing."

"Fine." I reluctantly agree.

Besides, why argue with my warden? I'll do what he says, whether I like it or not. I have this need to rebel against men pulling the puppet strings of my life. It started with my father. He smothered me with his intentions. I hate that his intentions for me to be a mafia wife align with Nico's intentions. I'm tired of feeling like I'm a pawn being manipulated. Even the years that I was away, living my so called own life away from the mafia, Nico was still moving me along his chess board. He still had control over my life. He was simply controlling me from afar.

That's why I have a hard time buying Anthony's promise to let me live my own life. He still has rules I have to follow. He will expect me to be the painted mafia princess turned mafia queen put on display when he needs me. I'm not naive or stupid. I know how the men are in the underworld, especially leaders. They literally ooze alpha male pheromones. They are dominant, controlling, and despicable even when they are being reasonable. Anthony is just giving me the same illusion that Nico did for the last four years. Men rule the world, and they reign supreme in the underworld. Women don't have as much power in the underworld as they do in the legal world. The underground world has an old world style of thinking. Women are property to be sold, bartered, and owned. I guess it's time to face the fact that the only way I'm escaping this underworld life is death. I'm not ready to die, so I guess I better find a way to navigate the inevitable path that has been chosen for me.

Chapter 11

Anthony

I have to admit, I was surprised Nico reached out to me. I thought for sure I was going to have to trap him into a meeting using Violetta to do so. However, it seems Nico is aware of the threat we face. That's a good thing because I'd like to avoid elimination, which is the only way that the other families of the underworld would be able to take our reigning position. So, if the two of us can come to some compromise where Violetta is concerned and have a united front, we might stand a chance of preservation instead of instinct.

Of course, this whole thing could be a trap, but somehow I doubt it. While the Ronka's and DeLuca's might not always see eye to eye, Nico hasn't personally attacked my family. His father has but my father was also guilty of attacking our so-called enemies. The problem is the Italians need to get over whatever fake civil war that has been going on for decades. Our enemies have noticed our divide and they are simply waiting to strike. The Russians love to attack when there is a change of leadership in any of the underground families. The fact that Nico and I will essentially be taking leadership around the same time raises concerns about our true enemies attacking.

The Italian faction of the underground has three main families, well, now mainly two since Calla's don't have many family members left. They have either been killed or died naturally. Violetta is one the last remaining Calla's in the city. She has family back in Italy, but we cut ties with the Italian mafia in Europe. I have no idea why, and from what I gathered a small group from each family escaped to the States and never looked back. My family has never even set foot in Italy and as far as I know neither has any of the Calla or DeLuca families. That makes me think that if we entered Italy we would be dead. So whatever the reason, our families fled and started their own faction of the Italian mafia in the States which suggests it's bad. I do know the DeLuca's do have property in the Mediterranean that isn't in Italy, which leads me to believe that Italy is the only country in the Mediterranean we aren't welcomed in.

The three families were united at first. It's how the Italian mafia came to be top dog among the underground world in the city. Then from what I've been told, the Don's of the families became greedy wanting what the other had. It started a mini civil war in the Italian faction that's gone on for decades now. Maybe we can end the civil war and have a united front once more. I guess tonight will either be the beginning of an official civil war or a truce that will preserve our position.

THE MAFIA LOVE CODE

I enter the dimly lit burlesque club. The stage is center and there are three girls performing a dance number to "Diamonds are a Girl's Best Friend". The bouncer immediately shows me the VIP booth with Violetta and Nico sitting next to one another drinking champagne. The VIP booths are along the upper level of the club that overlooks the stage and standard seats below. Violette almost chokes on her champagne as I approach them. Her eyes go wide with concern, I guess Nico didn't tell her they were meeting me. I'd be annoyed except the satisfied grin on Nico's face as he studies Violetta's reaction to seeing tells me he didn't tell her to surprise her.

"I'm glad you could join us, Anthony. Please, have a seat." Nico gestures for me to sit on the other side of Violetta whose face is now scrunched in confusion as she takes another swig of her champagne clearly unsure of what is happening. She does look cute when she is confused.

"Thank you for inviting me. I'm glad we could call a temporary truce to see if we can perhaps make the truce more permanent." I reply, as I slide into the half circle shaped booth.

"Wait, Nico, you invited Anthony, and you agreed, Anthony? I thought you two hated one another?" Violetta asks, baffled as she looks between us like we have lost our ever loving minds.

"Hates a strong word. More like we tolerate each other." I correct.

"That's a way to put it." Nico says with a grin before he focuses his attention on Violetta. "Look, while you were off playing normal person there's been a war brewing in the underworld for years. There are other underworld families waiting to take our spot as top dog. Anthony and I have called a truce because we want to see if we can negotiate a united front from all three Italian families." Nico informs Violetta while a waitress wearing a short black leather skirt and black lace corset in black heels delivers a champagne flute for me as well as a second bottle of champagne unopened on ice before she scurries away.

"The three main families? There's only two main families." Violetta states as her nose scrunches in confusion.

"There are three main families, Little Dove, your father never told you the truth about the Calla family. The Calla family escaped with the DeLuca and Ronka families to America. The three families were united but greed divided them. It took about a decade or so for the Calla's to be taken out of power. It's why your father was so hell bent on marrying you off to either Anthony or I. He was hoping to gain the Calla family status back, but in case that didn't work he had alternate plans to make sure the Calla family was the only one left. Many of your family members joined your father's cause, thus they ended up dead." Nico explains.

"It's true, Little Violet, the Calla family is a founding family of the Italian mafia in the American underworld in every major city. Sure, most of it started in New York but the American side has over time spread to other major cities. We also have to watch our backs from whatever Italian factions may come after us. We still don't know why our three families fled and broke ties with the Italian faction. That's why it's wise for the three of us to have a united front." I solidify Nico's point, hoping it will help Violetta understand why we are pulling her back into this world that she despises so much.

"Well, you did say I would like this surprise, Nico. You did throw me off with bringing me here. I thought you might make good on the threat about Madam Connie teaching me a lesson or two." Violetta remarks, satisfied with our explanation.

Nico and I both chuckle at her. I know Nico plans to take her to the brothel tonight, and I can't deny that I'm looking forward to it. I surmised Violetta was a virgin. Not that I really care if she is or isn't. I don't even care if Nico wants to take her virginity, which I assume he would. I also believe Violetta will be more comfortable with Nico because of their previously established friendship. Yes, I am a little jealous that they have an established relationship because it does make me the odd one out. The outsider intruding on their relationship. However, just sitting this close to Violetta has me craving her. That sweet rose and minty smell that perfumes of her in delicious waves has me adjusting the tent that is creeping in my pants. The black dress she wears shows off her large breasts. Her thick thighs peek from the dress slowly riding up in her seated position.

"Okay, so clearly you two know something I don't. I'm not sure I like this." Violetta pouts slightly, puffing out her lower lip. Shit that little bratty attitude is going to be fun to play with and tame.

"Are you going to tell her or should I?" I question, raising an eyebrow at Nico as I take a sip of my own champagne. Nico and I did end up talking briefly prior to our meeting about sharing Violetta. It seems our second in commands were quick to befriend one another and convince us sharing is best. Although, i suppose I'm about to find out why Nico needs to marry Violeta

Nico smirks. "Anthony and I have decided we are going to share you. You will marry me because I need a legal marriage in order to meet the will my grandfather left. My father is using that to hold the Don title over my head. I hope you understand, Anthony, this is nothing personal or some way to slight your claim to Violetta. If I could take Don without marriage, I would have zero problem agreeing to neither of us marrying her." Nico explains in a calm manner.

I absorb and quickly process the new found information. I'm quick on my feet when it comes to processing information and making precise decisions."I understand why you need to marry Violetta. You need to be Don of your family because we both know your father would never agree to a truce. However, I ask that I can spend the wedding night with you two." I reasonably negotiate.

"I agree to that. It's only fair. The three of us will probably end up all living together at some point. There's clearly logistics to figure out with kids because we both need heirs. However, I think that is a conversation for later. We need to survive whatever damn war is coming between the main families of the underworld. Heirs will mean nothing if we don't have an empire for them to inherit." Nico adds.

"I completely agree with that. We should probably figure out living arrangements and how we plan to eventually present ourselves to the world. You two need to get married first." I contribute before taking a sip of my champagne in an attempt to avoid touching Violetta.

"Wait just one minute," I interject. "You two are acting like I'm not sitting between the two of you. Don't I get a say at all about being shared and married to one of you. How the hell are you two so chummy and easily agreeable with one another? What the actual fuck is happening at this table right now?" Violetta bursts out frustrated, grasping her champagne flute a little too tightly that she might break it.

"Let me take that from you, Little Violet, before you break the glass." I say, taking the champagne flute from her hand. Nico chuckles at my action.

"Come on, Little Dove, Anthony and I are grown men. We can share and be reasonable. We both can see that logically it makes the most sense for us to be united.

The three of us all together in our own bond, we could be unstoppable, Little Dove. You just have to be willing to let it happen." Nico points out, and I agree with him. Although, I must confess, I wasn't entirely sure Nico could see reason. I'm glad to be proven wrong with this. I honestly have nothing against him.

"Great, I'm glad you two can play nice together in the sandbox. However, what about my say in things? You want a united front, so that means I can't be in the background as your faithful wifey who does what her owners tell her to do." Violetta argues, crossing her arms under her breasts making them pop at more. Fuck, she's tempting, and that brat attitude makes me want to choke her or spank her, maybe both.

"I'll make you an offer, Little Dove, one that Anthony has to accept as well. You give us complete submission when it comes to sex. We can touch you when we want and how we want. You have to give us each at least one child, and I know you like the idea of being a mom at some point so don't act like you don't. In exchange, you rule at our side. Two kings, one queen ruling the Italian faction. You can be in on every deal, exchange, meeting, and whatever else you want when it comes to the united family business." Nico offers, and I agree with his offer. It's slightly similar to what I offered her.

"I'm fine with it." I quickly state, so Violetta can't try to pit Nico and I against each other. Right now, she might benefit more if we aren't getting along. Maybe she counted on us truly hating one another so she could set us

THE MAFIA LOVE CODE

against each other and escape while we are busy fighting one another. It's a pretty good plan and she is smart. Truth is, we need her to make the united front stand so that our enemies can't pit us against one another.

Violetta sighs in defeat. "Fine, it's as good as I'm going to get. I agree to your offer." Violetta agrees.

I can sense she is a bit reluctant, and I'm sure there is a part of her that is hating this. However, I think Violetta is intrigued by being shared by the two of us. I have no idea how sharing her is going to work, but I'm willing to try it. Sure everything seems good now, but when we go to put this plan in motion, well who knows how it might go. I hope this is a good idea. I'm not opposed to it on any level. However, our preservation relies on this agreement working between the three of us. This should be interesting. At least if it fails, we'll be entertained along the way.

Chapter 12

Violetta

My mind has been blown from this evening. Completely blown. Never in a million years would have imagined that Nico and Anthony would be friendly with one another let alone forge an alliance where they share me. Fantasy wise, I'm down for being used by two powerful men in a sexual way, but I want freedom outside of sex. I want a say, a place at their side, and I definitely don't want to be shoved into the background like my opinions don't matter. They both have promised to treat me as their equal in that sense, but this whole thing is twisted in ways I didn't even know were possible. The worst part is, I want to believe their promises, but I'm not sure that is wise. Afterall, how much can I truly trust them?

Let's not add the fact that I found out the truth that my family truly is one of the main families that started the Italian American mafia. It explains my father's thirst for power. He was trying to reclaim what he thought belonged to our family. I don't care about the political bullshit of who should own what when it comes to Italian territory. The guys can deal with that, but I don't want to be kept in the dark about it either.

The dark is where I currently find myself sandwiched between Anthony and Nico who are enjoying the show of the woman currently pleasuring herself as she's spread out on some bed on a stage-platform like thing. I've seen plenty of dicks, breasts, ass, and vaginas as a nurse, but this is different. When I'm examining a patient or helping with a procedure while they are exposed, it's different because it's medical. It's necessary to touch that private part for a medical reason. However, watching a woman completely naked and her legs spread apart with a bar spreader while she skilfully fingers her clit with one hand while another pumps a silicone dildo in and out of her vigna is out of my scope of experience. Not to mention there's women walking around naked or in barely anything they might as well be naked.

I'm not judging these women. This is their chosen profession because every woman here auditions to work in both the burlesque and brothel. Yes, the brothel is totally illegal, but that doesn't mean these women are forced to be here. If this is what they want to do then so be it. I can't deny that this isn't a little erotic to watch this, but I'm a virgin and this just makes me want to have sex even more. Let's not mention the fact that I've probably downed an entire bottle of champagne myself trying to ease my nerves. I was not necessarily prepared for a sexual experience tonight.

We have terms mostly laid out, but there are some areas we need to figure out. Still, the entire thing shocks me to my core. Both of them get to have me and own my body. That's hot, I hate to admit that but it is. I can't pretend I've never thought about it. However, fantasy and reality are supposed to be two different things. So what the hell am I supposed to do when the fantasy turns to reality? I'm in way over my head with two experienced men at my side. Watching this woman fuck herself with a dildo is probably the closest thing I've come to sex. I'm twenty three. I really hate being a virgin. It's hard to relate to other women my age because they have had sex, one night stands, or at least some experience with sex. I have to lie and say I have experience so I don't get labeled the virgin nurse.

"Relax, Little Violet." Anthony whispers in my ear as his hand gently squeezes my thigh. I didn't even realize he put his hand on me because I was far too lost in my chaotic thoughts.

"She needs to get out her head. She tends to overthink." Nico adds, totally ratting me out to Anthony as he leans into me, his lips dangerously close to touching mine.

"An overthinker, well, I think we can handle that." Anthony's voice is husky with desire.

This can't be real I think to myself as Nico grabs my chin and forces my lips to his. Anthony moves my hair to one side before his lips fall on my neck to kiss and suck the sensitive skin. Anthony's hand on my thigh slides up and under my dress. His fingers play with the hem of my thong, teasing what he might do. Meanwhile Nico's hand is playing with my nipple through my dress and bra. I realize these materials are a lot thinner than I initially thought. The friction it provides sends tingles through my core. When Anthony slides his fingers between my legs and far too skillfully finds my clit, I suck in breath and moan into Nico's lips. Nico chuckles as he lets my lips go before Anthony pulls my lips to his.

What in the devil are these two doing to me? Nico moves my dress down so my lace bra is exposed. I should care that they are doing this to me in public, but we are in a brothel, I doubt anyone cares. They might even enjoy the show, and somehow that makes this much hotter. Nico plays with my nipples, pulling, pinching, and rubbing skillfully between his fingers. The sensations from the two of them have me moaning like a whore. Appropriate as we are in a brothel. Anthony's tongue darts into my mouth swirling with mine. Nico places delicate kisses on my shoulder. Anthony breaks our kiss before I find my lips recaptured by Nico's. Anthony rubs my clit in skilful circles while Nico continues his assault on my nipples. There is an intensity building in my core and before I know it my body quivers from the intense orgasm that temporarily takes over my body.

"When's the honeymoon," Anthony groans into my neck.

"Soon. Less than a month I say. We don't need anything fancy. A simple church wedding and a reception at an extremely fancy hotel. Violetta will be doing wedding stuff tomorrow." I hear Nico inform Anthony as I come back from whatever fever pitched ecstasy those two just gave me.

"Thanks for letting me know. " I bite sarcastically as I slow my breathing and come back to reality.

"I can give you an entire schedule tomorrow." Nico says, adjusting my dress as Anthony removes his hand from between my legs. Anthony licks his fingers.

"You should taste her." Anthony suggests, sucking his fingers clean of my juices. Somehow my cheeks heat even more. Nico takes Anthony's suggestion. His hand finds it way under my thong and between my legs. He teasingly rubs my clit before soaking two fingers in my juices. It's not hard. I can feel how fucking wet I am. To say I've never been touched like that is understatement. I thought I was good at touching myself but these two just proved I know jack fucking shit. Nico licks fingers like my juice is liquid gold. He groans his pleasure.

"Fuck I can't wait to eat you out, Littel Dove." Nico comments

Okay seriously I can feel the dark red flush heat my cheeks even more. For fuck sake, I don't know if being in a brothel makes this more erotic or just fucking crazy. It's only now I realize the girl who was playing with herself and the dildo are gone. Now there is a woman laying on her back while another woman sits on her face. That woman is sucking the cock of man while he is being anal fuck. What a freakshow brothel is this. I suddenly find my whole body heating with embarrassment. This is all a bit too much.

"Can we go now?" I ask, trying to hide the panic creeping in.

"Yes, it's been an eventful night. We shouldn't overwhelm you too much," Nico pauses, putting his arm around my shoulders. "Care to come back with us Anthony? It's my private condo, and I think you and I have much more to discuss about our alliance."

"What do you want, Little Violet?" Anthony questions.

"I want you to come with us." I answer sincerely. "I think having you both close is comforting." I confess because it's true. I know I'm safe with them from the dark enemies that might lurk in the shadows.

"Well that answers that." Nico concludes as the three of us get up from our seats.

We have Nico's driver take us back to Nico's condo. On the way, I'm sandwiched between Anthony and Nico. My head is resting on Nico's shoulders while I hold Anthony's hand. No one speaks as we are all lost in our own thoughts. It's funny to think the three of us have been fantasizing about us being together. I didn't think there was a way that would ever happen. I honestly thought that Nico and Anthony were sworn enemies. So color me surprised to find out the two dominating men can indeed work together and share me. What twisted fantasy turned reality do I find myself in?

Chapter 13

Nico

By the time we make it back to my condo, Violetta is half asleep. I think tonight was a bit overwhelming for her. It was fun playing with her, and Anthony and I are ready to have so much more fun with Violetta. However, as interested as Violetta is, she's hesitant. She was fun when we were playing with her but the moment her orgasm crashed over her she suddenly became very aware of where we were. Maybe playing with her in public like that was a bit intense for the first time, but she has to get used to it because I don't think either Anthony or I will be able to keep our hands off her in public or private. I might need to have one of Connie's ladies help Violetta to embrace her womanhood. It's not her fault her mom died when she was young or that I made sure men never went near her to keep her pure for my own selfish reasons.

Once we get inside, Anthony and I let Violetta settle in our room. I hear the shower pop on as Anthony and I leave Violetta be for a bit. She's overwhelmed, so it's best to leave her be to process everything. Her life has changed yet again and this time things are changing for the better even if she can't see that yet. I know how badly she wants out of this life, I can't say I've never craved a way out myself, but we were born into this life. This life chose us, and the only way out is death. Sure, you could change your name, fake your death, and leave the country. Sounds easy, but it's not. Even then you aren't entirely safe. You would always be looking over your shoulder terrified that your enemies have discovered you're alive. It's not how I want to live. I rather just face the fate that I'm meant to live my life in the underworld and not the legal world. Then again, it might be easier for me to embrace it because I'm a man and being a man in the underworld surely has its advantages.

Anthony and I end up in my study, drinking bourbon. We both sit on the black Italian leather sofa I have in front of the modern electric fireplace. I prefer a real fireplace but a condo in the city isn't where it's ideal. The countryside mansion is the perfect place for me to enjoy a real fireplace.

"So, now's the time for either of us to back out of the alliance." I say, breaking the neutral silence.

"I don't want to back out. Despite the fact that I should hate you just because of your last name, I've never really seen you as an enemy." Anthony answers. I like how he carefully chose the word enemy and not threat. He knew that if he said I wasn't a threat to him that I would take it the wrong way. So he went with enemy to show respect. I've heard of how respectable Anthony is, and now that I've interacted with him in person, I buy it. It actually makes me like the bastard even more.

"I don't plan to back out either. I was never sure if you were a true enemy like your father was. I'll admit I wasn't thrilled that you made a move on Violetta behind my back, but after I cooled down I realized I would have done the same damn thing. Meeting you tonight, playing with Violette together, I believe we can make this whole thing work. We have to be better than our fathers." I confess, taking a sip of my bourbon I enjoy the smooth burn down my throat.

I know our alliance and the fact that we want to share Violetta instead of fighting over her is insane. It's even crazier that Violetta was willing to be shared. I wasn't sure if she would be okay with that. I also didn't know if she was attracted to Anthony. I didn't know how I would feel if she was. When Jullian even bought up sharing Violetta with Anthony I wanted to punch him in the face. When I wanted him to get in touch with Anthony's second in command, I didn't mean for them to plot on how to get us to work together and agree to share Violetta so there wouldn't be a war. Our men don't want war. Many of my men have families or at the very least people they love and care about. Most of them are going home to someone at the end of the day. War means people are going to get killed, and no one wants to be the one going home in a body bag. I would never dare dream of putting my men in an unnecessary war. That would mean not fighting with Anthony over Violetta.

Neither of us wanted to give her up and there wasn't a reason either of us should. That's when I saw the logic and reason for what they were suggesting. It was the middle ground needed. The final piece was getting Violetta to agree because despite what she fears, she will always have a voice with me and as it turns out Anthony as well.

"I agree, we can't let greed divide the Italian faction anymore. If we do, we will end up swimming with fishes." Anthony jokes.

I laugh. "Fuck, I hate that stupid line. Normal people think it's so damn funny. I've never heard an actual mafia person say that other than to mock the movie."

Anthony chuckles. "Normal people love to think they know how we live our lives. Sometimes they aren't far off from the truth and other times I question how dumb normal people can be."

"That's why Violetta is addicted to reality TV." I comment, taking a sip of my drink.

"I must confess, I am a little jealous you have an established relationship with Violetta. You know her in ways I do not. I know with time I will clearly get to know you both better, but it's hard to deny the advantage you have over me." Anthony confesses, taking a sip of his drink.

"I will happily give you some time with Violetta to get to know her. I'll even help you with ideas for dates and such. I know I have an advantage you do not, and I might be smug about it at times. It's not on purpose, yet it is because I'm an asshole. So try not to take it personally.

Honestly, I want you to have a relationship with Violetta. I want the three of us to be united and to have our own bond. Shit, you and I should have our own bond. I'll tell you right now I'm straight."

Anthony chuckles. "I'm straight too, so no worries there. I know we are going to be enjoying a variety of sexual play with Violetta together, but I think we each should get at least a night or two with Violetta to ourselves. We can even have a night a month where you and I do something. I'm more than sure we have some things in common. We can obviously do dates together with Violetta too. It's a balance that will take some time to establish. We just have to be willing and open."

"I agree to that. We should do most things as a unit, but it would be wise to also nurture our individual relationships as well. We will probably need some type of schedule to keep track of it all. We can leave that for Violetta. She secretly loves schedules." I pause to collect my thoughts and to see if Anthony wants to interject his own thoughts. Anthony stays silent, nodding his head in agreement, so I continue. "At first we have to keep things to ourselves. My father is itching to stay in power even if no one wants him to be Don anymore. Most of my family worries about my dad and his choices. They are afraid he will do something stupid like kill off another underworld leader. Not you, he thinks you're too easy of a target. No offense." I inform Anthony.

"None taken. I'm just relieved I don't have to worry about your father trying to assassinate me." Anthony jokes, and we both laugh.

"I think the best time to announce our unity and alliance is after Violetta and I are married to avoid any issues from my father or anyone else under our leadership who might not be happy with our alliance." I propose, trying to figure out a new plan with Anthony.

"Sounds like a plan to me. I'm relieved to not do much in the way of planning shit. I'll have my little sister's wedding soon enough. That's if the idiot who knocked her up doesn't turn out to be a spy. I might come with my own family baggage." Anthony informs me.

"We all come with something. I'll be happy to help you with whatever you need concerning the idiot who was stupid enough to knock up your little sister. I know you are quiet and reserved, but that just means you are a dark fucker." I reply, finishing off my drink

"I am a dark fucker, just like you are an asshole. I have a feeling you have your own dark side. Mafia blood runs thick in both our veins. We are automatically fucked up." Anthony skillfully adds.

"I think we are going to get along just fine, Anthony." I darkly chuckle.

"I agree, Nico. I'm looking forward to getting to know you. Now, we should figure out where we are going to live, but we can talk that over with Violetta." Anthony replies, taking another sip of his drink.

"Okay, seriously what twilight zone, freaky friday shit have I walked into. You two are actually getting along, agreeing with one another, and I don't even need to be in the room?" Violetta bursts into the study in black silk nightgown.

Anthony and I both chuckle at Violetta as she plops herself between the two of us. "Shouldn't you be asleep?" Anthony questions.

"One, I'm not a child, and two, I work the night shift thanks to asshole number one here." Violetta nudges me playfully. "So, while I'm tired, my body thinks it should be awake."

"You had to be difficult about breaking free and doing your own thing, I had to punish you somehow." I answer casually.

"Yeah, well, you aren't the only man in my life now." Violetta states as she smugly crosses her arms against her chest.

"Oh no, Little Violet, I agree with Nico. You forget I watched you from afar for years. You were definitely being difficult." Anthony agrees.

"You stalked her?" I question, unsure of how I feel about that.

"Yes, and you would have done the same fucking thing if you were me, so don't try to come at me for it." Anthony skillfully counters.

"True." I concur, knowing he's right. I like that he isn't afraid to call me out on things. That's a good thing because I know I'll do the same with him.

"You two are not supposed to gang up on me." Violetta playfully whines. "Now, which one of you is either going to give me your drink or make me my own." She demands, eyeing my drink.

"Is she always so bossy?" Anthony questions.

"Yes, because she likes to think she is in control. However, I think you and I can fix that attitude of hers or at least try." I comment.

"I see. Then yes, we are going to have a lot of fun taming her." Anthony agrees as he polishes off his drink.

"Ugh, can you two not talk like I'm not in the room with you? I'm literally in the middle of you two." Violetta complains in her playfully bratty way that has me wanting to paint that ass of hers all sorts of pretty shades of red.

"You know we are going to do it now because we know it annoys you, right?" Anthony points out.

I snicker. "Anthony is right, you made an error in letting us know how much it bothers you. You should get some sleep, though, because you have a big day of wedding plans." I inform Violetta.

"Like what exactly?" Violetta questions, eyeing me skeptically.

"Dress shopping with my cousin Erica. I know you aren't her biggest fan because of how she acted under the influence of drugs. However, she's a lot different now that she is sober. I thought she was making shit up when she said it was the drugs making her a bitch. Turns out it was really drugs alternating her personality. Anyway, after that, you and I can go pick up your engagement ring. I don't have a wedding band picked out, so maybe Anthony can pick you out one. I know we will be legally married, but Anthony will be just as much your husband as I am." I inform her. I look over at Anthony who nods his head with appreciation. Who would've thought my ass could be so accommodating. Truth is, having Anthony around feels right and natural like it was always meant to be. It's almost strange how natural it feels, but it's a thing so I won't dwell too hard on it. Sometimes it's best just to take the win.

"I'd like that if that's okay with you, Little Violet. Oh, and maybe you can let my little sister, Sofia, tag along for the wedding stuff. She needs a good female role model or two." Anthony asks as he lovingly takes her one hand in his and kisses it.

"I like that idea. I also want to pick out bands for you two. I'm also thinking we need a tattoo. I might be a mafia princess, but I'm a badass too. I also like the idea of Sofia tagging along with Erica and I. I always wanted a little sister." Violetta agrees as she lays out her own, fair demands.

"Aw, she's cute thinking we don't already have tattoos." I comment, and Anthony chuckles. I have ink on my back, mostly fantasy inspired shit like dragons, warriors, and swords. I'm sure Anthony has ink somewhere himself. It's kind of a standard thing for mafia and outlaw bikers to have tattoos. I guess the movies do sometimes get things right.

THE MAFIA LOVE CODE

Watching Anthony with Violetta, I realize he's a romantic, and that's good because I suck at being romantic. Sure, I know what Violetta likes and dislikes, but I don't know how to make shit romantic. About the closest thing I get to romance is making sure that Violetta has her nonna's engagement ring. It was the one thing Violetta always said she wanted the man who was going to marry her to use as her engagement ring. When her nonna passed she left the ring to me to ensure it would end up on Violetta's finger and not pawned by Mario. Violetta asked about the ring, but I simply told her I didn't know where it was. It was always meant to be a surprise. Obviously, Mario was clueless as he was not in charge of the will, a lawyer was. However, that's it. I can buy Violetta just about anything her heart desires, but wooing her in a romantic way outside of sex is not something I'm good at. It does seem that Anthony is a romantic, and that is a huge relief. With Anthony and I sharing Violetta, we balance each other out. My weaknesses are his strengths and vice versa. That's a good thing because I have a feeling it's going to take both of us to handle the lively personality that is Violetta Amelia Calla.

Chapter 14

Violetta

As I stand in the mirror looking at myself in the most gorgeous gown I think I've ever worn, I'm not hating the idea of tying the knot. The ivory dress is a princess style gown, with a sweetheart neckline. Lace makes up the bodice while the skirt is made from tulle and lace. There's a gorgeous matching lace trim vale. The freight train of reality has struck me hard. I'm getting married to Nico, but I will belong to both him and Anthony. Equally their wife and queen at the same time. That thought excites and terrifies me at the same time. It's also not something I thought they would never agree to. I'm also grateful that they are not forcing me to stay a pawn and are instead making me their queen.

The fancy wedding boutique is something I would never personally pick, but I don't have a say with the shop. The dress has to come from this boutique because that's where all the ladies of the Italian mafia go. Probably because they launder money for us. Still, standing in the lavish boutique surrounded by dresses that don't cost under ten grand makes me a bit uncomfortable. I don't even want to know how much the dress cost. They don't put price tags on the dresses, but it's not hard to estimate that the dress I have on is easily twenty grand. I hate spending money like this on something I'm going to wear once and only for a handful of hours.

That's okay, after the wedding I will donate it to an organization that turns wedding dresses into a dress for parents to bury a child who died before their time in. It's cancer patients, gunshot victims, car accidents, and so on. It doesn't matter how the child died, but that they died before their time. Not to mention most families can't afford anything to do with burials. The free dress provides something for the grieving families. One less task for them to worry over. I believe the program also provides last pictures in the dress, a donation to the families choice of organization, and some other comforting and practical things that I'm all for. I learned about the program from a fellow nursing student who was recently married and wanted to do something good with her wedding dress. It's a beautiful idea, and while I hate dropping twenty grand on a dress, at least I know in the end it might ease some families in their grief.

"Damn girl, you are a fucking gorgeous bride." Erica comments, drawing me from my thoughts.

"You do look lovely! I can't wait until I get married." Sofia comments.

"Thank you. I feel like a princess. Um, sweetie, didn't you already kind of skip some steps?" I say gently. I was not expecting Anthony's eighteen year old sister to be knocked up and out of wedlock which, despite the modern times, does not go over well in a world where old school values reign supreme.

"I know, and Anthony won't let me get married to my Irish man until he is positive he isn't some spy. I get why he's protective, but it's annoying." Sofia pouts in her seat before popping one of the fancy French Macaroons in her mouth. The boutique offers champagne, cucumber water, and a variety of sweet treats to entertain customers while shopping and trying on dresses.

"Speaking of princess, Nico said you better have a tiara on." Erica informs me as she makes her way to my side with a couple of tiara options.

"Seriously, for what?" I question, gazing at the gorgeous diamond tiaras that I'm sure will cost one hell of a pretty penny.

"Girl, I don't know I'm just doing what the man says, okay? I love Nico, but he can be scary." Erica replies, shoving the tiaras more in my face as if I can't see them from where she is holding them.

"Since when do you fear Nico?" I question, raising an eyebrow at her as I look down at her from the pedestal I'm on while the tailor notes all the adjustments that need to be made.

"Turns out druggy me had iron balls, but sober me is a little bitch." Erica informs me and I can't help but snort. She giggles with me and Sofia joins in as well, but she clearly is just laughing to laugh because we are. Sofia has her nose buried in her phone as she makes googly eyes at it. She must be texting her Irish boy toy. Fuck, Anthony must hate that. Even worse because Sofia is pregnant. "I know, it's pathetic, but I'm a better person without the drugs. So, you want me to go pick out some jewelry options while you settle on which tiara will please Mr. Demanding Pants?"

"Sure, and you know what? You have better fashion sense than me so why don't you pick all my accessories out including the tiara. I trust you. " I offer.

"Oh, you won't regret it!" Erica squeals as she bounces off to where the accessories are.

I guess Erica has changed. A lot has changed since I left and came back. The life I thought I was going to live is totally different. I'm not talking about nursing career stuff. I'm talking about the fact that two men will own me, and I hate that I love the idea of it. Last night in the club was so erotic, and I want more. I want every damn sinful thing those devils are going to do to me. Those two Italian stallions better be ready for this stubborn Italian mare that will not make their taming task easy.

After the boutique we have some time before I have to meet with Nico, so Erica takes me shopping for some wedding night attire while Sofia searches for some maternity clothes to accommodate her growing belly. She's almost out of her first trimester. I can't even think about having a baby right now. I'm not opposed to it, but right now I need to focus on getting married and uniting the Italian family factions. It might be my first time lingerie shopping, and for some reason I hate to admit this. I do actually enjoy shopping for sexy stuff to tempt my two sexy Italian men with. I know I'm probably buying more than I will use in one night. Then again, I have no idea how long those two wicked men plan on keeping me at their mercy after the wedding. I have to avoid getting too turned on while I shop because this isn't just lingerie, they sell toys and other things for sexy fun. I've heard of these places, but I've never been in one before. I know, I sound lame, but the sex shop wasn't on the nursing school shopping list. Although, maybe it should have been.

Walking around the shop brings back memories of last night. Their hands on me, their lips equally intoxicating, and that fucking orgasm makes my pussy tingle just thinking about it. Maybe I should have paid a little attention to sex and things relating to it. I guess I never saw the point of talking about it with my friends or when the girls I was hanging out with would bring sex up. I knew that I couldn't have one night stands or even a relationship without risking the guy's life being threatened. Shit, if it wasn't Nico that would have killed the poor sap, it would have been Anthony who I didn't even know was fucking watching me from afar. It was easy to explain to my friends and co-workers that I was focused on my career and didn't want to date. In the underworld it didn't matter why I didn't have sex because I'm property. In the underworld sexism and racism is child's play. Women don't rule in the underworld, not on their own that is. Women in the underworld need a man to back them. In my case I have two, so that's its own power I suppose.

THE MAFIA LOVE CODE

 I haven't thought much about what my position means in the underworld. With Nico and Anthony at my side combined with the Italian faction of the underworld unified, we will be a force to reckon with. I have no doubt that both Nico and Anthony have set the proper wheels in motion. They have always been ten steps ahead of me. If I'm being honest with myself, I'm intimidated by the two of them. Not just with sex because they clearly have a fucking clue of what they are doing. Then there is also the fact that they have the advantage of having knowledge of the underworld. They know the underworld like the back of their hands. They have men loyal to them and who will die for them. They have connections, allies, and spies. I have nothing. A nursing degree.

 In the real, legal world my nursing degree means something. It's respect, a badge of honor, a way to do good in a cruel world. My nursing degree makes me a respectable person in society. That's great if that is the life I was going to live. The life away from the mafia that I have dreamed about for longer than I care to admit. I wanted to build a life that was mine. A life I controlled. Turns out I was the foolish one. I spent my time building my ideal life away from the mafia that I turned a blind eye to the fact that I was not truly free. I chose to live in naivety because I didn't want to admit my freedom was temporary. Even from afar Nico controlled my life, and in some way Anthony has had his own control over me as well. Anthony has stalked me, studied me, and he's ready to stake his own claim. Along with Nico who has been waiting for what I'm sure feels like forever to him for me. While I'm not hating being claimed by them I do wish I felt more confident in immersing myself back into the underworld.

I hate feeling like I've wasted my time with my nursing degree. I wanted so badly to do good with it. I liked my job at the hospital. I enjoyed helping people. The thrill of some of the things that would come through the ER doors would create an adrenaline rush I never knew existed. It was about saving lives. Now, back in the reality of the underworld. I'm helpless on my own. I need Nico and Anthony. I don't just need their power and influence, but most of all I need their protection. My father has many enemies. The fact that none of them have touched me since I lived on my own means that Nico and Anthony made sure it was that way. There's also the potential that my father promised me to other leaders of the underworld. They will not be as accommodating as Nico and Anthony that much I know. I've met members from the other factions. Sure, they weren't leaders, they were lower in ranks. Still, they were not friendly to me. I remember one of them tried to grope me. I'm way better off with the two devils I know.

Perhaps I made a mistake in my foolish pursuit of a normal life. Maybe I should have spent time learning the underworld better, forging my own connections, and having my own allies. Now, I've put myself in a position where I have no choice but to depend on Nico and Anthony for everything. I set myself up to be the one thing

THE MAFIA LOVE CODE

I didn't want to be and that's a fucking mafia wife. It was my fate. I should have accepted it instead of running from it. I guess it's time to accept the fact that I'm destined to be a mafia wife. Now, I just have to find a way to use that to my advantage.

By the time I make it to the jewelers I'm over the day. I'm tired of thinking. I'm also trying to resist the urge to run. Where would I run to? I have no clue. I wouldn't have money to run unless I stole it. Stealing from the mafia is not a smart move. What money I made as a nurse is certainly not going to cover the cost of what I would need to run and hide my tracks. While running is definitely an appealing thought, it's not a wise one. I would never be free and always looking over my shoulder for one reason or another. I have no way out of my fate. I can't fight it anymore. If you can't beat them, join them.

"There you are, Little Dove." Nico's silky voice reaches my ears, breaking my crazy train thought process as he beams one of his suave smiles at me.

I hate how sincere he and Anthony are being. It should make it easier, yet somehow it makes it harder that they are so accommodating. They will give me a place at their side to rule the Italian mafia faction together. I am happy about that. I have no doubt that I will have a good life with them. However, it's just that I want my dreams to matter too. I know I can't have a normal life, and I was probably foolish to try. I can't deny how lonely I was pretending to live a normal life. I had friends, but it's hard to get close to people afraid that my toxic, deadly world might consume the innocence of the regular world. Maybe I do belong at Nico and Anthony's side after all. Yet the urge to run is strong, but I lock it down knowing that running will only make things worse.

"Little Dove, focus. I know it's been a long day, but I just need your attention a bit longer. Then I promise you can zone out and get lost in the madness of your mind." Nico states, snapping his fingers in my face.

"Sorry, I'm a little tired. Erica dragged Sofia and I all over, and she's somehow more intense sober." I reply, trying to not let my irritation show because despite me being cranky from trying to adjust my sleep schedule and my maddening thoughts, I did enjoy my time with Erica and Sofia.

Nico snickers. "Yeah, who would have thought getting sober would cause such a major personality shift. Sometimes I'm not sure I buy it, but until I'm proven wrong I'm just going to assume she's sober."

"I don't think it's entirely Erica's fault. I haven't had a girls' day or night out in a while. Working the night shift made it a little hard to have a social life." I slightly lie. "I think I need to get used to being around people again. Plus, I'm adjusting my sleep schedule from night shift to day shift. So, I think I'm simply spent."

"Maybe I punished you too severely with the nightshift. I didn't mean for you to not have a social life." Nico's thumb strokes my cheek in a caring way.

"I missed you." I confess, letting the comfort of his touch soothe me.

THE MAFIA LOVE CODE

"I know and I missed you too, Little Dove." Nico kisses me sweetly on the lips. "Now, I want to show you the ring I picked out for you." he says, breaking our kiss.

I nod my head unsure of what to expect. Nico nods his head to the jeweler who pulls a small black square box from behind the counter and hands it to Nico. Nico takes the black box and opens it before dumping the ring into the palm of his hand. I barely have a moment to blink before Nico is slipping the oh so familiar ring on my finger. The gorgeous ivory pearl set in cushion of diamonds with a rose gold band. I stare at the ring in disbelief.

"My Nonna's ring. How?" I question, forcing my eyes from the ring to Nico's face. I thought the ring was lost or pawned off by my dad.

"Your Nonna left it to me to ensure it ended up on your finger. She knew how much you loved her engagement ring and wanted it to be yours one day. She knew I would make sure it happened. I believe in some way she knew I'd be the man to put on your finger." Nico informs me.

A smile forms on my face. I'm touched by Nico holding onto this for me. My Nonna trusted Nico with something that meant a lot to her. Something she knew I would need. "She did always love you and made her comments that I should marry you. Thank you for keeping it safe." I say before kissing him on the lips.

"Of course, Little Dove. Now, would you like to see what Anthony has picked out for us?" Nico questions, breaking our kiss once more. Damn, I really want to keep his lips on mine yet his words have me curious.

"He picked something out for all of us?" I question as Nico signals the jeweler once more who quickly moves to fulfill Nico's silent request.

"He did. It's actually very thoughtful of him. I hate to admit it, but I like him. I want to hate him, but I can't help but like the bastard." Nico comments as the jeweler walks over with black velvet tray containing three rings.

I pick up the thinner rose gold band. It's simple but it's the engraving on the inside that catches my attention The Italian Trinity NVA. Then I pick up the two matching titanium bands with a carbon fiber strip. They too have the same engraving.

"Anthony, is thoughtful. He might make us both look bad. Although, I think this could inspire our tattoos." I joke, making Nico chuckle deeply.

"I think he might make me look worse than you." Nico jokes back and we both laugh. Maybe it won't be so bad being the wife of two sexy Dons. They sure do set my body a light with desire in ways I've never experienced. It's addicting to say the least and I have to find the silver linings if I'm going to accept my fate as a mafia wifey.

Nico and I finish up at the jewelry store. I'm relieved when Nico sends me home to the condo because my social battery is low and I'm drained from a day of activity. Good activity too. I thought I would dread today, but despite my crazy thoughts trying to bring me down, I enjoyed being social again without worry of my past creeping up on me. One thing being back in the underworld is that I don't have to have the anxiety of when it will creep back into my life. At least being back in the underworld has some perks. Perks I might have missed if I'm honest. Still, I have to be proud that I did do something for myself with getting my nursing degree even if I'm unsure about what my nursing career's future is at the moment. I did something for me and there isn't anything wrong with that. However, I do feel like I have to pivot with my plans and that is frustrating.

One pivot I'm okay with is the fact that Antony, Nico, and I have entered into a poly relationship that none of us saw coming. Sure, I fantasized about it, but I thought it would stay a fantasy. While the fantasy coming to life is overwhelming in some ways, it's still an amazing thing that I'm looking forward to exploring. We still have some details to decide like on where we are going to live and how kids will work. Sometimes I can't believe the three of us are actually doing this. It's insanity, yet it's completely logical at the same time. It's also something we all want and desire making things that much crazier to believe this is all real. Part of me is afraid I will wake up and find this all to be a blissful dream, but deep down in my heart and soul I know this is real, and for the first time I'm excited for the future to come.

Chapter 15

Anthony

It's been a couple of weeks since Nico, Violetta, and I have all agreed to be a united force to reckon with. It seems insane to think the three of us are going to do this let alone make it truly work. In the normal world what we are doing, being in this poly type relationship, would probably be frowned on by most people. However, this is the illegal underworld and there aren't many rules if any at all. There's an advantage to being in the underworld, one that I don't think VIoletta fully appreciates yet.

Speaking of Violetta, both Nico and I are a bit concerned about her. She's adjusted back to a regular sleep schedule, but without her job she doesn't have much to entertain her. It's clear she misses her job because of her clear new obsession with medical dramas. I might not know Violetta well, yet, but I know that isn't really her. She's not one for TV unless it's reality. Even the books she reads are non fiction. It's almost as if she can't stand the fact that she lives in a world that people write about, make films of, and even documentaries of. Regular people are interested in the underworld. They want to study us from afar and create their own versions of how we live our lives. Violetta is the opposite. She's interested in normal and normal is not something she will get in the underworld. However, Nico and I are going to help her realize the potential the underworld has.

On top of Violetta acting a bit odd, I have my sister to worry about too. She's blinded by love for this boy, but I don't trust him. I do hate that I have to be skeptical of the boy she is interested in, but she is unfortunately an easy target that could be used against me. So, I have her living with me at my town home. Nico, Violetta, and I need to figure out an official living situation. Then there is the fact we have to consider that I might have to have my sister live with us to make sure she is safe because I still do not know the Irish boy's motives. Sofia thinks I'm paranoid, but she doesn't realize I'm that way for a reason. I want her to be safe, and I'm not thrilled she is pregnant at eighteen and unmarried. I promised her I wouldn't control her life and I would allow her to have her own choices, but I worry she doesn't have the right female guidance in her life. I hope that can change with Violetta being in Sofia's life.

I push thoughts of my sister aside for the moment and focus on my current task. Nico has invited me to some clinic that hasn't even opened up. I look at the name on the door that reads Angel Clinic. I'm intrigued in what Nico is scheming. Nico is a good businessman. His understanding of financial investments is impressive. The three of us each bring a strength to our trinity. The Italian trinity that is going to make sure we solidify our place in the underworld.

Entering the clinic the waiting room is a decent size filled with chairs, two Tv's hang on opposite sides of the room. To the left it's more set up for kids with toys and games to entertain them. On the right is set up for adults and teens with magazines, books, and other things that would perk an adult's interest. The check in window is a standard doctor's office set up. Nico comes out from the door that I assume patients will either enter or exit from.

"Welcome to the Angel Clinic." Nico says as he greets me.

"What exactly is this? I mean I can gather where you are going with this in regards to Violetta, but other than that I'm not sure where you are going with this." I confess as I follow him through the door he exited out of.

We walk down the hallway which breaks off into a couple other hallways. Reading the signs I see the hallway to the right is for lab patients. The hallway to the left is patient rooms. We head straight past a nursing station and a doctor's personal office. There's a small break room at the end of the hallway that we enter. There's a door that clearly leads to a little outside area that from the brief glimpse looks like there is some patio furniture for staff to use. The break room itself is fairly standard with a long foldable table that has foldable chairs around it. There's a little kitchenette with a fridge, sink, microwave, coffee machine, toaster, and cabinets that I imagine are stocked with utensils, plates, and other things along those lines.

What does grab my attention is the door on the right side that has Authorized Personnel only.

"As you can see this is a medical clinic. I'm going to open it as a nonprofit so we can help those who can't afford medical bills. Free visits and medicine. Just because we are in the underworld doesn't mean we can't do some good for the regular community we use to hide behind." Nico explains as I keep my focus on the one door that sticks out. Well, it sticks out to me. To a regular person they would simply assume there were chemicals, oxygen, or something like that would need to be kept locked up for the safety of others. However, I'm not a regular person and I know that the door conceals something illegal.

"That's lovely and all, but what I care about is what is behind that door." I point to the door that has been holding my attention since we entered the breakroom.

Nico forms a smug grin. "I knew you were smart. Come on, to the real business." Nico says as he puts in a passcode to the keypad on the door. I should have noticed the keypad, but I'm honestly trying to take in whatever crazy shit Nico has going on.

I follow Nico through the door. The door leads to a square hallway that has an elevator. We get in the elevator and go down one floor that leads to a hallway with double doors that mimic a hospital. Following Nico through the double doors I find myself in an entirely different clinic from the one upstairs.

"Welcome to the Angel of Death Clinic where we help you find death on your terms." Nico smugly says the slogan like he's brilliant. I mean he is, but I'm used to being the only smug one. However, we are two cocky men and a stubborn woman, we don't bow too easily. That might just make us unstoppable.

I let his words process in my brain as I look around the clinic. There's a check in desk, a nursing station, and from what I can tell further into the clinic private rooms. I'm sure there's more that I don't see because we are only in the front part of the underground clinic. Nico is setting up a clinic for terminally ill patients to commit suicide, or as they see it, going out on their terms. It's totally illegal in the States. Some countries have it legal, but it crosses a lot of moral lines so it's not something I see becoming legal in the States. That means we would be a top choice because then patients don't have to leave the country. People will come from all over the States and maybe even North America. Even better it's something that doesn't involve drugs, sex, guns, and what all our enemies are always fighting over.

"You're dangerously brilliant, Nico. You plan to let our enemies fight over the typical underground ways of making money like guns and drugs. Meanwhile, we have a fucking cash cow that I'm assuming feeds the free clinic upstairs." Shit, I'm impressed. I did not know Nico was this clever.

"You have the general gist. This clinic helps everyone of any class. There are levels for different patients. Just because they are poor doesn't mean they don't deserve the right to end something horrible on their terms. Everything is carefully monitored and screened. Non disclosure agreements, a lawyer, and other important shit. I have several funeral homes around the city willing to help with cremation and prepping the bodies for proper ground burials for the clients that want it. I have five doctors on board. Doctors over the way medicine is run in this country and want to take matters into their own hands. Two of the doctors are willing to do house visits for those that want to die at home. They have all been screened and verified. Everyone involved knows if they speak a word of this to anyone outside of the trusted circle they are dead. I've been building this for the last three years or so when it became apparent that Violetta was going to stick with nursing. I wanted something for her in this life so that she didn't have to give up something she loved." Nico informs me.

"Okay, you are a lot more thoughtful and caring toward Violetta than I originally thought. I guess I wanted you to be this horrible man so that I would look better to her. It was bad enough you already had a friendship with her. I wanted a reason for her to hate you." I confess.

Nico shrugs his shoulders at my words. I'm glad I don't have to worry about him flying off the handle at my words. Looks like Hot Head Nic has learned to be level headed. I guess stubborn Italian Stallons can learn new tricks. I've always been able to control my anger, it was never a struggle for me. My struggle was with my enjoyment at hurting others. It's not normal for someone to enjoy inflicting pain on others in the worst ways possible.

Power is dangerous and somehow killing allows me that power without letting the power of Don go to my head. In my twisted mind it makes sense.

"That's completely fair. I would feel the same way if our roles were reversed. Hell, I would be lying if I said I wanted you to be a bad person so that Violetta wouldn't want to run to you to escape whatever fate she thinks I have waiting for her. It's hard for her to not associate male dominance in a negative way thanks to her father. We both know Mario was an idiot to say the least." Nico pauses, gathering his thoughts. "Yes, I do care very deeply for Violetta. I love her, but I know I can't give her everything she deserves. I'm not romantic like you are," he pauses. I go to remind of the engagement ring, but as if reading my train of thought, he raises his hand to stop me. "Before you give me credit with her nonna's engagement, her nonna left it to me to make sure it ended up on Violetta's finger. She essentially is responsible for the whole gesture. Her nonna was fond of me, and I think, on some level, wanted Violetta and I to end up together. Mario's own mother didn't trust him." Nico confesses. "I'm good with sex, and I might know a lot of what Violetta enjoys yet I have no clue what to do with it. We both bring something different to the table for our woman." Nico reasons. The way he casually mentions Violetta as ours feels so right. Right in ways I'm not sure I'm ready to face.

"Does this ever seem insane that the three of us have somehow come together and formed our own relationship through an alliance?" I question, knowing I can't be the only one who thinks this is insane.

"It defies logic, but I think that's why it works because the three of us want to make a name for ourselves. The best way to do that and make sure the Italian mafia stays on top is to form one hell of an unconventional alliance. It's self preservation, yet it's more than that." Nico suggests.

"Stranger things have happened I suppose. Now, I want to know how you think Violetta is going to go for this whole angel of death thing?" I point my finger and circle it around gesturing toward the clinic we are standing in.

"She is going to be in charge of this whole operation. She can see patients in the clinic upstairs. She doesn't have to interact with the patients down here if she doesn't wish to. There is plenty of paperwork and scheduling she can hide behind if she wants. I will work with her when it comes to this clinic, but the important thing is I want her to have something so she can still see patients because we both know that's the part she cares about. So even if she works mostly upstairs, she will still be in charge of what goes on down here. I don't want her to feel like her only purpose is to be a perfect obedient mafia wife her father only believed she could be." Nico explains.

"I was going to offer her something similar before we joined forces. Although, I will say that mine was certainly not as well thought out. Then again, you know her better than I do. You know what she needs to help make this transition easier for her. I am glad we are on the same side, Nico. We can do better than our generations before us." I concur.

    The two of us spend some time talking and even end up grabbing a bite to eat. The three of us are keeping our relationship secret, but we aren't afraid to be seen together. Our enemies need to see we aren't at war. Let them draw their own suspicions and then after Nico and Violetta are married in just under two weeks we will announce our unified relationship. The three of us are basically living in Nico's condo when I'm not at my townhome with Sofia. We are shopping for a home that feels right for all of us or we might end up buying land and building. We are weighing our options and figuring out what will work best for us and what we want for our future like kids. We are definitely going to have children. Violetta knows she wants to have at least two children, which means at least one for me and one for Nico. After that, it's up to her if she wants to have more or not. We agree to raise the kids together as well. Everything is slowly falling into place even if Violetta is a little stubborn, but I have a feeling she will adapt as she accepts the world around her. I'm glad the three of us are unified, and I'm pleased to find that Nico has thought of something for Violetta. This is all the honeymoon phase, though, because there is no doubt a power war that is about to be waged in the underworld. I hope the Italian trinity can weather the storms that are ahead.

Chapter 16

Violetta

The wedding is soon, and I'm oddly looking forward to it. I can't believe I'm looking forward to marrying Nico and Anthony. Well, Anthony I won't be legally married, but that's just semantics. Those two possessive men will be all mine just as much as I will be theirs. As much as I'm looking forward to my life with Nico and Anthony, I still wish I had some purpose other than being their wife. I know kids are in our future, and while I want that, it's not all I want. I'm allowed to want a life outside of being a mom and wife. Nico and even Anthony have to know it's important for me to have more. Maybe when the time is right I'll ask them about going back to work as a nurse, or something along those lines. I hate to think I wasted all those years getting a nursing degree for it to end up collecting dust. There's also the option to take the time to go back to school and further my degree. I have some options I need to consider before I bring anything up to the guys.

However, I have to admit there are perks to the mafia life. Call me a pampered mafia princess but I can't deny it's nice living with an indispensable wallet. Part of the reason I wanted so desperately to live frugally while on my own is because it was a suggestion from my Nonna. She was a hard working woman and she made sure she taught me how to cook, sew, and that helping others is the best thing a human can do. Maybe it's why I went into nursing in the first place because I knew it was a great way to help people. Plus, I've always been good with science, math, and bodily fluids never bothered me. I'm solid in the profession I chose for myself, which is why I would hate to watch it fall to the wayside.

    I push my troubled thoughts away and focus on the fact that Nico and Anthony are taking me back to the burlesque club and I know we will end up back in the brothel part. While I enjoyed our fun last time, I'm embarrassed to admit that I'm not on that level yet. I want to be because I enjoyed it, but with very little experience to guide me, I feel prepared. In the moment it was hot, but afterwards I felt overwhelmed. I don't have experience like Anthony and Nico making them incredibly intimidating. I've debated about watching porn or trying to look stuff up on the internet but somehow I feel like it won't be enough.

    Anxiety eats at me as Nico's black town car drops us off. We enter the burlesque club, which is packed with people. I know we have a VIP table spot so getting in and finding a seat won't be an issue. Another perk of mafia life is access everywhere and anywhere. I can't believe I'm counting being in the mafia a perk, but maybe I should stop fighting my fate and find a way to make some good out of it. That thought will have to wait as Nico and Anthony lead me to the brothel instead of the VIP table in the burlesque club. My anxiety spikes as we go down the stairs leading to the lavish brothel.

"Relax, Little Dove." Nico whispers in my ear as he leans while he leads me through the brothel with Anthony on my other side.

"That's not helpful." I seeth back at him, causing Anthony to snicker.

"You weren't lying, she really is like a caged animal when she is on edge." Anthony comments.

"I do not like you two talking about me behind my back." I stop walking, and stomp my foot to make a point that I'm not moving. "I'm really over surprises when it comes to sex stuff. It's also not fair that you two have way more experience than I do. I hope keeping me a virgin was worth the break down I'm about to have trying to keep with you two. I have no damn clue what I'm doing pleasuring a man and I have not one but two to keep happy in bed." I snap at them as my nostrils flare.

What really grates me is the snickers I get from Anthony and Nico. "You are worried about the wrong thing, Little Violet. We are already ahead of you." Anthony counters before he tosses me over his shoulders and starts walking.

"Are you serious, Anthony!" I smack him on his back, his muscular back for being ridiculous for tossing me over his shoulders like a sack of potatoes. It's not fair that they both have the bodies of gods.

"Oh, Little Dove, we have a lot of work to tame that pretty ass of yours." Nico says as he walks to the side of Anthony. What I don't expect is the smack across my ass from Nico that causes me to yelp, making both men chuckle.

I can't really tell where they are taking me because my current view is of the black marble floor. Seriously, black marble in a brothel? They take being upscale to a new level. The next thing I know I'm being tossed on bed with dark red silk sheets. I push the hair out of my face and try to gather my bearings. My view is currently of the two handsome mafia men who look amused at my current state. I glare at them.

"Little Dove, I'm well aware you might feel a little out of control because you are a virgin with no experience. Yes, keeping you a virgin is worth it because you have always belonged to me and now you also belong to Anthony. I kept you a virgin because I wanted to train you myself, and now I get to share that training with Anthony. We both picked up on your panic after last time. You were fine in the moment but when you crashed back down to reality you freaked out because it was overwhelming." Nico explains.

"In hindsight we probably should have had our first time playing with you in private, but we are men and we don't always think clearly when it comes to you, LIttle Violet. We are eager to have you and play with you, so forgive us for rushing. Nico talked with Madem Connie and she suggested we have someone essentially prep you for what we are expecting of you. So Madam Connie has decided that Dedra or her stage name Bubblegum, will be a good advisor of what to expect. Nico and I have some particular tastes that Dedra can help you with." Anthony continues to explain.

"I don't even know what to say." I confess. "What tastes are you talking about?"

"Complete submission, a non-consent sexual relationship with both of us, bondage, wax play, and discipline when you want to be a stubborn Italian woman." Anthony answers, and I have no idea how to take any of that.

"I can't pretend that none of that peaks my interest, but do I get any say in what I want with sex?"

"Of course, Little Dove, we aren't total monsters. We also are willing to take things off the table if it truly makes you uncomfortable. We aren't going to force you to do anything you aren't comfortable with. Dedra is going to go over everything with you as well as help you explore what you might be interested in. We want this to be a good experience for all of us." Nico explains.

"You know it's really hard to be mad at you two when you're reasonable, which is somehow even more irritating. However, I'm fucking relieved that I don't have to watch hours of porn to try and figure out how to please you two." I comment, causing both of them to laugh.

"Oh, Little Violet, tainting your innocence is going to be so much fun." Anthony comments.

"It's going to be more than fun, it's going to be satisfying too." Nico adds. "Now, we are going to leave you for a bit and attend to some mafia business upstairs. Before you ask, it's something for you. A surprise that I promise you will love and adore. I'm asking you to trust us."

"Despite my better judgment, I do trust you both." I confess, letting my guard down. Being vulnerable around them is becoming easier as this relationship moves forward morphing into its own unique thing.

"Good. Behave, Little Dove." Nico warns as he and Anthony leave.

As Anthony and Nico leave, a woman with golden curly blonde hair to her shoulders in a sexy bubblegum pink lace one piece suit with black fishnet stockings and black heels strides into the room. Confidence and sex ooze from her like the glitter that dusts her skin. She's got a nice pair of perky breasts, and I'm not sure if they're real or fake. Her makeup is a bit dramatic for my taste, but she is sex worker so it suits her and adds to her sex appeal.

"Are you my unicorn?" The woman asks, shutting the door behind her.

"Unicorn?" I question in confusion.

A smile comes across her pink painted lips that match her body suit. "Oh, you are definitely my unicorn. A virgin slowly approaching her early twenties, honey, that's what makes you a unicorn. It's rare to find someone like you so perfectly preserved, but then again I shouldn't be surprised as you are the desire of not one, but two powerful and influential men. Now, Nico and Anthony have told me what their desires are, but I want to know what you desire in your sexual relationship with them?"

"I don't know. I never really thought about it." I confess.

I was always too busy trying to fight against the grain, against my status in the mafia as a pawn, and determined to make my life away from the underworld. I never once put a thought into my life as a mafia wife to Nico, and now Anthony. I certainly didn't give thought about sex. Fantasies, sure, but I also never thought the two powerful men who are supposed to be enemies would actually form an alliance and bring my fantasy of being shared by both of them a reality.

"Oh, sweetie, we have more work than I thought, but that's okay. I've worked with a lot less before. I'm a sexual consultant. My job is to help women embrace their sexuality and discover their inner goddess. I help the women in the burlesque club and brothel find their confidence with their sexuality. So, you are in good hands. I will help you get ready for your wedding night and to help you afterwards because the wedding is only ten days away. It's not as much time as I prefer, but we will make it work. Tonight is all about figuring out what you might like, and to get you to feel comfortable. I can tell you are a natural submissive, but you won't be easily tamed by your Italian stallions. Good because they will enjoy the challenge when your brat side acts up." Dedra explains.

"This is such a relief. I've been so anxious about sex with them." I confess, feeling the weight of my anxiety lift. I felt pathetic with my panic about sex. I was half dreading the wedding night yet looking forward to it at the same time.

"Honey, you are in good hands with me." Dedra states with a confident smile.

As much as I want to fight the underworld life, I can't deny that it is sucking me back in ways I never expected. I don't know how I feel about it either. Part of me is thrilled for it because the life I thought was planned out for me in the underworld as a mafia wife is turning out to be different than my assumptions. The guys are going as far as to basically get me sex lessons, and are doing what they can to make me feel comfortable. It's really hard to hate them and resist their plans when they are being reasonable, accommodating, and caring. Maybe things won't be so bad. I assumed my father's vision was also Nico's. While I wasn't sure about Anthony I had assumed he would have a similar vision. However, they are proving they are not my father. Perhaps my trust in them isn't misplaced afterall.

Chapter 17

Nico

While Violetta is getting her sex lessons from Dedra, Anthony and I are off to meet someone a little unexpected. I've conducted plenty of business in the burlesque with my dad, but never with him being the party I'm negotiating with. Anthony found what I needed to confirm suspicions that something wasn't right with my dad. His health has declined, and for good reason. The asshole has colon cancer. He's hiding his cancer treatments that aren't working. The doctors even told him not to bother with treatments because the chances of it working are slim. However, my father moved forward with the treatments in a desperate attempt to keep his pathetic ass alive.

"Before we go up against my father, are you positive of the information you have?" I question as we settle at the VIP booth that is basically mine because I always sit here, and the club never lets anyone else sit in the booth.

"I am," Anthony confidently states as a waitress immediately brings over glasses filled with wine along with the bottle on ice.

"Good. It's not that I don't trust you, Anthony, I just don't want to give my father a reason to poke holes in our alliance because he will. He will be furious with our union, but he's ill and we can give him what I know he craves most; a peaceful death." I know my father fears death, but even more he fears a painful death. I'm hoping I can use that to get him to see reason. I need everything lined up for me to take Don. Nothing can stand in my way. I'm set to marry Violetta, and I'll be damned if my father stops me from being Don because I'm aligning myself with Anthony.

"I'm positive. We have him, Nico. I have an extremely vested interest in making sure you are the Don of the DeLuca family. I wanted to make sure your father didn't find any reason to snub you of becoming Don in case he found out about our alliance. I don't trust your father. I'm a man who likes assurances." Anthony answers.

"You are right not to trust my father. I've been concerned he might try to pull on over me and some ensure he stays Don. He doesn't care that everyone is ready for new leadership. I'm sure your men like my men are tired of their friends and family coming home in body bags." I add.

"Exactly. So let's go nail your father to the early grave he is so desperately trying to avoid." Anthony adds as he pulls out to cigars

"It would be my absolute pleasure to do just that." I reply, taking one of the cigars Anthony is offering.

Anthony and I choosing to be united and forming an alliance has been an interesting, unexpected experience. Anthony is like the best friend and brother I wish I had growing up. I wanted a brother so badly. I hated being an only child, and it was the same for Viollette. She was the only damn good thing that came out of me being an only child because it bonded us. Jullian is my best friend, but there is still a boss and employer relationship between us. With Anthony we are equals so it's easier to talk to him about certain things. Anthony also understands the pressure of being Don. We can be each other's strength with our pillar of Violetta between us.

We enter the VIP area of the burlesque club. It doesn't take long for eyes to land on my father sipping a whiskey. His dark hair is now thin and white. His once youthful skin is wrinkled and he's far too pale. His dark blue suit is loose from the amount of weight he's lost. Anthony and I casually stride over to him and take our seats on either side of him.

"What is the enemy doing here?" My father spits.

"Anthony Ronka is not my enemy. Maybe yours, but certainly not mine. Now, I'm marrying Violetta Calla in ten days. Once I'm married, I become Don right then and there. My wedding ceremony is also to celebrate and announce me as Don of the DeLuca family." I demand.

My father gives a mocking laugh. "I won't give you Don if you have made friends with the enemy."

"I thought you might say that, but here's the thing: you're dying from colon cancer. All the money you are wasting on the treatment is only making you worse. You won't live another year, maybe not even six months. A painful death awaits you as the cancer destroys your body. If you die before handing me Don then someone could challenge me to be Don. Is that a risk you are truly willing to take especially when I can offer you the peaceful death you wish. A death that you have a say in." I defend.

"You have made nice with a man that is not to be trusted, Nico. Maybe I should let someone challenge you for Don because I'm not so sure you are the right choice. I let you get away with saving Violetta with the promise that you would make her a worthy investment. I'm not so sure that investment has paid off either. You do not have your priorities straight, Nico." My father poorly defends.

"Should I kill him like I did my father so I could become Don?" Anthony ponders out loud, puffing on his cigar with an eerie ease that sends a wave of chill up my spine making me glad he is my ally and not my enemy. "See, my father was much like you, Mr. DeLuca. Stubborn and set in the old ways. Tell me, do you even know why I am the enemy? What have I personally done to you to have earned the title of your enemy?" Anthony skillfully prompts.

"You are your father's son, and that is enough." My father spits back.

"Wow, you couldn't even give me an educated answer. I didn't realize you were a teenage girl with a petty view of the world." Anthony retorts with such suave and confidence it's hard not to be impressed as he slays my father with his intelligent insults.

"How dare you insult me! I am a Don, your elder by many years. You are disrespectful, and that is enough to hate you." My father attempts a comeback.

"Oh, I promise, Mr. DeLuca, this isn't me being disrespectful. Disrespectful would be chopping you to pieces until your body shuts down from the trauma and then dancing on your unmarked grave. I'll make your death so fucking painful you won't even know what the word disrespectful means. Now, for once in your pathetic life, do the right thing and make your son the Don of the DeLuca Family or you will not walk out of here alive. If you think Nico will stop me, think again." Anthony threatens, making me realize he is one dark fucker that I'm glad I choose to make an ally out of.

"I won't stop him. I'll fucking help him. I'll enjoy listening to you scream in agony because you have made my life fucking difficult for no damn good reason. Everything is a battle with you. Nothing pleases you, and you enjoy a power you don't fucking deserve. You have put obstacle after challenge in front of me to prove I'm worthy to be Don. No matter how many times I prove to you I'm ready, you hold on to your fucking position. I'm trying to be respectful and give a peaceful death we all know you don't deserve. So, do we have a deal?" I prompt.

"No. I will not give in to your foolishness. Anthony has corrupted you somehow. It doesn't matter if you marry Violetta or not, I will not give you Don."

"I do so love it when fools choose the hard way." Anthony comments with an evil grin.

"Let's see what damage you can do." I say to Anthony as I wave Lorenzo and Jullian over to us. Anthony, Lorezo, Jullian, and I are all working together to ensure I end up married to Violetta and Don of the DeLuca family. We are determined to make this alliance a permanent fixture in the underworld community. The Italian trinity is coming, and no one is going to stop us, especially not my dumbass father.

"Jullian, you would disgrace your family and betray your Don?" My father's questions appalled.

"You aren't my Don, Nico is. I follow his orders, and only his orders. I'm not the only one who feels this way. You will find very few allies among your own constituents. We want Nico. We want to stop having friends and family come home in body bags over a civil war that no one knows why they are even fighting anymore." Jullian boldly answers. I will always be thankful for his loyalty.

"Last chance, Dad. Will you give me Don?"

"Over my dead body!" My father declares slamming his fist on the table, which he instantly regrets as his I can hear his frail bones crack from the force. My father howls in pain.

"That can be arranged." I say as Jullian and Lorenzo haul my father out of the VIP area.

They will take him to the one of the safe torture places Anthony has. I knew my father was going to be a problem. His reaction proves he was never going to give me Don when I married Violetta. I'm going to fix that with Anthony's help. Now that my father is hauled off, we will deal with him later when Violetta is safe and home with trusted eyes on her.

Chapter 18

Violetta

Dedra is making things so much easier for me where sex is concerned. I've only met with her twice and both times we simply talked. It feels good to have someone validate my feelings about sex. I'm nervous. I know I shouldn't be, but I am. I'm intimidated by Nico and Anthony with a lot of things. It's not just with sex, it's life in the underworld. They have power, influence, and men to back them. I hate feeling powerless because that's exactly how my father made me feel. I appreciate that they are trying to be better than my father. Anthony and Nico aren't my dad, nor are they their fathers either. They are trying to do better, and I want to be at their side helping them do just that.

I'm going to my third session with Dedra. We meet late at night while Anthony and Nico are off conducting business that I'm positive I want nothing to know about. I will confess there are parts of this life I definitely don't want to know about. I like that they are giving me the option to pick and choose what I want to be a part of and have knowledge of. They are trying to create a place by their side. Two kings and their queen, so why does that thought terrify me? Why does the thought of being intimate with them overwhelm me so much? It can't just be because I'm a unicorn, as Dedra so endearingly refers to me as.

The first two sessions I discovered my anxiety is related to me giving control because control means acceptance of my role. The role I've spent a good portion of my life fighting against. However, I made assumptions, and I let my father get in my head when I shouldn't have. He was grooming me to be what benefited him. I've had my father's damn voice in the back of my head feeding me lies to not trust Nico. I didn't think my father still had a hold of my thoughts and emotions but it would appear he might. I need to let go of my father's voice in my head and listen to what my own voice is telling me. Nico and Anthony are a safe and good choice.

Dedra is slowly making me realize that a lot of my fears with sex and my role is something I have to let go and embrace. I don't know how to embrace it, which is part of my problem. I'm going to do everything I can to embrace my new life in the underworld because I do want both Nico and Anthony. Our time so far together is amazing. I know I'm lucky that my fantasy and desire to have them both is now an official reality that I haven't fully wrapped my head around it. I'm just glad the guys were smart enough to recruit Dedra to help. I confess I was skeptical, even if I felt relieved. In two sessions with Dedra, I feel a bit more confident, and all we've done is talk.

I'm sitting in the familiar room on black satin sheets on a circle shaped bed. Dedra struts into the room after the guys leave, her confidence comes off of her in waves just like her sweet, fruity perfume. "There's my unicorn!" She beams at me as she shuts the door.

"What are you going to call me when I'm no longer a virgin?" I question, raising an eyebrow. I still don't know if I find the nickname endearing or insulting. Maybe both.

"Oh, bringing the sass early tonight, I see." Dedra retorts.

"What can I say? It's a trait I learned watching my Italian Grandmother talk to men." I reply with a shrug.

Dedra giggles. "I would like her. She sounds dominant, so how did you become so submissive?" Dedranow raises a perfectly plucked brow at me.

"Eh, I admired my Nonna and her strength. She taught me so many things before she passed away. I don't think it's so much that she was dominant, but that she knew how to play dominant men. She was always a step ahead of my father and his schemes. She was observant as she would play the part the men around her expected her to play." I answer.

"Definitely a woman I would have liked. Men have power from birth because of the penis between their legs. They have what I call superficial power. Women have manipulative power for so many reasons, and it's how you choose to wield that power that is up to you. Your nonna used observation, I use sex, some use their bodies in other ways, voice, mind, words, submission, and so on. You, my unicorn, you are a combination because you have two roles. You are a wife, and in the role, your submission and body are key. However, you aren't just a wife. You are a mafia queen. You need to use your observation, mind, and words. Nico and Anthony are doing something rare. They are giving you a place at their side as their queen, and you better use that to your advantage as much as you can. You have the queen part handled because your nonna was clearly preparing you for that, even if you didn't know she was. I'm going to help with the wife part, specifically sex and getting over your fears. One downside to being so perfectly preserved as you are, Unicorn, is that you suffer from what I like to call the purity curse." Dedra explains. I swear she's got some hidden psychology degree because she is damn good at.

"Purity curse?" I question.

"Yes, purity curse. You are brainwashed to think that sex is bad, that way you aren't tempted by it. You probably didn't even know it was happening. Think about it. Think about what you were taught about sex that didn't come from your nursing degree, friends, or anything before you went off to college." Dedra challenges.

My mind goes to before college, to high school, middle, and elementary school. It's easy because it was all the same. An all girl private school that I know was not cheap. I never gave much thought about the school choice because it's where my father sent me. I didn't have a choice, and after he died Nico's father just continued to pay for me to go. Looking back at it, the school was meant for wealthy girls to go so they would be kept virgins, not tempted by things they shouldn't be, and were taught to be trophy wives. Sure, we got an amazing education, but for what? Most of my graduating class didn't go to college. From the last social media stalking I did of my graduating class, most of them are married to high profile men in politics or business. I'm one of a handful of girls that went to college, and even then out of that handful, only half graduated from college. Our sex education was basically abstinence which makes sense when our fathers are trying to preserve them to barter off.

"It's not a great sex education, I'll give you that. It almost made sex feel dirty." I confess.

"The religious approach. I'm familiar with that myself as a Catholic school girl. Sexual repression is a weapon that men like to use against women. Lucky for you, you have two men who don't want to repress you. They want to explore with you, and that is gold, so don't take it for granted. Not all women are so lucky."

"I won't, but first I need to get comfortable in my own skin when it comes to sex." I observe.

Dedra smiles proudly. "That's right, Unicorn. So, get naked. Don't worry about making it sexy. All I want is for you to simply get naked in front of me." She instructs.

Taking a deep breath, I stand up from my position on the bed. I slowly start peeling my clothes away from my body. It's not like I haven't changed in the locker room with girls in school. Somehow, Dedra being a female is making this easier. Fuck, how did I get so screwed up sexually, and how did I not even realize it until now? I have desires, I do, but I guess I've been ignoring them. I haven't masturbated in so long. Everything has been focused on getting my nursing degree and building a life outside of the underworld that I denied myself pleasure, not just with masturbation, but with everything. I denied myself luxury and in doing that, somehow I denied myself sexual pleasure too.

"Good." Dedra compliments when I'm completely naked. I try to not shift uncomfortably as she stares at me. "Now get on the bed. Head on the pillow and lay on your back." Dedra gently directs.

With another deep breath. I lay on the bed as Dedra directed. "I feel exposed, so how do I distract my mind from that?"

"It's not about distracting from your exposure. It's about embracing your exposure. Explore your body, Unicorn. Start simple like your belly region or arms. It will help if you spread your legs and bend them because that is a position you will be in often. This is your base position so to speak. The position that you can feel comfortable in." Dedra explains.

"Can I close my eyes?" I question.

"Yes, but just this once. Just to help you embrace that exposed feeling you have. Exposure isn't a bad thing. It can be elating, self-discovering, and more. You just have to think of it as a positive thing and not a negative one."

Closing my eyes, I lay my hands on my stomach and then adjust my legs, making sure they are spread as wide as I'm willing to let them be while having them bent. I take slow breaths as my hands glide from stomach to my breasts. I cup them gently before I lightly squeeze my breasts. I squeeze in different levels from soft to hard, finding that I like it more hard, maybe even rough, but I'm going to leave that for another lesson. My fingers slide on either side of my nipples and naturally pinch them. I start off lightly but I pinch a bit harder each time, enjoying the tingles that spread through my core. The tingles encourage me to move my right hand down my belly and between my legs. I cup my pussy and even play with lightly trimmed hairs. I've always been anal about having myself groomed everywhere. I always left a little bit of hair on my pussy because I hate being bald down there.

After some time, I can't take it any longer and my fingers slide between my lips to find my clit. My hand on my left breast switches back and forth between the right and the left as my fingers rub my clit. It feels good, way too good. Fuck, what have I been denying myself? I let small moans escape my lips. They feel foreign at first, but soon they become the melody that I touch myself to. The tingles that I felt building in my core finally explode as my orgasm overtakes me.

Clapping drags me back to reality as my eyes fly open to meet Dedra's sparkly blue ones. "How'd that feel, Unicorn?"

I can feel my cheek heat. I forgot I had an audience, but I guess that was the point. "I want more." I confess as I sit up.

Dedra gives a full belly laugh. "Oh, Unicorn, we are just getting started.

I can't help but relax into the bed as I enjoy the last little bit of orgasm. I would masturbate at home, but somehow I think the two men in my life might have something to say about that. Plus, I'm not sure I'm even ready to do anything sexual near them besides kiss. Although, I say that but our first night together in the brothel did prove they are good distracting me. At least I won't be clueless come my wedding night. Shit, Dedra's right, I am a damn unicorn.

Chapter 19

Anthony

I'm not surprised that Nico's father is being difficult. He is still refusing to give Nico Don. At this point, Nico has to make the choice to end his father's life. I know that it is hard for Nico to make that call. I can tell he still has respect for his father. I don't sense a love between them, much like there wasn't love between my father and I. Something I plan to do differently with our children. I want the three of us to be present parents. Somehow I have a feeling they will want to be present parents as well. The three of us are striving to do better than our parents. To do that we have to weed out the bad apples.

We have a week until the wedding. Nico and I are using Violetta's sexual goddess lessons to help her emerge into what our play in our relationship is going to look like. I think it's adorable she needs help embracing her sexual side. Dedra is right when she calls Violetta a unicorn. It's not Violetta's fault either. The men in her life made sure she was a unicorn, and I'm one of those men and so is Nico. I'll give it to Violetta, she was smart and avoided other men who attempted to pursue her. However, some of those assholes didn't take her no for an answer and would be a bit too persistent. Between Nico and I, we took care of them one way or another. It would seem Nico and I have always been working toward the same goal; we simply didn't know it.

"So, what do you want to do about the old asshole?" Nico asks as the driver pulls away from the spot we are holding his father. Another night of him refusing. I thought my father was stubborn but Nico's father takes the cake.

"Sometimes mother nature takes too long to do the job and we have to move things along. Take matters into our hands." I answer.

"You really are a little psycho like the rumors say," Nico gives a soft chuckle. "I'm glad we are on the same side. I didn't think I'd like to have a partner in crime. However, I must confess you are one hell of a partner in crime to have."

I chuckle. "I'm a little crazy, but I'm control crazy, which probably makes me more terrifying to my enemies. I never minded the idea of a partner in crime. I knew I needed someone to be my Watson to my Sherlock so to speak. Before you get all Alpha, Watson is underrated for his wits and street smarts. Sherlock is crazy and well, I'm crazy so it works. Point is, you are the partner I needed to make sure the Italian faction stays on top. We have the same goal. Rule as much of the city as we can without becoming greedy. Greed was our ancestors' downfall, and we are doing better than them. You have your faction's support to be the next Don. You don't need your father to truly hand it to you. You are fulfilling your end by marrying Violetta. Once you two are married, being Don is your right. So, we get your father to record a video explaining his health has taken a turn and he can't make it to the wedding, but he gives his blessing. Once we get that video daddy dearest can go off into the afterlife."

"Shit, you're even poetic in the way you speak like Sherlock. I'm going to leave the video recording, and how you get it in your hands. Have fun. I don't want to be involved in my father's death. The respect he's beaten into my brain just won't let me end him. That asshole knew what he was doing when he fucked with my mind."

"Do I want to know what you mean by fucked with your mind?" I prompt.

"My father tried doing hypnosis therapy to get me to be more obedient because I was too wild. My father did a little bit of damage before I got my grandfather to lay down the law as he was Don at the time. My grandfather was always on my side. Honestly, I think my grandfather hated my dad. When my dad wasn't around, my grandfather would call him an embarrassment. So, make it hurt when you kill him." Nico explains.

"It will be my pleasure. I'll make sure he knows it comes from you." I reply with a smug grin.

"So, how do you want to do this? The sooner the better we both can agree on that." Nico prompts as we draw closer to the burlesque club.

"Yes, let's pick up Violetta and get her ass home and tucked in bed. Doesn't she have wedding shit tomorrow?"

"Yes, she does." Nico answers.

"Good. Once we get her in bed, I have to go check on Sofia and then I'll be taking care of your father." I answer.

"Sounds like a good plan. I know I'm in charge of finding us a home, and I wanted to ask you if you want that home to have room for Sofia and her baby? I don't trust her Irish boy toy either. Violetta will be able to help. She's already expressed her concerns about Sofia and her naivety towards her Irish lover. If Violetta is picking up on off vibes, we need to keep your sister safe." Nico explains.

"Here I was unsure how to ask the two of you if it would mind Sofia and her baby living with us. Yes, I want her safe and her baby. There's something I don't trust. The whole situation feels off. I have Lorenzo on the Irish lover." I reply as relief floods me.

"Hey, Sofia is our family and so is her baby. We will keep her safe. I'm really good at keeping people safe. Violetta has called me her warden in the past for a reason."

I laugh. "That's reassuring." The car pulls up in front of the burlesque club. "Shall we go get our girl?"

"Yes, let's go retrieve our little submissive. Fuck, I can't wait until Dedra gives us the all clear to play with her." Nico rubs the palm of his hands against his dick that's at half mast.

"I feel you there, brother, I don't think I've ever had such bad blue balls. I know it will be worth the wait, but fuck I'm itching to get my hands on her." I agree as we both slide off of the SUV to go get Violetta.

I'm eager for the wedding for many reasons and I know Nico is as well. The thing I'm most looking forward to is the wedding night. I know I'm not the only one. Violetta is eager to know what it's like to ours, and we are ready to claim her. In the meantime I will distract myself by killing Nico's father. It's not that I enjoy killing. It's simply a necessary evil that I'm willing to use when the situation calls for it.

Chapter 20

Violetta

The wedding is five days away. While I know our wedding cake is going to be a cannoli cake with cream cheese frosting and pretty chocolate designs that will be dusted in gold, that was apparently the easy part. I might know what our wedding cake looks like, but trying to confirm what topper to go on the cake is a whole other story. The three of us agreed to come out in a poly relationship at the reception. So, I want the cake topper to resemble that. I find it ridiculous that I can't decide on a damn cake topper from the catalog in front of me yet I can make life or death options in a split second as a nurse within a heartbeat. It figures I would over think the simplest option yet quick life or death choices are a piece of cake. Ugh, cake only reminds me that I have to pick out a damn topper soon. It shouldn't be this hard.

"Can I weigh in?" A sweet voice from my side draws my attention from thoughts.

Sofia tagged along with me today, and I'm happy to have her with me. She's a sweet girl who is a little naive, but she is still young with plenty of years to grow especially since she is going to be a mom in a matter of six months give or take. I must confess I was surprised to see a fresh eighteen year old who is thrilled to be pregnant. I do worry that Sofia thinks having babies and being a wife is all she is allowed to do in life.

When I first met Sofia, I was upset. Not at her, but at how easily I could have been her if I hadn't fought for my independence. Well, and that Nico made sure I was allowed to have that independence because he knew it was something I wanted and needed for my own sanity. It sounds old fashioned to say that, but the underworld is still deeply rooted in old values. Old values that I realized Anthony's father would have pushed on Sofia. Anthony only recently gained guardianship over her, and it's not even a real guardianship because she is eighteen. Eighteen in the underworld means she is ripe to be a pawn for whatever the men in her life decide for her. Thankfully, Anthony is not doing that to his sister. He's protecting her and trying to give her independence as well as support. There's no way of knowing if Conor is sticking around for a variety of reasons. Sofia very well may end up a single mom.

"Sure. I'm clueless." I confess, feeling defeated by a stupid cake topper.

Sofia beams a warm smile. She has long hazel brown hair that is pulled back in a high ponytail. "You should go with an infinity symbol in gold and you can customize it by adding your three names." She flawlessly suggests.

"That's actually a good idea. Thank you for the help." I reply with a smile as I wave the baker over to let her know I've made my choice.

"No problem. It's nice having an older sister. I love Anthony, but he doesn't understand girl stuff. I could never go to him with girl stuff like sex." Sofia says as the baker joins us.

"Yeah, I could see where that might be awkward." I comment, and we both giggle. "I will happily be your older sister and friend to help with whatever you might need."

I quickly place the order for the cake topper and fill out the form that's needed. Then I grab some Italian cookies and coffee for Sofia and I before we leave to go for a walk. Sofia is starting to open up to me, and I want to hold on to that. I want to help her, and it's clear she has things she needs a woman to talk to about. I understand that because when my Nonna died I felt like I had no one to talk to about female stuff. Erica and I weren't close at that point, and she was really the only other girl in my circle that wasn't out to make a connection to further themselves or didn't see me as competition. Thankfully, my Nonna was alive when I got my period, but she died shortly after so I went through most of puberty on my own trying to piece together what I could. I want to be a positive female role model for Sofia because I know how lonely it can feel when you have so much bottled up inside and have no one you can relate to.

"Thank you for the coffee. Anthony is insistent I can't have it." Sofia states as I hand her the cup of coffee as we leave the bakery.

"You can have caffeine while pregnant, just not a lot. It's best to avoid it if you can or do decaf if possible, but a little bit here and there isn't harmful. Anthony is just being protective. He cares a lot about you." I comment as we begin to walk down the street confidently, knowing Nico and Anthony have men tailing us to ensure we are safe.

"I know Anthony cares. He's honestly the best big brother. It's nice to have a sister, and I guess I gain another big brother too with Nico. I think it's really cool what the three of you are doing. It's progressive, something the underworld needs." Sofia adds, taking a sip of her coffee.

"I agree the underworld does need to drop some of its old fashion values. It's not always easy being a woman in the underworld, trust me I know. It's easy for us to feel forgotten or like pawns in a bigger game that we have no control over. The nice thing is that Nico and Anthony are striving to change some of those old ways. One way of making change is them having me as their business partner and not just their wife. I'll be a queen with two kings on my side that will give me a voice. We are lucky to have two men willing to let us be more than what our fathers would have wanted." My little speech makes me realize I truly am lucky that Nico and Anthony are doing what they can to give me a true place at their side instead of shoving me in the background. I must confess I feel valued, loved, and appreciated by them. I have a voice, and they both know how important that is to me. I really am lucky to not have just one but two men who will lift me up and let me rule at their side.

"See you get it. I know Anthony isn't happy that I'm pregnant so young. The truth is, I want to be a mom. I'm totally okay with this. I kinda made sure it happened." Sofia confesses.

"What do you mean?" I question.

"I told Connor to not wear a condom. He insisted we should, but I begged him not to wear one. I wanted to get pregnant." Sofia's confession shocks me a little. Here we thought she was pressured into sex and the pregnancy was a result of it. We thought it was all Connor to blame, but he isn't the one to blame.

"Why would you want to be pregnant at eighteen?" I question, trying to understand because I was certainly not thinking about having kids at eighteen.

Hell, I've only started thinking about having kids since Nico and Anthony have totally overridden everything I thought I knew or wanted. So, for me to hear Sofia confess she wants a baby at eighteen is not something I understand. While I might not understand her reasoning, I want to try to see her point of view. I also want her to feel seen and understood because that was something I desperately wanted from the people in my life. Nonna, Nico, and now Anthony as well as Erica and

Sofia are the only people in my life that have ever made me feel like I was seen for who I am and what I desired.

"I've always wanted to start having babies young. I want to start young because I want eight kids. I know that's ambitious and probably won't happen, but I want as many kids as I can have." Sofia answers casually.

"Eight kids is a lot, Sofia. I'm not saying women don't do it, but medically speaking your body might not be able to handle it. Now, I want to address something that is more of present concern. Do you plan to have your children have the same father? What if Connor doesn't stick around?" I'm trying to be realistic with her. I'm glad she seems confident in what she wants, however, I also need to be sure she has properly thought this through. I feel a sense of responsibility for Sofia as an older female role model. I want to be the role model for her that I wish I had in my life. My mom died when I was two, I have no memory of her and while I adored my nonna, she was raised in the thick of old fashion values. She is one of the ones who would have told me to get married, have some babies, and then think about nursing school. It's not her fault, she had a slightly different mindset than me. It also doesn't ever take away the fact that I would do anything to just sit with her on the swing that sat on her back porch and spend our time simply chatting about everything and anything. I miss her terribly, but I'm so happy I have her ring. I can never express to Nico how much him keeping it for me means.

"Ideally, I would like my kids to all have the same father, but I also understand it might not happen that way. I would be content if Connor and I got married, but I would also be okay if I married someone else. I don't care about having a husband per say, but you know as well as I most women in the underworld who come from high ranking families have a high rate of arranged marriages for one reason or another. I have always assumed I would have an arranged marriage and I'm fine with it. I want kids and I don't necessarily need a husband for that even though I'm sure I will be married at some point. I also know Anthony will make sure that if I don't end up with Connor, and I have to marry someone else, he will ensure that me and my baby are a packaged deal. I have a lot of faith and trust in Anthony." Sofia answers so confidently, I have a hard time finding my next words.

"It seems you've thought this out. I'm glad to hear you trust Anthony. I trust him too, and I haven't known him as long as you have. As your older sister, I want to make sure you are happy and be there for you for whatever you might need. I hated being an only child, so to finally have a sibling is the best part of this whole arrangement."

"I'm flattered, but we both know Nico and Anthony totally top me as the sweeter part of the deal. I am glad Anthony picked a pretty amazing woman to be with. It's nice knowing that I have an additional sister and brother to look out for me. I know that no matter what happens with Connor, I'm going to be okay because I have three awesome siblings looking out for me and my baby." Sofia sweetly says as we reach the home supply and decor store that we are going to so I can do a wedding registry.

"I think we are going to be amazing sisters, and that is why I need your help with this wedding stuff. You are really good at party planning and decorating." I compliment as I hold the door open for her, and we walk inside the store.

"Thank you. I might turn my love of planning events and interior decorating into something, but I haven't gotten that far yet. It's defiantly something to think about because while I want to be a mom, I want to have something that is my own."

"I completely understand that. I'm happy to help or support you where I can. Now, let's get this over with so we can grab some lunch."

"Oh, I'm so down for some food." Sofia agrees as we head the guest service section of the massive and expensive home supply and decor store that only those with money shop at. I can't deny the money of the underworld is a totally perk of this life.

I can't deny that there are perks and things I do love about the underworld life. I guess you can take the girl out of the mafia but you can't take the mafia out of the girl. I must confess coming back to the underworld hasn't been as horrible as I once imagined it would be. In fact, I don't think I could have ever pictured my current arrangement though. I never would have seen this outcome and it's one hell of an outcome that makes me feel a bit foolish for being so concerned with escaping my fate. I left the underworld and when I was finally dragged back, I found that the underworld is changing, and I'm about to be a part of that change in the underworld. A change that is going to help bring the underworld into a modern mindset where limitations are nothing more than insecurities that we have overcome.

Chapter 21

Violetta

Excitement brims in me as we head down the stairs into the brothel. Tonight is what I've been waiting for, and I finally feel a bit prepared. I have to accept that on some level the guys will simply always have a bit more experience with sex than me, and that with time, I will have my own experiences. However, the important thing Dedra's taught me is that it's not about what came before our partnership, it's the relationship the three of us build from here on out that matters.

There is a level of training that I will go through with the guys as I learn to be their submissive in the bedroom. Honestly, the whole submissive thing should piss me off given how verbal I am about making sure I have a place helping them lead the family businesses, however, it turns out I don't like to have control when it comes to sex. I also think I'm so comfortable being a submissive to Nico and Anthony because I know they actually give a damn about me. I can never deny how much those two care and love me. So, giving them control is easy because I trust them. Even if they can grate my nerves, they are still the two men I'd rather end up in bed and have a life with. There is no denying they hold my heart captive, and I want nothing more than to please them.

Dedra is waiting for us in the room. She has a prideful smile on her face. Underneath my excitement is anxiety that I'm going to over react or do something wrong. I push the anxiety down and focus on my excitement. I'm ready for this. I've been eagerly anticipating tonight. I know we won't have sex until the wedding night, but I'm just eager to have their hands on me again. I'm much more confident than I was before and as Dedra so lovingly reminds me almost every session is that it's natural to feel shy or nervous with sex especially if you are a unicorn like me.

"So, tonight is about the three of you getting comfortable with one another. Violetta, you are going to be blindfolded to help you focus on their touch and pleasure. If they do something you don't like, say stop and we will go from there. It's important to keep in mind that all three of you are learning together how all of you can enjoy your sexy time as one and not three individual people." Dedra explains before she ties a silk blindfold over my eyes. "Now, the guys are going to undress you and have a little fun touching you. They know what they're doing, so follow their lead. They are in control. Do you two have names you want your submissive to call you?" Dedra questions as anticipation of what they have come up with builds along with anticipated touching that I know is going to send me to my own personal bliss.

"We've thought about it, but ultimately we want Violetta to be comfortable with them too. I thought she would call me Warden. Afterall you love so much to call me that." Nico teases as I feel his hands slip under the hem of my dress before he gently pulls it over my head, careful to not to take the blindfold with it. I can't help but giggle at his name choice. I've called him that on and off since he and his father took over my care when my father died. I usually called him that when I was trying to rebel against something I didn't want to do for whatever reason. I guess this is his secret payback because now I have to use it while obeying him during sex. At least it will be sexy payback.

"I like that one for you, Nico. Warden it is. Anthony?" I question, reaching my one hand to him in memory of where he was last standing next to me. Anthony takes my hand in his, pulling me into his arms. My hands fall on his chest, feeling the smoothness of his very expensive suit.

"I'm thinking of something more on the classic side. I was thinking Dom. Simple." Anthony suggests as his free hand pops my black lace bra off.

"That suits you." I reply, leaning into his touch as his hands land on my hips turning me to face Nico who is already doing away with my thong. Nico helps me slip out of my black pumps while Anthony helps me balance so I don't fall, successfully removing the only thing that was left on my body.

Anthony remains at my back and Nico at my front. Anthony's hands land softly on the curve of my hips. I feel

Nico's warm breath on my right ear. "Do you trust us?" Nico questions with a firmness that leaves my legs feeling a little jelly like.

"Yes." I answer without hesitation but my voice is on the softer side. Anticipation for their next touch has me mesmerized.

Nico's one hand lightly wraps around my neck. He's not restricting my breathing, however, his grasp isn't light either. His grasp is just enough to make me uncomfortable and I like it. I even crave it a little tighter but I'm not in charge so I'm not going to list demands while I'm supposed to be learning to be a good submissive. Now is not the time to let my Italian stubborn side out. "Even now?" Nico questions once more his tone just as firm as before.

"Yes," I answer without hesitation once more but this time I strain my voice to be heard due to Nico's grasp becoming firmer as I answer. How did he know I wanted him to choke me harder? I shouldn't be surprised because it's clear these men know how to play my body like a fine instrument that leads to a melody of pleasure.

"Good girl," Anthony and Nico compliment at the same time and can't help but rub my thigh together.

Nico lessens his grasp before his lips eagerly and roughly fall on mine. Nico's force is a little much, causing me to have to lean back on Anthony for support, which he happily helps by securing my back to his chest. I feel the fiber of his smooth, almost silk like suit, against my back, making me wish they were naked as well. However,

I'm unsure if they are getting naked with me this round or not. I wasn't told much of what they would be doing other than playing with me. I didn't even know about the blindfold until Dedra mentioned it the moment before she placed it on me.

Anthony secures my wrists behind my back with his hand while Nico's hand around my neck tightens slightly as he removes his lips from mine. "And now, Little Dove?" Nico questions in my ear before he nips it.

"Yes." I mange out in a raspy voice.

"That's our girl." Anthony compliments as he kisses my left shoulder while Nico's lips forcefully claim mine once more.

Nico loosens his grip around my neck, but Anthony does not let go of my wrists that he has bound in one hand. Nico's kisses keep me temporarily captivated before he pulls away once more. Nico releases his hand around my neck as Anthony releases my hands. The two of them gently and carefully lead me over to the bed. One of them lays me on the bed so that I'm on my back. The next thing I know I feel a weight shift on either side of me on the bed. Their warm bodies enclose me between as my anticipation grows.

I don't know who is on either side of me, but I'm not sure it matters because when their hands land on my body the only thing that matters is the pleasure I know these two are going to give me. A mouth lands on my left nipples, sucking and nipping it as a hand lands on my right breast playing with my nipple between his fingers. Another hand finds its place between my legs as it slides up from my knee to my inner thigh and lands right on my pussy where fingers skillfully find their way to my clit. My breath hitches as the pleasure builds in my core from their touch.

Someone's lips land on mine. I think it's Anthony because he tends to be a bit more on the clean shaven side where Nico likes scruff and even sometimes has a light beard. Honestly, it's hard to tell who is who without seeing them. Not that it matters which one is doing what to me because the combination of pleasure these two are giving me has me chasing an orgasm. However, when I get close they each let up on their touch to a point to where I'm afraid their touch will disappear. Thankfully, they don't ever fully stop touching me. I think they are edging me. Dedra explained what edging was to me and that while it might feel like torture while they do it, the orgasm that comes from edging is apparently very intense. I think I'm going to find out how worth it edging can be because I don't doubt Dedra or the guys knowledge when it comes to sex, kinks, and really anything relating to sexy time.

After several minutes of light touches, they go back to roaring my pleasure back to a full blaze. I'm lost in their touch as it's completely amplified on a level I didn't know was possible. I know moans are leaving my lips that are sometimes captured by lips. I don't know what one of them is doing but their combined magical touch is more amazing than I remembered. While we technically have an audience, I don't mind Dedra being here because I'm comfortable with her. Not that I can maintain a thought long enough for it to matter as Nico and Anthony play my body like a fucking musical instrument as they practice edging me. I've lost count of how many times I've almost orgasmed at this point, but I do know I haven't had one. Maybe a mini one if that's even a thing. I can feel the orgasm building in my core threatening to burst out of me and this time my controlling men finally let me cum

After I catch my breath, I remove my eye mask. "We didn't say you could take that off." Nico comments.

"Sorry, but I wanted to see you guys. As erotic as it was being blindfolded, there was a part of me that didn't like not seeing you if I wanted to. Without the blindfold I can close or open my eyes at will." I explain as they help me sit up.

"That's fair, but it did help you get out of your head." Anthony comments.

"The blindfold was more or less a tool to help you learn to feel comfortable being touched. It's not something you three have to use in your play all the time. Part of this is learning what all three of you enjoy and how to mesh that into pleasure for all three of you. I'm here for them as much as I'm here for you, my sweet unicorn. They need to learn to work as your doms together because they aren't used to sharing," Dedra explains.

"It's true, Anthony and I are used to being doms by ourselves and not having to consult co-doms where our submissive is concerned. This whole dynamic is new for all three of us. You might have more of a learning curve, but you aren't alone in needing guidance with how this dynamic works." Nico adds. I hadn't thought about this being a new dynamic for them. Sure they have sexual experiences but this is something new for them.

"There's no rush to figure everything out before the wedding, especially where sex is concerned. We don't have a huge amount of time to train before the wedding so training will naturally also take place after. There are a lot of dynamics and parts to our poly relationship. We all have to be patient and understanding because this could easily blow up in our faces as it could lead to our success." Anthony contributes.

"Exactly. I'll be here every step of the way and even when the day comes when you don't me, I'll still be around. I like you, Unicorn, so I better have visits after you no longer need me." Dedra asks.

"I have a feeling we will be here as often as we can for business and pleasure." I reply, leaning my head on Nico's shoulders as I take Antony's hand in mine and rest it on my leg.

The four of us talk some more about the dynamics and things to try at our next session. By the time we leave, I'm beat. I'm more than content when the three of us get into bed together. It's strange this little Italian love triangle we built, but it's the missing piece I didn't realize I needed. Is it crazy to think I can enjoy my life in the mafia underworld or I'm just painting a delusion I can live with?

Chapter 22

Nico

We are in the final days before the wedding. Anthony has successfully recorded my father's approval video for the wedding reception. I'm honestly relieved Anthony was able to get the video and I don't want to know the details of how he got it. I do know my father is dead, and we will bury him in the family plot in the cemetery outside the city. He doesn't get a funeral or anything along those lines. Maybe that seems disrespectful, but it was his wish and I will honor that, mainly because it makes my life a hell of a lot easier. Not only that, but most of us in the underworld prefer low key funerals if one has a funeral at all.

I've been focused on the Angel Clinic and our not so legal Angel of Death Clinic. We are getting ready to open the legal portion to the public, but the not so legal part has a few more things we need to have lined up before we can start with actually seeing patients. We have a listland for us to build our house of potential patients already so when we are ready to open we shouldn't have to work too hard of a time booking appointments.

Anthony and I are preparing to take Violetta and show her the clinic on the night of the rehearsal dinner. She is still obsessively watching her medical dramas as much as she can when she isn't occupied with wedding stuff. I hope she embraces both Angel Clinics because I did create them for her. Sure, it lines the mafia's pocket with money, but that's just a bonus. My goal was always to create something for Violetta to have that was her own.

With everything slowly falling into place, I've made arrangements to purchase land that is just outside the city limits for us to build the house of desires.. Plus, I like the idea of our everyday home outside the city. I adore the city, but it's noisy, and the older I get, the more I crave a place outside the city. Violetta also likes the idea of us having a home outside the city limits because there will always be a part of her that craves space from the underworld. Anthony is Mr. Easy Going. He tends to go with the flow, but that doesn't mean he won't insert his opinions and thoughts where he needs to assert it. Anthony is quiet and reserved so it balances the impulsiveness of Violetta and my anger. The three of us fit together in a strange yet beautiful puzzle that I could never have imagined. Now that our trinity is formed, I don't think I could live without it, without them.

While on the personal front, things are heading in the right direction, the underworld part is gearing up for a possible war. I don't want war, especially not a turf war. However, with Anthony and I showing a united front along with Violetta at our side our enemies might not be happy. Our enemies want nothing more than for us to tear each other apart, so like the vultures they are, they can pick apart the carcass of the Italian Mafia. Our union throws our enemies a curve ball they were not expecting. This curveball will put them on edge and they might try to come for us anyway. So, to avoid our enemies getting any type of advantage and because we need allies in the other factions, I've got Connor, Sofia's little Irish boy toy, waiting for me at the office in the casino. I'm going to find out what this little punk is up to and if I can use it to my advantage. Afterall, Anthony asked me to handle this while he handles shit with my father. He delivered, now it's my turn.

It's possible this kid has zero links to the Irish mafia, but those chances are very slim. Nothing is an accident or coincidence in the underworld, and the sooner you learn that lessen the better chance of survival you have. Entering my office, I find Connor sitting in one of the black leather chairs on the one side of my desk. His flaming red hair gives away his Irish heritage as well as his fair complexion and the light freckles that are speckled across his cheeks. I take the single seat on the other side of my desk. I stay silent observing him. He has a little sweat on his brow while he grips the arms of the chair tightly to where his knuckles are white. He's nervous. Good because he should be.

"So, we can do this the hard way or the easy way, Connor. Just be honest. I don't want to have to hurt you, especially because Sofia cares about you," I pause to observe him. A bit more sweat graces his brow. I don't think his knuckles can get any whiter. Time to go for the million dollar question. " Do you work for the Irish mafia?" I bluntly ask. No sense in sugar coating why we are here. Sugar coating is for the weak, and in the underworld you have to have a thick skin or else you'll be eaten alive.

"Finally!" Connor tosses his arms in the air as he goes from nervous to releasing frustration as his hands flap down onto his thighs. "I've been waiting for one you Italian fuckers to confront me. At least you didn't tie me up or some shit. Look, I don't just work for the Irish mafia. I'm Shamus McCormic youngest son. I started dating Sofia to try and get close to Anthony so I could tell him who I was. That the Irish want a treaty. We know there is war brewing in the underworld, and my dad wants to be allies. I didn't expect Anthony to be so difficult to talk to, but I won't lie, he's a scary fucker." Connor immediately answers.

"I see. So, Sofia was, what, a fun time while you attempted to cozy up to her brother?" I question, starting to feel my own protectiveness over Sofia. She is Anthony's baby sister and that makes her family to me.

"No, it's not like that. Not even a little. I genuinely have feelings for her. I didn't mean to catch feelings, but I did. I never meant for her to get pregnant. I want to do right and marry her and my father would like to use our marriage as an alliance with the Italians. If war is coming, you know allies are important. Currently the Russians and Mexicans seem to have a mini war going on, and it's unfortunately possible that their war can spill on to our doorsteps. We have no idea if the winner will come for us next. The Mexicans are known for being greedy and even more shady than the rest of us. The Russians are so kept to themselves that it's impossible to know what those fuckers are up to." Connor explains.

"Okay, I'm not disagreeing with what you are saying as far as war is concerned. Why not just come talk to Anthony or I? You've plenty of moments. I get Anthony might be intimidating especially since you got his baby sister pregnant, but what about me or our second in commands?" I question.

"I thought about it, but so much started happening with Violetta, you, and Anthony it didn't feel right. I figured you had to have your suspicions and one of you was bound to confront me. I didn't think it would take so long, though. Either way, we are here now." Connor states with a shrug of his shoulders. He's much more relaxed now that the elephant in the room is out of the way, which is understandable especially for someone his age who is trying to find their footing in the underworld.

"Fair." Connor is clearly young and his father tossed his ass to wolves and hoped for the damn best it would seem. Not totally unexpected in the underworld. "When does your father want to meet?" I Inquire.

"After your wedding. He doesn't want to intrude on your special day." Connor answers.

"Good. Set it up and let me and Anthony know when to show up. You also need to break the news to Sofia that you are in the Irish mob and what your marriage would mean. It's an alliance, meaning you two can never get divorced." I caution him. Connor is young and so is Sofia for that matter. He's nineteen and she's eighteen. However, there are other factors at play.

"I know I need to tell her the truth. I wanted to talk with you or Anthony first. I will talk to her the morning after the wedding, and I will let you know when the meeting with my father will be. I'll make sure it's neutral territory."

"Good. Get it done. Now, scurry along. I think you have an ultrasound appointment to get to with Sofia. If you are going to do right by her and marry her then you better show up for her too. Don't be just words, Connor. Make sure you follow your words up with actions that match." I advise. Connor nods his head in agreement before he scurries out of my room.

I know Jullian is already on his tail to keep an eye on Connor until we know if he is trustworthy. He doesn't seem like he has malicious inventions. He honestly comes off as a kid trying to please his father while trying to find his way among this crazy underworld we live in. I empathize with him. Especially because he is the youngest, and if I remember correctly Shamus has five sons, meaning Connor is more than just a spare heir, he's almost disposable to Shamus. I'm not saying Shamus thinks that way, but most ruthless mafia leaders would.

I go about my business for the clinics and inform Anthony about Connor, which has him a bit relaxed where Sofia is concerned, but I know he fears Connor's intentions with Sofia aren't true. He's looking at this more from a big brother's perspective, which is why he is having me handle it. It's the same reason I preferred him to handle my father. Sometimes being too close to the person or situation can be harmful and having another set of eyes is helpful. I just hope Violetta isn't triggered by Sofia and Connor's marriage being an alliance. She's really big about her and Sofia not being used as pawns in our mafia games, but she has to understand that arranged marriages for alliance is part of the world we live in.

Anthony and I would never consider them pawns in our games. Sofia will be able to have a choice if she wants to marry Connor. I honestly think she will because she seems so in love with him from what I've observed of them together. Sofia is a bit opposite of Violetta in the sense that Sofia has no problem accepting her role as a pawn because she knows that's her place. Of course, that is very much of the old way of thinking, and I believe women can rule in the underworld as well as men. Sure, it's harder for women to be seen as more than just a pawn, a sex object, or baby makers because the old ways are still embedded into the underworld, however, there are those of us working to improve the old ways like our newly formed Italian Trinity. Not just because we are in a poly relationship, but because Anthony and I are letting Violetta rule at our side as our queen who has a say in everything she desires to have a role in. Violetta was never meant to be a pawn. She was always meant to be a queen and that's exactly what she is and her two kings are happy to give her a voice because together we can make changes that future generations will benefit from. Just because it's the underworld doesn't mean it can't evolve, and that's exactly what we plan to do as the Italian Trinity.

Chapter 23

Violetta

Rehearsal dinners are an annoying tradition in my opinion. It makes no sense why couples have to practice getting married. It's not that hard. Bride walks down the aisle, the bride and groom get married, they kiss, and that's it. We aren't doing a crazy long or intricate ceremony, but Nico insisted the rehearsal dinner was necessary. Who am I to argue with my warden or dom? Besides, Nico promises he and Anthony are going to show me something that will help me get back into the medical field. I guess they took my hint that I missed it seriously. It wasn't actually intentional at first. I was bored as I'm used to having a schedule and errands to run. Sure, I'm busy with the wedding, but that by no means takes up my entire daily schedule. Turns out I have a limit of how much reality TV I can watch in one sitting. So, I switched it up with medical dramas to give me a taste of what I was missing even if they aren't totally accurate. I sometimes make fun of how inaccurate they are, but I'm addicted now. I have to admit I was curious to see if either of them noticed my new TV addiction. Turns out they totally noticed.

I think it's cute that they are concerned over it. It means they care. They both know how to make despicable look reasonable, and it's not fair. They both have such a hold over me when they shouldn't, but I'm reliant on them now. Surprisingly, I'm not as upset as I was about having to rely on them because they love and care about me. They seem to have my best interests at heart. Plus having Sofia and Erica in my inner circle helps me as well with being pulled back into the underworld. In truth it was only a matter of time. I think I feared it so much because I was afraid of being a pawn as my father led me to believe. However, I'm not a pawn to my kings. I'm their queen and with them at my side anything feels possible.

To my delight the rehearsal at the church goes smoothly and then we eat at a very upscale Italian restaurant. Anthony is with us, although no one knows we are in a poly relationship yet. That announcement is for tomorrow during the reception, and it's something no one will see coming. I won't pretend I'm not looking forward to people's reactions when they do find out. Nothing like this has been done in the underworld to show such solidification and unity. Sure, marriages for alliances happen in the underworld, just as they do in the regular world. However, being poly allows us to be united in ways the underworld has never seen before. It seems silly that something so simple could hold so much power, but it does. The entire Italian faction united in polyamorous relationship is the ultimate alliance that no one has used to their advantage. Their loss is very much our gain.

After the rehearsal dinner, Nico and Anthony take me to my surprise. I am indeed surprised as my brain tries to process the fact that we are standing in a hidden clinic inside of a basement of a regular clinic. I have to admit I did not see this coming. I should have, though. Shit, I really am out of touch with mafia life. Several weeks ago, I thought that was a good thing. Now, well, I might be just as morally grey as the two men who own my ass.

"Say something, please, Little Dove." Nico begs, looking at me nervously.

I stay silent, soaking it all in as I realize this is my path in life, and I'm honestly alright with it. I'm maybe even a little excited because we get to do good and help our community in ways that my heart swell. Helping others is all I ever wanted to do as a nurse. I think it was my way to try to do good for the world considering the underworld I live in is flooded in sin. Although, that was my old perception of the underworld. A perception my father wanted me to believe because he wanted me to feel weak, a pawn, incapable of doing anything without a man. Now that I'm back in the underworld after years away, Nico and Anthony are opening my eyes to how empowering the underworld can be as a queen that has my view completely changing and erasing whatever lies my father wanted me to believe.

"Little Violet, you are making us anxious." Anthony informs me as if I don't know the two of them are sweating bullets, afraid I'm going to flip out over this, and I might be having a bit of fun keeping them on edge.

Maybe there was a time I would have thought this whole thing was horrible and wrong, especially as a young teen, but I'm older now and I have some adult experiences as well as nursing experience. I know that sometimes assisted suicide is truly desired by patients. Sometimes, a patient doesn't get a good diagnosis and there are some medical conditions that can make end of life horrible for patients. I understand why someone would want to go out on their own terms versus waiting for some terrible disease to do it for them in some slow, painful way. I'm not as naive as they think I am, and while I have a good heart that doesn't mean I don't support some morally grey things.

"How long have you been pulling this together, Nico?" I inquire, keeping my tone even to not give away how I feel. I can't help but keep them on edge. I know opportunities like this won't come around often, and I'm going to enjoy it for as long as I can.

"Since I realized you were taking nursing seriously. I wanted you to have something, so you didn't feel like you had to give up everything to marry me." Nico answers, honestly. For a moment I don't know what to think because I never considered Nico had been thinking about what I would want in this underworld life that I'm learning to embrace in a positive way.

When emotion stands clear among the variety of swirling emotions inside, and that's love.I bridge the small gap between us and kiss him on the lips. "Thank you for thinking of me." I say after I break our kiss. I'm truly touched that he planned a future where we both were happy. This whole time I thought he was being selfish by forcing me to marry him, but he wasn't being selfish because he thought about me and wanted to ensure I was happy with him. He created two entire clinics just for me to have something that was mine, something I could be proud of.

"Does that mean you are okay with all this?" Nico gestures around to the hidden clinic we are standing in.

"Yes. Assisted suicide is something that many patients would love to have as an option when it comes to a horrible disease or terminal diagnosis. I've met so many patients, whether it was terminal cancer, Parkinsons, Alzheimers, and other sickness or situations that have left people facing hospice care doped up on morphine so they don't feel the pain of their body failing them in the most horrible ways. Not to mention the money from this will help fund a free clinic, so there is access to medicine for those who can't afford it is amazing. I can justify morally grey when it's suitable. Also, I think it's sweet that you thought about me. I think I might have not given you enough credit, Nico." I confess.

"We just want you to be happy in this life with us," Anthony adds as he comes behind me to wrap his arms around my hips while Nico holds my one hand. Their embrace makes me feel safe, desired, and loved.

"Exactly. We don't want you to hate your life. I never wanted you to hate being my wife because you were restricted. I watched your father restrict you and push you toward his goals. I want to be better than him because you deserve better." Nico replies, and it's at this moment that I realize how much love he has for me and how we have always loved one another. It's a little overwhelming as the love I have for Nico rushes through me. It's always been there, but I've been keeping it locked and tucked away, but that is no longer the case.

"I love you, Nico, and I'm sorry that I didn't give you enough credit." I express as I kiss him on the lips.

"I love you too, Little Dove." Nico replies as we break our kiss.

I quickly turn on my heels in Anthony's arms because I don't want him to feel like a third wheel because he isn't. "I know that I don't know you as well as I do Nico. I'm sure you feel like you have disadvantage, but I promise you don't. I love getting to know you and I feel deeply for you already. I know I'm not ready to say I love you to you yet, but I know it will come soon because having you in my life is just as important as having Nico in it." I seal my promise with a kiss.

Anthony cups my check in his hand when we break our kiss. "It's okay, Little Violet. I know you need time. I love you because I have watched you for years, but I understand that it's different for you. The fact that you even acknowledge that I mean something to you and have agreed to be with me is enough. I could be a jealous man and hate what you and Nico have. If I'm honest, maybe I did hate Nico for what he had with you at first. However, the three of us came together and formed our own unity. All I wanted was acceptance, and that is what you two have given me." Anthony confesses.

"Why do I sense there is something more there?" I inquire to Anthony as I put my hand on his that rests on my cheek.

"Not now, Little Violet. Another time. I do not want the shadows of my past to cast darkness on our happy occasion tomorrow." Anthony replies.

I smile and nod. I won't push him. Anthony clearly has parts of his past that are painful, and he will share them when he is ready. I know it's best to not push and let him come to us when he feels comfortable. As much as I want to know what pains him so I can make it better, we simply aren't there yet. The three of us have a lot of growth ahead of us and challenges that I have no idea if we are ready for. Nico and Anthony filled me in a bit with what is going on with Connor and his ties to the Irish Mafia, him and Sofia getting married, and the alliance between the Irish and Italian mafias so we have a fighting chance against whatever war might blow on our front doorstep. War is ugly period, but a war in the underworld, where rules don't apply, war can be a death sentence.

Chapter 24

Nico

Today I finally get to marry my Little Dove. I never pictured I'd be sharing her with someone let alone the man I should consider my enemy. However, Anthony has proven he is far more valuable as an asset. I have no problem admitting I like Anthony and our alliance. Anthony and I might not have sexual relationships due to us both being straight, but we connect on a social and emotional level. Not to mention sharing Violetta with him adds an erotic, enticing, and enjoyable factor that I certainly didn't anticipate. The three of us have come together to form our own love alliance, so to speak, and it's going to shake the underworld a bit. That's okay, I'm all about making jaws drop for the right reasons, and this is one hell of a reason.

Anthony, Jullian, Lorenzo, and I are in a room inside the church getting ready with final touches to our suits and such. Lorenzo and Anthony are very similar to Jullian and I in the fact that our second in commands are our best friends. Meanwhile, Violetta is with Erica, Dedra, and Sofia. Violetta wanted Dedra at the wedding and reception. They are forming a bond, and I'm happy about that. I love watching my little dove spread her wings and build friendships for the next phase of her life.

"So, I bought some imported Italian cigars to celebrate." Anthony announces as he hands us each one.

"See this is why I like him, he's classy." Jullian comments as he takes a light from Lorenzo to stoke up his cigar. I chuckle at him.

"Are you trying to say I don't have class?" I question.

"You do, but it's a modern class where Anthony has more of an old school class." Jullian answers as he puffs on his cigar, making me shake my head.

"It's why they mesh so well." Lorenzo adds.

"I must confess you two seem so accepting of our alliance and relationship. Can I ask why?" I question, letting my curiosity out. I'm happy that our right hand men are on our side with this, and not resisting. I guess I didn't think they would be so accepting at first.

"Honestly, most of us don't see the point in being enemies with our own faction. The Ronaka, DeLuca, and Calla families should have always remained united and maybe we wouldn't have the issues we have now." Jullian answers.

"I second that. We have bigger enemies than ourselves to fight. Plus, no one has pulled off an alliance with a poly relationship before and as a gay man who is open to a lot of shit, your relationship isn't a shock. I think you will find more shock among older generations than the younger. We need all three families unified if we plan on surviving whatever bullshit the Russians and Mexicans are doing with their own mini war. Those fuckers are insane and their morals are questionable even for the underworld." Lorenzo adds.

"There is power in unity. Our enemies are counting on our divide to use to their advantage. No doubt they will try to pin us against one another, eliminating half of the threat for them. At least, that's what I would do if I was trying to win a war." Anthony contributes, and he's not wrong. I would plan for something similar. It's an age-old tactic that can truly only be countered if we are united therefore there is no divide and no one is us taking out the other one to make things easier for our enemies.

"Our enemies don't expect us to be united, let alone solidify that unity with a poly relationship." I agree. "With that being said. Anthony, I know you agreed to sit in the front row when we originally started planning the wedding. However, after talking with Violetta we would like it if you stood next me. I know it might be awkward but you technically are marrying her too even if it's not legal in the eyes of the organized government. It is up to you as we want you to be comfortable." I offer.

"Really? I mean, isn't Jillian your best man?" Anthony questions as he puffs on his cigar.

I know he is keeping his composure but I also know he's shocked and hiding it. Anthony hasn't given us too much into his upbringing, but what he has mentioned makes me think he has lived a lonely and possibly isolated life. I also believe it's why he wanted Violetta so bad and even stalked her. He simply wanted to feel connected to someone. It makes me care more about him in a platonic way that I haven't experienced before. Sure, I have Jullian who is my best friend and has been through so much with me, and while I care about him, it's somehow different with Anthony because we are in a poly relationship, sharing the one woman who captivates both our hearts. I'm building a life with him and Violetta. They have become the two most important people in my orbit. That's why Violetta and I have made our goal to make sure Anthony feels accepted and loved by us.

"Look, I'm still up there. I truly don't care that much. Besides, it will be more fun having you up there. I'm looking forward to the gossip that is going to come from this whole spectacle of an event." Jullian intervenes before I can answer.

"Well, when you put it that way how could I say no. It also feels right to be standing next to you rather than in the front row." Anthony answers.

"Violetta will be happy. Speaking of her, you know we need to come up with a pet name that we both use for her. I mean we can clearly keep our individual pet names, but don't you think we should have one that we both use? Especially where sex is involved." I suggest taking a puff on my own cigar.

"I've been thinking about that too. Do you have any ideas?" Anthony ponders, puffing on his own cigar.

"See you two think alike in so many ways." Lorenzo adds pointing his cigar between the two of us. We all chuckle at his comment.

"It's true we are weirdly synced," I pause as a joint pet name comes to mind. " I do have a suggestion. Butterfly since we are helping her emerge from the cocoon she has put herself in." I suggest.

"I don't think I could come up with anything better so Butterfly it is. I suggest we tell her tonight when we finally get to claim her as ours."

"I like that idea." I agree.

The four of us talk a bit more and finish off our cigars before it's time for us to take our places for the wedding ceremony. Anthony stands next to me at the altar. I can't focus on anything other than the fact that Violetta is the most beautiful bride I've ever seen. She walks down the aisle with grace and a wide smile on her face. I knew she would be happy that Anthony was next to me.

The wedding ceremony is about thirty minutes long. I'm glad when it is over because I'm looking forward to the reception and wedding night. We do go take some wedding photos with Anthony and our bridal party before we head to the wedding reception where everything will officially unfold to the public that the Italian mafia faction is united instead of divided.

Chapter 25

Anthony

The wedding ceremony was sweet. I'm happy Nico and Violetta wanted me up there with them. I didn't really want to sit in the audience, but I also didn't want to impose on them knowing they have a special bond. They did grow up together. It also felt easier to go with the flow than to push my own agenda on them. When Nico asked me, I was shocked, but in a good way. Standing up there with them truly made me truly feel accepted by the two of them. I must confess there are moments where I feel I'm a third wheel, but today being next to Nico at the altar made me truly feel like in some weird way all three of us got married. In many ways we are married, especially in the eyes of the underworld. We don't necessarily need a certificate from the government that says we are married. The underworld has its own laws. Contrary to popular belief the underworld is not a free fall of anarchy.

The three of us finally arrive at the hotel ballroom where the wedding reception is being held. We went more intimate with the ceremony and all out with the reception. The reception is the important part. It's where Nico officially announces our Italian Trinity as we have dubbed ourselves. Our poly relationship is going to certainly turn heads. The whispers already started at the ceremony with me standing up there next to Nico. By all rights, we are supposed to be enemies so me even being at the wedding is mind blowing. I have to admit, it's fun keeping people on their toes. It's good to keep people guessing.

The three of us walk in together. Nico and I are on either side of Violetta, our arms linked with hers as the three of us stride into the center of the dance floor. The room falls completely silently, shocked at the sight that shouldn't be. Whispers slowly start as the DJ walks over to hand Nico a microphone. Nico clears his throat and puts on one hell of a confident smile as every person in the room is now officially staring at us. The whispers die down as Nico begins to speak.

"Thank you all so much for attending our wedding reception. This is not just a union between man and woman we celebrate tonight, but of two men and one woman forming a unity to unite the Italian factions. Anthony Ronka is to be acknowledged as Violetta's husband as well as she his wife." Nico pauses to pull my wedding band from his suit pocket. He hands it to Violetta who slips it on my left ring finger. "The three of us are a unit, the Italian Trinity, if you'd like to call us. So, let's celebrate happy unions and to once again be a united Italian faction." The three of us are handed champagne flutes from one of the waitresses. The three of us raise our hands in the air as does everyone around us before we all take a sip of our drinks.

Nico hands the microphone back to the DJ who invites everyone to help themselves to their seats so dinner can be served. The three of us head over to our designated spot. The bridal party table is composed of Erica, Sofia, Connor, Jullian, Lorenzo, and Dedra. Dinner goes by smoothly and it's already hard to ignore the gossip ringing throughout the ballroom. We have certainly cast a spotlight on ourselves, but it's important that our enemies know they can no longer divide us

After dinner there is a small moment where speeches are given and the video I forced Nico's father to make. Then there is dancing and drinks flowing freely before it's time for cake. After the cake we linger a bit more, but the three of us are eager for tonight. We have been waiting patiently to properly claim Violetta, and she is eager to be claimed. She practically begged us to fuck her at our last session with Dedra. Dedra has been wonderful helping us with Violetta and finding our groove as a throuple. I chuckle inwardly at the thought, shit, I never thought that I would be in a poly relationship. Especially not with Nico who is supposed to be the enemy. I am relieved that we are no longer enemies. I'm confident in our union. Even as we socialize with others, we have a smooth flow like we have been together for years.

THE MAFIA LOVE CODE

I must confess I wasn't sure I would be able to find a place with Nico and Violetta, but I have. I feel accepted by both of them. They do everything they can to make sure I feel included and not like a third wheel that I was afraid I would be. Tonight is the start to our future empire together. Two kings and one queen in charge of the Italian mafia. It's our kingdom now. No parents in our way or anyone to tell us what to do. We have our men at our side and a possible alliance with the Irish. We are making the right moves with the two clinics. We are moving pieces in our favor. I do look forward to a couple of days of not worrying about business and strictly focusing on pleasure.

Chapter 26

Violetta

After showing our faces, dancing, eating, and socializing with our guests, I finally make my way to the hotel suite that the three of us will be staying in for a couple of days since we will do a honeymoon vacation later on when war isn't being threatened. We need to have our alliances solidified and be sure war isn't coming our way. Plus, I'm fine with several days and nights holed up in a hotel suite with my kings.

I have Dedra coming up with me to help me get out of my wedding dress and into something sexy the guys picked out for me to wear. They are downstairs finishing showing their faces while I get ready for them. I'm slightly nervous, but I honestly anticipated the nervousness. Dedra and even the guys told me it's totally normal to feel some nervousness my first time. Even though there is a hint of nervousness underling my excitement, I'm determined to embrace this night for everything it's going to be. I want to have sex. I've had such a taste playing with the guys at the club with Dedra's guidance. I've learned to suck their dicks the way they each like. NIco is all about the under shaft and tip area that he enjoys my tongue. Anthony enjoys deep throating with more focus from my lips than tongue. I won't lie, them teaching me how to please is its own erotic pleasure.

Dedra helps me out of my wedding dress, undergarments, and accessories. I clean the makeup off my face and wash the hairspray out of my hair before quickly combing and blow drying it. I do a quick once over to make sure my bits that I liked shaved and groomed are good to go. I slip into the cream colored sheer teddy. No thong or panties, I'm not surprised. Dedra looks me over as a smile crosses her face.

"You are ready, Unicorn." Dedra beams her approval.

"Thank you for helping me, Dedra."

"Of course, it's my job, Darlin. Don't tell the other girls, but you are my favorite that I've ever helped. I don't think I've formed a friendship with a client before, but I'm glad it happened. Now, tonight you know the guys will be all about your pleasure and making you comfortable. After tonight, well, that's up to them." Dedra advises.

"I know. I guess you should probably tell them I'm ready before they bust down the hotel suite door with their impatience." I joke and we both giggle, knowing full well they would do it if they felt we were taking too long.

"Probably a good idea. They are eager to make you theirs. Good luck, sweet unicorn!" Dedra says as she blows me a kiss as she leaves.

I go sit on the giant king sized bed while I wait for them. We have talked about positions I should be in when we are in sexy time, but we haven't officially decided yet. I'm sure the guys will let me know when they do. They have been very good at keeping me in the loop with things. Well, most things. There are certainly things I prefer not knowing especially if it's related to violence, murder, or anything unsavory along those lines. They seem to know what I'd be okay with knowing and what I can certainly live without. I will do my best to help them carry the burdens of being leaders in the underworld, but ultimately I'm glad they have one another because they both need someone who can understand the entirety of the underground world. This life can be brutal at times and to shoulder it alone is even harder. I'm happy that the guys can be there for each other in a way I can't.

The beep of a key card being scanned catches my attention. I leap off the bed as Nico and Anthony come striding into the room. I stop in my tracks over to them because the predatory looks they are giving me freeze me in place. They don't stop in the pursuit of me until they are on either side of me. My breath hitches in my throat as they each lay a hand on me. Nico's is on my right shoulder and Anthony's is on my left upper arm.

"Are you ready to be claimed, Butterfly?" Nico questions as he leans in so his mouth is close to my ear causing a slight shiver of anticipation to course through my body.

"Yes, Warden. Butterfly?" I can't help but ask where the new pet name came from. Nico has never not called me Little Dove.

"Butterfly is what we have decided to call you when we are being intimate with one another. It will be easier for all of us." Anthony explains his own breath on my shoulder sending shivers down my spine before he plants a soft kiss on my shoulder.

"I like it, but why Butterfly?" I question, unable to help myself.

"Because you are finally emerging from your cocoon. You're not Violetta Calla anymore. Today you are officially Violetta Amelia DeLuca-Ronka." Nico answers as the reminder of my name change sinks in.

I plan to legally go by a new name as well. The hyphenated last name shows that I am both their wives. We truly do not care about the legal aspect of Nico and I being legally married. Honestly, the legal, regular world has no say in the underworld. I belong to both of them now, and strangely I'm at peace with the direction my life is taking.

"I guess I am emerging into the underworld society. I did successfully avoid it for a handful of years, but I guess this was inevitable." I answer.

"I'm not sure any of us could have pictured this exact situation." Nico comments, causing us all to laugh.

"No, but I'm glad it's what happened." I answer as I'm now sandwiched between them. Nico is in front of me and Anthony behind me, my back against his chest.

"Time for us to claim what is ours." I hear Anthony's deep baritone voice behind me as his hands land on my hips almost as if he is steadying me or bracing me for something.

"I agree." Nico's silky voice fills my ears as his one hand grabs me a little roughly around my neck as he pulls my lips to his while his other hand slips under my cream teddy to my thighs as he teasingly rubs circles on my inner thighs to where his fingers might go next.

Everything becomes a haze as their hands are all over my body as I take turns undressing them until they are both naked like me. I lost my teddy quickly. I'm not sure why they had me in anything at all, but I honestly think it was to help ease my nerves. I can't even think of being nervous as these two men make my body feel like jelly. Nico's light choke around my neck with his demanding kisses have me in a captivated hold. Anthony's lips kiss every inch of skin his lips can find fueling my body's burning need to have his lips on my body. These men of mine are intoxicating and the hold they have over me is something I crave.

They have brought me out my cocoon and helped me embrace life in the underworld. I'm their butterfly, their queen, and I want nothing but to be theirs. That's what tonight is all about as they set my body a blaze with desire and passion as they move closer to the bed. Anthony's hands on my hips guiding me while Nico's fingers dance their way between my legs as his fingers start to rub my clit. Nico's hand around my neck is not tight enough to cut off my breathing, but tight enough that the threat is there. I shouldn't be turned on by being choked, but I am. I'm a mafia princess, I'm bound to be into things I shouldn't.

Anthony moves from behind me as he gets onto the bed as Nico releases me. "Come to me, Butterfly." Anthony commands.

Nico helps my short ass climb the bed to Anthony. I crawl to him and the moment I'm close enough he pulls me to him. I straddle him, his hard dick against my pussy. His lips find mine as each of his hands goes to a breast. I feel the bed dip behind me before I feel Nico's hands on my body. Nico pulls my arms behind my back and holds my wrists together with one of his hands. His other hand snakes around my front to go back to playing with my clit while Anthony's hands massage my breasts while his fingers skillfully play with nipples. Pleasure courses through me as they leave me merciless to their touch.

My pleasure builds and I know I'm close to the edge, but I also know I shouldn't cum without their permission. It's the rule, and while I'm sure rules might be bent for tonight, I don't want to risk it. "Please, Warden and Dom." I beg between Anthony's kisses.

"Tonight, you can cum when you want, Butterfly, but only tonight." Nico informs me. With that information I allow myself orgasm, sending me into a sweet hazy bliss. They don't stop playing with me until I've cum a couple more times. "I can't wait for you to do that around my cock." Nico says as he kisses my shoulder.

"I think she's ready." Anthony says as he breaks our kiss.

"I think she is too." Nico agrees as he releases my wrists.

Nico helps me off Anthony as he moves over to lean his back against the headboard in a seated. Nico positions me so I'm on my back laying next to Anthony. I part my legs as Nico settles himself between them. Nico lines his rather thick cock up to my entrance. Both my guys have great cocks or so I've been told by Dedra because I honestly have nothing to compare it to. Either way, I'm a lucky woman to have two men who are sexy who are well endowed.

My nerves start to pick up a bit, but Anthony takes my hand near him. "It's alright, Butterfly. We will be gentle this time." He says kissing my hand while his other hand goes to grab his hard cock. Nico lines himself up and I feel the head of his cock near my entrance. My attention goes to Nico. His lips fall onto mine as a good distraction as he slowly pushes himself inside of me. It's fine at first but the moment he pushes past my resistance, pain erupts. I squeeze Anthony's hand a bit. Nico attempts to distract me as his lips move from my lips down my jaw and neck to my breasts where his lips find one of my nipples causing pleasure and pain to mix.

Nico moves in and out of me slowly letting me adjust to him while his mouth tortures my nipples in the best tantalizing ways. The pain and pleasure is a combo I do like and to be honest the more Nico moves in and out of me the better it feels. I'm more than sure I'll be sore afterwards but I don't care because the soreness is going to be a good reminder that I'm not a unicorn anymore. Although, I'm pretty sure Dedra is never going to let me live down that nickname.

Anthony lets go of my hand and leans a bit forward as his hand moves between Nico and I so his fingers can slide to my clit. He begins to rub causing my attention to shift to him. My free hand goes to his cock that has his other hand around it. He grins as he lets his cock go as my dainty hand wraps around it. I stroke Anthony's cock to the rhythm of Nico fucking me. Nico's mouth is still working on my nipples as Anthony plays with my clit all of that combine with Nico fucking me has me spiraling into a fast orgasm. My walls clench around Nico causing him to groan in pure satisfaction.

Nico begins to pick up his pace making it a bit harder for me to keep up, but Anthony stops me anyway. I know he doesn't want to cum yet. They both are determined to fill me with their seed until I'm pregnant. I'm actually okay with it because I feel secure in our relationship. Plus I'm a nurse, I promised myself I'd be done having kids by my early thirties. I like the idea of building a family with them and we are going to have so much intoxicating fun along the way.

Anthony stops rubbing my clit. I think they are getting ready to switch. These two have this night planned out, I'm simply along for the ride and that's how I like it. Turns out I'm a natural submissive with sex making it damn near perfect that I'm with two very dominating personalities with sex and in life outside the bedroom. I swear they both have a suave about them that is unmatched. It makes me crumble at their authority. Being claimed by them both is exactly what I want. Nico moves faster gaining my attention as his lips move back to my lips. He nips my lip as I feel him explode his own orgasm.

"Your turn, Anthony," Nico says, rolling off to the side.

Anthony wastes no time lining himself up at my entrance. His lips fall on mine as he enters me in one swift motion. Nico moves his hand to play with my nipples as Anthony furiously moves in and out of me. Anthony reaches his fingers between us to play with my clit. These two are sending me into endless orgasmic bliss with their touch. Anthony's tongue darts in my mouth swirling with mine. I arch my back slightly as an orgasm surges through me as my moans are captured by Anthony's furious kisses. Neither of them stop what they are doing and I cum once more. I don't know how many orgasms I've had at this rate but just when I think my body can't take another one they manage to pull it out of me. Anthony finds his release before he rolls to the other side of me.

All three of us are taking a few moments to catch our breaths. Damn that was good. "Is it wrong that I want more?" I question, breaking the brief silence.

They both chuckle. "In good time, Butterfly. We will happily oblige your request, but I'm sure you are tired from the day." Nico informs me as he rolls to face me while

Anthony does the same. I'm sandwiched between them just the way I like it.

"I am a bit tired." I confess, not wanting to admit I feel worn out. I feel zapped on all fronts.

"We figured as much, and to be honest, we are a little tired ourselves. Today was a big day for the three of us." Anthony says before he kisses my temple.

"It was a big day. We certainly shocked the underworld tonight. Our union isn't usual, but we can write our own code of love." Nico adds, stroking some of my hair to the side.

"That we can. I need you both in my life." I say, my hands gripping one of their hands.

"We know that now. I'm glad stubborn Nico saw sense enough to share you with me." Anthony kisses my hand that is in his. We all chuckles at his joke.

"I figured starting a war wouldn't be wise. I guess it's a good thing I have some sense after all, considering our enemies are waiting to strike in our weakness. It's almost like the three of us were meant to be together, bring unity when it's needed the most." Nico adds before he kisses my other hand.

"I never thought I'd hear Mr. Logical talk about fate." I tease as I slightly bump his arm. He chuckles at me.

"Watch it, Butterfly. I don't want to punish you on our wedding night." Nico teases back as he leans in to nip at my jawline.

"Fate or whatever it was that brought the three of us together, I don't really care what it was. I'm happy I have you two and a chance to form the family I've always wanted." Anthony adds, leaning in to kiss my shoulder. I hum my approval.

"Okay, we need to got to sleep or we are going to end up fucking again. We have the next two days to ourselves to fuck as much as we want. Let's get some rest." Nico suggests as kisses me sweetly on the lips.

Nico then pulls me into the crook of his one arm. Anthony then plants his own sweet kiss on my lips before he lays his head on my plump breasts as I place my arm to rest on his back. The three of us are finally officially married in the eyes of the underworld. I can't believe I'm the queen to two kings in the underworld. We are marking our territory and standing strong. Our unity is going to make us a powerful force in the underworld. I never thought I would look forward to my life in the underworld yet here I am not just looking forward to it, but I'm ecstatic about it. I have my own clinic! I'm a lucky woman to have two men who want me to rule at their side and not be shoved into the background to just produce heirs for their empire. They have made me their equal, and that is something I will always be grateful to them for.

Chapter 27

Nico

The two day honeymoon was bliss. Anthony and I broke in our butterfly. We tandem fucked her hard, and it was amazing. We do plan on doing anal with her so we can fuck her at the same time, but it's a process to get to that point. Violetta just got her cherry popped, and while we love how eager she is to try everything, we both know easing her in is the best way. Dedra also agrees. Dedra will work with us when the time comes. She has been a gift to us in helping us navigate our poly relationship sexually.

With our blissful honeymoon behind us, it's time for things to move forward. It's about a week after the wedding, and we sure are the talk of the town so to speak. Part of it is good because it's important that everyone knows the Italian faction of the underworld is united. Everything is moving forward for us on a personal and business front. We have an architect who is helping us design the house. I have purchased the land. It's nice to build a home with my two companions.

I never thought I would want a male companion, and I'm not talking in a sexual way. I didn't think I could share the crown, but it feels better to share the crown. The burden isn't solely mine and that's a relief. I believe Anthony finds the same relief as I do. I care about him and his family. He has a place in my life that I never thought I needed someone to fill. I always believed Viloletta would be enough, and in many ways, she would have been. We could have done this without Anthony as was my plan for so many years. However, I don't want to do it without him now that he is with us. I enjoy sharing Violetta with him. The three of us have found our own piece of happiness that I'm sure will face challenges along the way.

While things are solid on the personal front, our business front is about to take off. Violetta has met with staff. Erica has agreed to work the front desk of the Angel Clinic while also doing receptionist work for the Angel of Death Clinic. The Angel Clinic is scheduled to open in a month, and Violetta is currently printing up flyers to have our lower ranked guys to hand out as well as email blasts and so on. She's on top of it and I'm very proud of her for how she is embracing her life in the underworld.

I must confess, I was afraid Violetta would have cold feet and try to run, or something crazy along those lines. I worried that she wasn't truly happy. It was my own fear of losing her. Those years without her near me were hard. Maybe the hardest years of my life because I felt empty without her nearby. However, I knew I had to respect her wishes to spread her wings a bit. I wanted

Violetta to find something she could be passionate about. I always knew she wasn't going to be a stereotypical mafia wife and perhaps that was her appeal. The reason no one else could capture my attention the way she did. Now, I don't have to worry about my dove flying away forever. She's mine, well, rather ours. My little dove is happier than I've ever seen her before.

While things are going good with the clinic we do have the Irish to work things out with. Connor has set up the meeting with his father. Connor is doing his best to earn our trust. Sofia, of course, is blindly in love with him. She seems happy and content with her circumstances. From what I understand, Sofia has completely decorated Anthony's townhouse that he gave them. It's funny trying to watch Anthony navigate his sister. He tries so hard to not be the stern, older brother but he is in his own way. He genuinely cares about and loves Sofia. It does show he is going to be a great dad. I have a feeling we will be different dads, but still united in our parenting. It's nice to think about the future, but right now I need to focus on current business stuff.

An alliance is going to be helpful with a potential war against the Russians or Mexicans who seem to be having their own war. While they are currently at war with one another that doesn't mean their war won't spill onto our front door. It's happened before and I'm hoping it doesn't happen again. It's been years since a true faction war has taken place in the underworld. If a nasty war is coming our way, it's good to have allies that can add security. Security in the underworld is an armor of protection that is important to have if you can obtain it.

Sure, there is a risk of meeting with Irish, as it could be a trap, but I doubt it. Connor seems very determined to prove this is a peaceful meeting. Connor and Sofia honestly have done a lot of the hard work that comes with these types of alliances. She's knocked up, and them getting married willingly saves a lot of the negotiation process, making fortifying our armor that much easier. War is messy, expensive, and often not worth it. Unfortunately, sometimes it's out of your control if war shows up on your doorstep and that's when being prepared with allies and weapons as well as blackmail and other resources come in hand. Our kingdom might be newly formed, but that doesn't mean we are weak. We are strong and armor is about to become even harder to pierce solidifying our newly formed kingdom.

Chapter 28

Anthony

Tonight, we are meeting the Irish at a neutral location, which happens to be a famous steak restaurant in the city. The restaurant has several awards and shit I couldn't care less about. Lodge SteakHouse is in neutral space. There is an entire section of the city that the underworld is never allowed to touch. It's an unspoken agreement we have with the legal government of the city. So, we use this piece of the city to do meetings. No one, not even the Russians, would dare harm someone in what the underworld calls Switzerland, the part we are sworn from infecting.

We enter the restaurant as I go into defensive mode. While there is no worry of a trap now, I still worry about how the meeting will go. Alliances like this haven't been formed in the city for a couple of decades now. It might even be a risky move because it could piss off other factions making us a target. There's several ways this can go south, and I'm trying to not overthink it. Normally, I'm not so edgy about meetings, but this involves my baby sister. I have to protect her and make sure whatever union between her and Connor is something she is okay with. I don't want to force her into a marriage she doesn't want. She can be a single mom. I would support her if she chose that. Sofia is also attending with Connor because they should have a say in their future. I am glad to have Violetta and Nico with me to help me remain calm because when it comes to my baby sister, and now Violetta, I'm quick to kick ass and take names later.

As we follow the waitress to the private room with a large table where Connor sits with an older man whose ginger and white hair and beard indicate he is Shamus, Connor's dad. The guy sitting next to Shamus looks very similar to Connor but with a longer face. I assume that's Conall, Connor's older brother who will be taking over as leader when Shamus either dies or passes it off to him. The four of us take our seats. Sofia is seated next to Connor. I'm on her other side and Violetta is sandwiched between Nico and I just the way we like it.

"Thank you for meeting with us, Shamus." Violetta says sweetly with her pearl winning smile.

"The honor is ours. Congratulations on your union and creating the first ever poly union. You clearly play by your own code, and I think we can work together. After all, my son did knock up Anthony's sister. It's only fair that we attempt to do right by them." Shamus explains.

"Thank you, and yes, we do play by our own code. We also believe that we can work together. Especially because it doesn't help that the Russians and Mexicans are a potential threat with their civil war. It's certainly a concern for both of us. You know just as well as I that their war can easily blow to our front door." Nico adds.

"That is also true. There is a benefit to Sofia and Connor getting married." Shamus agrees.

Violetta puts her hand on my leg and pats it gently. She is letting me know she is here for me. Nico and Violetta know I'm struggling with this meeting and my concerns for Sofia. I never pictured I would be here bartering my sister for marriage. I know it's not exactly like that, but it's what it feels like to me. I suddenly understand Violetta's strong feelings toward the shitty feeling of being used like a pawn in a bigger scheme of things. I feel as if I'm using my sister as a pawn to secure our alliance with the Irish. Granted, I know it's a totally different scenario since Sofia is pregnant and seems like she is happy and eager to marry Connor. Still, there is a part of this that makes me a little uncomfortable.

Our waitress comes over and takes our drink and appetizer order. The conversation turns casual and a little less business which I'm thankful for. Nico is smooth with how he talks with Shamus, something I'm not sure I'd be able to do because this involves Sofia. I'm realizing now that my protectiveness over her makes it hard for me to be objective. Violetta is sweet and charming when she speaks while making sure I'm alright. Sofia is too busy making puppy eyes at Connor, who is struggling to divide his attention between the conversation happening and attending to my sister's demands. Conall remains neutral and more observant. I remain calm and participate in the conversation where I need to.

By the time dinner is served, the tone changes to more business. Connor and Sofia both give their acceptance to their marriage. They are okay with it and know that it's a good way to establish a treaty. Duty and love seem to align, and I suppose I can't ask for a better turn out for my baby sister. I don't fully understand my sister and her willingness to marry Connor so easily. Part of my issue is that I still look at her as a child in many ways when she is clearly a grown woman.

I'm still not solely thrilled that my sister is a part of this treaty, but since she is willing it makes it an easier pill to swallow. Connor seems like a decent guy, and I should give him the benefit of the doubt. He is trying to do the right thing by Sofia and their baby. I can't say the kid isn't putting an effort in trying to get in my good graces as well as Nico and our second in commands. Plus, Shamus seems like an honorable man. Not that I'm sure any of us can claim honor in the underworld, but there is honor among thieves. Still, the alliance is a good thing. For the last couple of decades, treaties in the underworld among factions. I'm unsure of why but if I had to guess it would have something to do with greed or pride.

By the time we are finished dessert, Sofia and Connor are officially engaged and their wedding is going to be taking place in less than a month. The sooner they are married and we have an alliance with the Irish the better. We are going to need allies if war is coming our way. We still don't know what is fully going on between the Russians and Mexicans, but in case their war overflows into other parts of the underworld it won't hurt to have allies.

Now that we have an alliance in the works with the Irish our business side of things are looking excellent especially where the two clinics are concerned. We already have clients starting to line up for the Angel of Death Clinic as I've been working on this for years and many were simply waiting for us to open our doors. The regular Angel Clinic will have enough patients to service and is the legal part of the operation. The community seems to have a positive response to the clinic from the advertising we have done. It's the best option many will have. Hospitals are too expensive even for the public and supposed affordable ones can easily run someone thousands of dollars. The Angel Clinic is going to be popular, and depending on how popular, might mean a second location. Meanwhile, the Angel of Death Clinic will expand in its own ways. Home services are in high demand and with only two doctors willing to do home visits, we might need more doctors, which Nico is already on. Nico has a lot of connections that I never really knew he had. I thought I was well connected but Nico is even more connected than I am. I think it has something to do with his business mind set.

There is a lot happening on all fronts, business and personal. It can wear you down, making me glad when the evening is finally at an end. I want nothing more than to go home, play with our butterfly, and get some rest. The three of us have been sleeping in the same bed. Violetta doesn't want to sleep without either of us. We can't deny her anything it seems. We might be the ones in control but she has us wrapped around her fingers in her own ways. Exploring with Violetta and Nico is more fun than I ever thought it could be. I don't think my fantasies could have prepared me for how wonderful the reality is. Violetta and Nico have become strong figures in my life that I now need. They are the drug that keeps me sane and happy. We have indeed written our own code to love, and it's proving to be the best damn decision we have ever made.

Chapter 29

Violetta

E rica and I are currently setting things up in the clinic. It opens in less than a month now, and I'm so excited to have patients again. I still feel so lucky that Nico built this clinic for me. Even the assisted death part is something I'm okay with. I know it's illegal and certainly a morally grey area, but I do believe people have the right to choose how they want to go out when they are given a terrible diagnosis. I also adore that Nico took those who aren't rich into consideration with both clinics. After all, the legal clinic is essentially a nonprofit and people will pay what they can afford. Even the not so legal part will take patients who might not be able to afford it because there are going to be those that definitely can.

I never really gave Nico much credit where his kindness is concerned. Nico has always been someone to look after the less fortunate. I used to think it was for show to make him look good, but now I know it's because he has part of him that is kind and good. Growing up, Nico would insist on buying Christmas gifts and taking them to the hospitals to sick kids and to lesser fortune areas where gifts were a dream. He has always had a big heart for helping others even if he hides it under his tough, mafia man personality.

While Nico might be a caring soul, he can be equally cruel where it matters. Nico loves to punish those for their sins, but I think Anthony might love it a bit more. Anthony is his own dark soul. I haven't fully figured out what tortures him exactly, but part of me wonders if I ever will. Anthony is open with us, but there is a darker side he keeps hidden from me, perhaps as to not scare me. Whatever it is, it's clear he doesn't hide it from Nico, and that is somehow okay with me. I think it's nice they confide in each other with things that maybe they can't share with me. They have their own bond that I find sweet.

The three of us are happily finding our groove. Building our home has been fun. Some of our ideas feel a bit out there like the play dungeon the guys want to build for us to play in. It will be attached to our room with a key so our future children don't end up scarred for life. I never thought I'd have a play dungeon in my dream home, yet it's there now. I chuckle inwardly at the thought of how much my love life has drastically changed in the best ways possible.

Erica clearing her throat gains my attention from the supply closet I'm supposed to be organising. "I thought you might be ready for lunch? I order from the Indian food place you secretly like but will never admit." Erica jokes.

"Indian food is my dirty little secret, okay? I love Italian food, I do with my whole fat girl heart. However, I like foods from other cultures too. No offense to Nico or even Anthony for that matter, but how they eat Italian and American food every day is crazy to me. Don't they want a change up?" I ramble my thoughts out loud about my men and their damn eating habits that sort of drive me insane.

Erica chuckles. "God, tell me about it. Nico's ability to consume pasta and bread is impressive. I want to know how the hell he isn't a million pounds." Erica jokes back, and we both giggle.

"It's all the gym workouts. You know his father made sure Nico stayed in shape. It seems Anthony is the same way. They are now weight lifting bros and want to build a personal gym in our house." I inform her as I give up trying to organize the one supply closet and follow her to the break room where said secret food is.

"Oh, I don't even want to begin to picture what that leads to." Erica comments as she heads to the table with the bag of food.

"You know they don't fuck each other right? They only fuck me. I don't think they have ever even touched each other's dicks." I inform Erica as she pulls out containers out of the big and places them on the table.

"I don't need to know anything you three do. I have my own sex life to worry about." Erica retorts.

"I wasn't aware you had a sex life to worry about. Isn't the first rule of NA is to not be in a relationship within the first year of being sober?" I question as I grab some paper plates from the freshly stocked kitchen cabinets.

I know some things about NA and AA as a nurse. Most nurses take the time to educate themselves on these programs to further help patients. I know there are rules that they are supposed to follow but I don't truly remember how long those rules are enforced for. With Erica growing up she was certainly not a rule follower. In fact, I think she did almost anything she could to break the rules. With her reformation from addict to sobriety I don't know how much of the rules she chooses to follow. Yes, she is definitely a changed person there is no doubt about that, but that doesn't mean she still isn't a rule breaker. After all, this underworld where rules are often meant to be broken.

"You are correct, except I'm going on two years sober, so that means sex and relationships are on the table." Erica informs me as she opens the containers.

"Shit, sorry, I didn't realize. When Nico told me you were sober he made it sound like it was more recent." I apologize, hoping I didn't offend her when we finally have a shot at a real friendship.

It was hard to be friends with Erica when we were younger. She was often in trouble and rebelling. I found it was safer to not be around her unless I wanted to find trouble. In our teens Erica started using drugs which drove a wedge between her and just about everyone in her life. Now that she is sober, and we are more mature, it's been nice getting to have a chance to be true friends.

"It's okay, girl. Nico is shit at communicating that stuff, and I never told you how long I've been in recovery. Now, can we get to sex part of things?" Erica questions as I join her at the table.

"Yeah, I assume that's what this lunch is for. A bridge to talk about something you need to get off your chest." I surmise as we take our seats.

Erica even got us iced chais, so she must really be trying to butter me up for whatever she is about to tell me. I'm very curious about what is going on with her. I also totally accept her lunch bribe too. Not that she had to buy me lunch. I would happily talk to her without bribes, but we did grow up in the underworld. Bribes are sort of a thing for us even for silly things like lunch just to have a conversation.

"Am I that transparent, huh?" I nod my head as I spoon some of the basmati rice onto my plate. She sighs before taking a deep breath. "It's Jullian. We hooked up drunkenly after your wedding. It was supposed to be a one night thing. One whoopsie we were drunk and it was a wedding that was our excuse for one night of passion. Except it wasn't just one night. It was the morning after, that afternoon, and the following evening. Basically, the entire two days you three were off on your honeymoon tour of each other's bodies. Jullian and I were doing the same thing, but it was only supposed to be once." Erica rapidly spills to me as if the words coming out of her mouth were on fire.

"Woah, slow down. Jullian as in Nico's best friend and right hand man? Okay so what is the nature of your relationship?" I inquire. This lunch just got a whole hell of a lot more interesting. Blame my love reality TV and now medical dramas, but I love me some juicy shit like this. Does this make me a basic mafia wife? Yes, but ask if me if I fucking care. We all have something basic about us and the best part is we get to choose it.

Erica stays silent for a moment trying to gather what I imagine are her racing thoughts. I can only imagine how anxious she is with this regarding Nico. Erica doesn't have to say it, but I know she doesn't want to be looked at as the fuck up anymore. She's worked hard to break that stigma around her as the wild child, fuck up, problem. Hooking up with Jullian is something that may not paint her in the best of light to Nico, but that might not be the case depending on where Erica and Jullian want things to go. There's two ways I see this going. One is bad, and other is good. I hope it's that later.

"I don't know. That's the problem. I'm in my mid-twenties. I don't want to fuck around town anymore. I did so much of that in my druggie days. Getting sober is supposed to be about embracing life and a fresh start. Part of that fresh start is to find someone I can settle down with. However, Jullian isn't exactly someone I can be with freely due to his relationship with Nico. They have such a strong bond. I don't want to fuck that up by starting a relationship with Jullian. Nico would be pissed if Jullian broke my heart. I'd almost be afraid to break up with

Jullian if it came to that because of how Nico would react. Yet at the same time, I like how Jullian makes me feel. He's so supportive and respectful. He's a considerate lover, which is something I've never had. I hate that I can see the stupid dream with him. You know the marriage and kids dream? What if I take this chance with Jullian and it all goes to shit?" Erica unloads as she piles her plate with food. I'm not sure she's even paying attention to what she is putting on her plate.

"If Jullian makes you happy then you should go for it with him. It's worth the risk, and I can help talk sense into Nico if need be. You deserve to be happy, Erica. You made a huge and positive choice when you decided to get sober. You've come really far from the girl I remembered when I left for college. I'm proud of you and you deserve happiness. So, if Jullian makes you happy then give it a shot. It's worked out well for Nico, Anthony, and I so far. Sometimes the risks are worth it." I advise her while she eats some of her food.

"Shit, when did you get so wise?" Erica jokes, and we both giggle. "Seriously, thank you, Violetta. I needed someone to talk sense into me. So before I lose my nerve I'm going to text Jullian right now that I want to seriously date." Erica declares as she pulls her phone from her pants pocket and quickly texts Jullian. I shake my head at her as I giggle at her actions.

"Good for you, Erica!" I say and put my hand up for a high-five. She smiles as her hand gently smacks mine in the air.

"So, is Sofia driving you crazy with wedding plans yet?" Erica changes the subject as she picks up her drink to sip it.

I laugh. "A little. I can't say that I'm shocked the guys saddled me with wedding planning with Sofia, but I need help balancing that girl out. I don't know if it's her hormones she is high off of, but that girl's head is in the clouds right now. She's just starting to show and she just entered her second trimester. She wants this wedding to be special and huge. She wants it on a fucking ferry cruise boat thing that goes up and down the river at night."

"Damn, that's high class shit for sure. I bet Anthony is sparing no expense either. So, you want me to help you balance the innocent eighteen year old who is high off pregnancy hormones?" Erica asks with a giggle.

"Yes, please." I love Sofia, I do, but I'm finding her a bit hard to manage when it comes to wedding stuff or anything that involves setting up her life with Connor. I love that she is excited and I understand why she is. However, I'm not good at event planning. Sofia is clearly good at it, and I think half the time I'm just there for supervision.

"Done! Just send me the details of your next wedding thing and I'll be there."

The rest of lunch is nice as we talk. I really am enjoying getting to know Erica now. I'm genuinely proud of her for how far she has come. I'm also glad she decided to take a chance with Jullian. I think they will be a solid couple. Nico might have some reservations at first, but I can help soften him. Erica deserves to be happy, and I will not let Nico and his thick skull ruin it for her. I'm also glad I will have someone who can help me balance Sofia. I love that sweet girl, but I didn't realize how high maintenance she is. I'm used to high maintenance women, but she is family and pregnant so it's a bit of a delicate situation that I'm glad Erica will help me with. My life in the underworld is turning out to be pretty damn sweet, and that is not something I ever thought I would be able to say. I guess embracing fate or whatever this is worked out after all.

Chapter 30

Violetta

Sofia and Connor's wedding is less than a week away and the clinic opens in two. Life is crazy busy preparing for these two major events. Even with help from Erica and Sofia I'm swamped with work, but I don't mind it. I don't do better if I have too much time on my hands. I like staying busy, however, I do enjoy a break once in a while. I haven't had much of a break lately, but I'm hoping that when the two big events are over things might settle for a bit even if the threat of war lingers over our heads.

I will confess that I feel more fulfilled in the underworld than I thought I would. I thought the only way I was going to have a fruitful life was if I left the underworld. I was wrong. I had a narrow view of what the underworld life was. I was groomed to be a mafia wife. Proper, pretty, loyal, and faded into the background. I made the mistake of thinking Nico would be the same as the many powerful Dons before him. I convinced myself that Nico didn't truly care about me, and I was nothing more than a prize. I think I convinced myself of that because it made walking away easier There was always a part of me that didn't want to let go of Nico. Yet, I felt like I needed more.

Now I realize the more was Anthony. Anthony adds uniqueness to our relationship. He balances Nico and I where we need it. Antony struck me the moment I saw him. I didn't want to admit there was something about him that drew me to him on a level I didn't understand. My heart felt torn between an old love and the potential of a new love. Thankfully, my heart didn't have to stay torn because my old love and new love came together. They forged a path where I get to be at both their sides. They have become everything I desire and want in my romantic life.

That's why I'm thrilled that the three of us finally all have a night together. We all have been busy and while busy is somewhat normal we'd normally be able to have time together. However, two major events and the threat of war have the three of us scrambling around in different directions. So, tonight our different directions will finally lead us all home. I'm looking forward to spending time with both of them. It's been one or the other and I don't mind that change up because I do enjoy my individual time with them. However, I enjoy having them both with me. I feel safe with them and in the underworld feeling safe is a rare gem to hold on to.

Erica and I finish locking up the clinic and head outside. We get escorted around the city for safety reasons. We each have assigned drivers. Erica hops into her car while I get into mine where I find a pleasant surprise of Anthony and Nico waiting for me. That explains the SUV. Usually, if it's just me it's a sedan but when it's all three of us we take the SUV for more room.

"What are two up to?" I inquire as the SUV takes off. I was under the impression we all were meeting at home.

"We have a surprise and then we are going to take you to a nice dinner. After that, it's home to play until we pass out." Nico casually informs me.

"Oh, do I get a hint at what the surprise is?"

"Something to make our union more permanent." Anthony hints.

"Permanent as in like a tattoo?" I question, trying to not get too giddy. I know they have tattoos. Nico has most of his tattoos on his chest and some on his back. Anthony has less tattoos and his are only on his back.

I suggested to the guys that we should get little tattoos on our left ring fingers now that we are officially together and out in the underworld with our poly relationship. I got the idea from one of my reality TV shows. A couple did, and I thought it was cool and sweet. So, I suggested it to the guys randomly during our little honeymoon getaway. At the time, they didn't really answer me yes or no. I think they were more shocked at my suggestion. I've never been one to voice my liking of tattoos. It's my dirty little secret.

"Yes, Little Dove." Nico answers.

"We are going to get a simple butterfly and the antennas will make a V." Anthony informs me.

THE MAFIA LOVE CODE

"I love that!" I beam as I happily clap my hands and they both chuckle at me.

"You get to decide what you want to get for us." Nico adds.

"Something simple. A heart with an N and A inside it. Do you two want to get something for each other?" I question, curious.

"We thought about that. We will put an A or N in the butterfly wing." Nico answers.

"You two thought this out. I'm really excited." I beam a giddy smile.

We arrive at the tattoo shop, and we each get our tattoos at the same time. I have a female tattoo artist as does as Nico. Anthony has a guy doing his. Neither of them flinch while they are getting theirs. I can't decide if I love the burning session or not. I know my face twisted in pain a few times, but I think that's to be expected with getting a tattoo. Once we are done, they tell us how to take care of the tattoos, and we head out to dinner.

The guys take me to one of my favorite pizza places in the city. I love sharing things with Anthony that come from Nico and my past that we can now include him in. I enjoy bringing Anthony into our relationship, and I know Nico does as well. Even now as the three of us are laughing over pizza and wine, it's as if Anthony was the missing piece Nico and I didn't know we needed. I'm genuinely happy right now and I'm enjoying a nice evening out with my kings.

I think it's so sweet they made a nice evening for us in our busy schedules. I also can't believe they went with my tattoo idea. They are proving they are nothing like the mafia men I'm used to. I might be a trophy mafia wife so to speak, and I can't say there isn't a part of me that enjoys the attention when I'm on my men's arms. I have the best of both worlds in my opinion. I can be the trophy wife and I can be a career woman at the same time. Who ever said women can't have it all? Whatever fears I had about being a mafia wife have completely faded.

On the way home the three of us have fun playing with one another in the car from me sucking their cocks to them finger fucking me. These two know how to make my head spin and I'm starting to think the wait for sex was completely worth it. I was so intimidated by them having so much more knowledge than me but it's turning out to be perfectly fine. So fine as an orgasm escapes me. Shit, I'm hot and bothered, and I can't wait to get back to our bedroom because I'm ready to have them fuck me into oblivion for the rest of the night.

Chapter 31

Anthony

The moment we get home we waste no time heading to our bedroom. I can't wait for our house to be built because our sex dungeon is going to be so much fucking fun. For now we have Nico's condo which we make work. It's certainly not a permanent solution, but for now it doesn't matter because my focus is entirely on our butterfly who is now completely naked.

Violetta is touching herself, putting on a show for Nico and I as she rubs her clit with one hand while her other hand plays with her nipples. We both enjoy watching her touching herself and she enjoys putting on a show for us. I love watching Violetta spread her wings both in the bedroom and out of it. Nico and I are naked standing in front of the bed watching Violetta. Playing with her before we got home on the way back was fun. She sucked both our cocks but neither of us came. Turns out we like edging ourselves along with edging Violetta. It's been making for some serious mind blowing sex that I didn't even think was possible.

When we started this little poly journey Nico and I both didn't think we could gain any new ways of pleasure. We both knew what we liked and could train Violetta to please us both. Neither of us expected that we would find ourselves finding new ways to bring ourselves pleasure. Violetta thinks she is the only one learning about sex, but just because Nico and I have experience doesn't mean we have experience with sharing the same woman. Needless to say Dedra has been a great guide for all of us.

Violetta is so close to cumming. I look at Nico and he nods his head proving he is ready like I am. "Cum for us, Butterfly." I command, and her body shakes as her orgasm crushes over her.

Her hands fall to her side as she catches her breath. I climb onto the bed and position my pulsing cock up against her clit teasingly before I slide inside of her enjoying her tight walls on my cock. I move in and out of her slowly at first because I truly enjoy how she feels. Violetta's eyes close as she enjoys my tease. My lips land on her shoulder as my one hand goes around her neck just tight enough that it is slightly hard for her to breathe. Violetta loves being choked. Even now she's getting wetter just from my fucking her and choking her at the same time.

"Fuck, you're beautiful." I say in her ear as Nico comes over and sits on the edge of the bed.

"That she is." Nico boldly states as he begins stroking his cock. The two of us enjoy watching one another fuck

Violetta. Once again our poly relationship brings a new light to sex because I never thought I would get off on watching another man fuck a woman. However, it's completely different with Violetta because she belongs to both of us.

I pick up my pace a bit more feeling the need to chase my own release. As I get close my lips fall to hers before I remove my hand from her neck so she can easily breathe again. I thrust harder and faster into her as my lips furiously attack hers while capturing her moans of pleasure. She's soaking fucking wet making her feel even more amazing making it that much easier to find my release.

"I love you, Anthony." Violetta declares as we break our kiss, completely stunning me.

"You do?" I question, nuzzling my nose to hers.

"Yes. I love you both." She says nuzzling me back as her one hand reaches for Nico.

"Well, I just showed you how much I love you, so now it's Nico's turn." I say, kissing her sweetly on the lips before I pull out of her.

As Nico and I switch places he gives me an I told you so look. He knows I've been eagerly and patiently awaiting Violetta to say those three magic words to me. Watching her say it to Nico that night was almost a nightmare come true, but then she quickly recovered the situation. I understood where she was coming from. I've never been blind to the advantage Nico had. Now, it's evened out making me feel a little lighter with concerns that she would never love me.

I will commend them both for their valiant efforts to make me feel just a part of this as they are. They have shared their favorite places with me, told me countless stories from funny to more serious from their past, shown me pictures, and have done everything to incorporate me in their life and in our relationship. I love them both for it. Their consideration means so much to me. Probably more than they will ever know.

I lay next to Violetta and enjoy watching Nico fuck her. I realize how they have become two of my favorite people and the most important people in my life, besides Sofia. They make all the trauma my father put me through worth it. They are the two people I get to build the rest of my life with, and I wouldn't have it any other way. I know none of us saw this future for ourselves, but it's one none of us would trade.

Nico finds his release and rolls on the other side of Violetta who looks beyond relaxed and content like a cat who just had warm milk. She always ends up in the middle of us. Violetta rolls into me laying her head on my chest while I move my arm so she can snuggle more comfortably. Nico rolls one his side and places an arm over Violetta's stomach.

"I'm glad I have you two, and you have shared a lot of your past with me to help me feel included. I appreciate that, and it's only fair I tell you a bit of my past. I don't talk about it much and to be honest this might be the only time I ever talk about. My father was mentally abusive. He wanted me to be emotionless. He would waterboard me as punishment. He was brutal, and he fucked me up in the head. It's why I can kill and it have it not even phase me. I'm completely desensitized when it comes to killing because that's the beast I was made into. My first kill was at eight years old when my father made me kill a man who couldn't pay his debt. I don't and can't go into more detail than that." I attempt to explain something I've never explained to a living person before.

My past has always been something I've kept to myself. Not even Lorenzo knows all the details of my past. He's my best friend and has been in my life since my early teens. I've tried opening up to Lorenzo about my past with my father, but I always choose to keep it to myself. However, Nico and Violetta make me want to heal that part of my past and finally look forward to the future with hope instead of only duty.

"You don't have to go into any more detail. It's your past and that's where it can stay." Violetta says lovingly as she snuggles more into me.

"We are your future, Anthony. We can make happy and better memories that will make you forget about the horrors of your past." Nico adds, peeking his head over Violetta. I nod my acceptance to him.

"That's exactly right." Violetta echos Nicos thoughts.

The three of us fall into a comfortable silence knowing we are all beat from the day and our end of night play. For once my mind is at peace before sleep.

The fact that I even shared a portion of my past with them has me feeling a bit freer. They are right, we are forging new and better memories. I'm sure it won't be all blue skies, but wherever storms I may have to face, I'm glad I'm doing it with Violetta and Nico.

Chapter 32

Violetta

Things feel busier than ever as I help Sofia with last minute details to her river cruise wedding. At first, I thought the river cruise was over the top, but it's grown on me and I'm actually looking forward to the day. Sofia is positively beaming with joy. She found a beautiful flowy dress that hides her small baby bump. The girl is on top of it with plans and even baby stuff. I'm very proud of Sofia and her embracing mafia wife life. Watching her embrace it with such fervor makes it even easier to accept my role as a mafia wife.

I still can't believe I'm a mafia wife to not one but two Dons. I fought so hard for years against marrying one Don and now I have two. Two Dons, my Kings who share their power with me. They will not let me fade into the background. I love them for giving me a place at their side. It's clear I'm not the docile mafia wife that is happy to shop and spend money. Sofia is totally content to be that type of mafia wife and it's what clearly makes her happy. It goes to prove that even mafia wives can be different. I had this false assumption that all mafia wives were the same, but I was happily proven wrong. It's nice to have a variety of us because it shows that we don't have to be forced to fit into a box. The underworld may still be steeped in old ways and lines of thinking, yet slow changes are being made. I get to be a part of that change making it something I'm proud of.

My mind shifts to the clinic and the fact that it opens a week after Sofia and Connor's wedding. I'm so excited to have patients in the clinic. It's going to be so great seeing patients again. I really do love being a nurse. I've even thought about going back to school to become a midwife. I haven't broached the subject with my kings yet. Mainly because I haven't fully decided if it's something I want. I have a couple of paths I could take. Becoming midwife is one of them. Once I have made up my mind, I'm going to talk it over with my Kings and see if something we can make happen. I'm not even worried about them telling me no because they have both proven they are supportive of my dreams. The clinic alone is proof of that. There's also our tattoos. I don't doubt them on any level and that makes me feel even more secure in our relationship.

"Hey, Girl!" Erica's voice grabs my attention from the wedding checklist I'm going over.

Erica and I are meeting for breakfast. I beat her here and grabbed us a spot at the cute little French cafe that has the best crepes in the city. Erica has become my food buddy in exploring other cuisines that don't come from the Mediterranean since my kings are a bit particular when it comes to food. Erica grabs her seat across from me. I went with an outside table since it's nearing summer and it's warming up enough to actually want to embrace the outside.

"Morning," I greet back as our waitress comes over. We place our coffee orders before our waitress heads off again while we look over our menus.

"So, everything ready for the second big day for our family in less than three months?" Erica probes.

"I think so. Sofia is pretty on top of things." I answer, deciding on the wildberry crepes.

"Good. So, Jullian asked me to be his date to Sofia and Connor's wedding." Erika informs me with a confident smile.

"Does that mean things are going well with you two?" I probe a bit. I've been curious on how things have been going with them, but didn't want to overwhelm Erica with questions. I figured it was best to let her bring it up.

"It does. Jullian thinks it's a good test to feel Nico out. We want to ease him into us dating. You know how protective Nico is over the women in his life." She reminds me as our waitress comes back with my lavender latte and Erica's melon matcha tea. We place our orders and our waitress bounces away to help another table.

"I think Nico will be okay with you guys being together. I mean, he knows Jullian, and he knows he's a good guy. It's not like you have to introduce some guy from outside of our life to Nico. It could be worse. I think you two should give Nico a bit more credit. I know he will definitely give Jullian a stern talk as your older cousin who cares about you, but Jullian can handle that. They are best friends." I advise, hoping to alleviate some of her anxiety over telling Nico.

"Yeah, you are probably right. Well, the wedding will be a good test. He won't make a scene, so there's that. I think part of me fears Nico sees me as fuck up. The druggy girl. Maybe it's how I still see myself. I thought being sober would fix everything. I mainly thought it would fix me, but it only helped a little. Jullian is a good guy and I don't feel worthy of him." Erica confesses.

"Self doubt is a tricky beast to fight. It gets the best of us, but we have to remember our value. You are not your past, Erica. You have changed your life around. I love getting to know you. I'll be honest, I stayed away from you before I went off to college. You were right, I saw you as trouble. I almost didn't believe Nico when he told me you were sober. Now, I don't see you as trouble anymore. Now I see you as my friend, and you are turning into a beautiful person that I'm proud to have in my life."

"Well, damn, girl, when you put it like that," we both chuckle. "Thank you for that. It's easy to get caught up in who I used to be. I really didn't like who I was strung out on drugs. I hated myself for so long and finally love myself even if it's not a hundred percent." Erica shrugs, taking a sip of her drink.

"I don't think anybody can say that they love their entire self. We all have parts we don't love and maybe can't change. We are all a work in progress, we are simply in various stages." I reply, taking a sip of my own drink.

"College definitely made you wise." She jokes, causing us both to laugh.

We enjoy our breakfast as we bond more as friends. I honestly didn't know what to expect when Nico dragged me back to the underworld. I had some false ideas of what coming back to the underworld would be like. I certainly never imagined what I've actually come home to. Home, I never really felt like I had one. Living with my father, he certainly never made our house feel like a home. Then I was the warden to a man who held my very life in his hands. When I went off to college, I tried to make a home in the apartment I rented, but it never truly became my home. Perhaps because deep down I knew it was temporary. I finally found my home with Nico and Anthony, and with those around us from Erica and Sofia to Dedra. I'm happy with my life in the underworld. That is certainly something I never thought would happen

Chapter 33

Anthony

I can't believe I'm at my little sister's wedding less than three months from my union. I still don't fully know how I feel about her marriage being used as an alliance with the Irish. I suppose I thought I was better than that. Better than using my sister as a pawn, although she does seem like a willing pawn. I suppose her being in love and happy eases whatever strange guilt I might feel. I'm not even sure why I feel so guilty about the arrangement. Maybe it's because I feel she should be older or maybe I'm thrown off by her wanting this.

Even now, Sofia is beaming as she dances her first dance with Connor. Everything, even the ceremony took place on the ferry. This whole river cruise is elaborate and totally on par for my sister. None of this is a surprise to me. Sofia has always been a hidden diva. She kept it hidden because I think she was afraid of being judged by our father. She was always eager to please our dad, and in some ways, I was like that too as a child until I started receiving his less than ideal parenting style. Sofia knows nothing of what our father did to me. It's better that way.

She was his princess, and he treated her as such. I was his heir and weapon. We didn't have the same childhood, but just because mine was less than ideal doesn't mean I will ruin the ideal childhood that Sofia had. I don't hate her for it either. It's not her fault our father treated us differently.

Sometimes I forget Sofia is an adult, a freshly minted adult granted, but an adult nonetheless. She is happy to be starting her family and is content to be with Connor. I'm not sure if they love each other, but they do seem genuine with their mutual feelings of affection. I think that's the bare minimum I can ask as her guardian. I certainly didn't think she would marry so young, but then again I think there was a part of me that will always be in denial that my baby sister is grown. I'll probably be the same way with my own kids.

I do love the idea of kids. It was always more for duty than desire. Something I knew would be expected of me as the next Don. Heirs and spares are important in the underworld. If you don't have someone in line to take your place, it can become a bloodbath for the position. It's always best to have an heir or someone lined up and ready to take the position of Don, that's if you want leadership to stay in your family lineage. So, I knew kids were always a part of my future. A duty that had to be done. However, Nico and Violetta, make me genuinely want a family.They have helped me to see how positive and wonderful having a family can be. Kids are so much more than duty now. They are something I get to share and experience with two people I have come to not be able to live without.

"Can I have a dance with my brother?" I hear Sofia's sweet voice reach my ears, breaking my thoughts.

"Of course, you can." I reply with a smile as I lead her out to the dance floor.

Nico and Violetta follow behind us as well as Erica and Jullian, who came together because they are in a relationship that apparently stems from our wedding months ago. Nico is happy for them and told them both they worried for no reason about telling him. I think they were afraid he would overreact with how overprotective he can be and his known anger issues that I now know he has under control. We take our places on the dance floor as music begins to play as our cue to start dancing.

"You look so beautiful, and I'm so proud of you." I beam as I sway Sofia across the dance floor.

"Aw, thank you. I'm proud of you too, Anthony." She replies with her own sweet smile.

"You are?" I question as I spin her.

"I am for doing what makes you happy. Nico and Violetta. You three are making good changes in this crazy underworld life. I'm so thankful that you are my big brother. You have always taken care of me even when Dad was alive. You've always looked out for me, and I'm grateful. I'm also glad you gave me a brother and a sister. I mean most people only get one, but you made sure I got both." She declares as we twirl around the dance floor to a song I'm not even paying attention to.

I chuckle. "I have an amazing little sister, and she deserves the world."

"See that's the kind of stuff that makes you the best brother ever." She giggles, and I chuckle, shaking my head slightly at her. "By the way, thank you for the townhouse. Connor and I are really making it a home."

"You're welcome. I'm glad you guys like it. It can be your place in the city. Nico bought you the land next to ours in the suburbs so you and Connor build your own dream home." I inform her.

"Well, now I don't know, you might have some competition with Nico for best brother." Sofia jokes, and I laugh as the song ends.

"What's that about me and Anthony competing for best brother?" Nico says as he and Violetta walk with us off the dance floor.

Sofia giggles. "Thank you for buying us land next to you guys. I love keeping our family close. I want our kids to be best friends."

"That was the idea." Nico replies. "Plus, I'm an only child. I finally have a sibling to spoil."

"You will hear no complaints from me." Sofia says as she kisses Nico on the cheek.

"Thank you, guys, for making today amazing for me. Now, I need to go to mingle a little. Bridal duties and all, but I love you three very much." Sofia declares, kissing me on the cheek before she hugs Violetta and Nico.

Sofia heads off to mingle while Violetta and I have a dance. Once the river cruise ends, Sofia and Connor are off to some winery bed and breakfast combo thing in the mountains for a couple of days. It was a gift from Connor's family. I'm not really sure why they decided to send a pregnant woman to the winery, but apparently they have a non-alcoholic options. Still, a strange gift, yet Sofia and Connor were elated over it.

    The three of us head back home, tired from the last couple of days. Weddings are exhausting, and I would totally be fine if we have a nice gap until the next wedding. Once we are home the three of us strip out of our fancy dress clothes and shower. Violetta does take time to remove her makeup and pins in her hair because it was up in some elegant updo. The three of us end up in bed, Violetta sandwiched between us. Normally, we would play a little before bed, but we fooled around at the wedding. There were little nooks that we took advantage of. Sex would be an option but all three of us are craving sleep which means the chances of morning sex fun are much higher. Morning sex can be a great thing to wake up to, and I look forward to what the morning will bring.

Chapter 34

Nico

I pop the champagne as Violetta passes out flute glasses. Both Angel Clinics opened today and we are celebrating at the burlesque club at our VIP table of course. The Angel Clinic for low income families and really anyone who needs medical care is a true success. The papers even wrote a glowing piece on the Angel Clinic and the positive impact it already has on the community. Meanwhile the Angel of Death Clinic is scheduling patients. The best part of all of this is watching my sweet Little Dove, my Butterfly glow with happiness. She has such a passion for helping people and she chose to do that by becoming a nurse. Knowing my ambitious Violetta, she is already plotting to further her career somehow.

The clinics aren't just great for Violetta. They have turned out to be a great place for Erica to thrive as Violetta's assistance. I also love how they are forging a friendship. I'm proud of Erica and how she has completely turned her life around. She even snagged herself a good man in the form of my best friend. I don't care if they are together. They seem to make each other happy, and that's good enough for me. I trust Jullian. I don't have to worry about him hurting Erica. Honestly, them being together is a relief to me and makes my life easier because now I don't have to threaten some poor schmuck who wouldn't last a day in the underworld.

I'm not entirely sure why they were afraid to tell me. Apparently, Erica was afraid I would be angry and do something irrational. In fairness, a much younger me might have done that. I was certainly more aggressive and a hot head in my teens and early twenties. Then when the prospect of becoming Don was closer, I shifted my attitude to be more mature and patient. For the aggression part, I run, box, and workout. Anthony and I actually box together as it's something we both enjoy. Anthony certainly has his own aggression to work out. After Anthony opened up a bit about his past it made a lot of things click for me as I finally put some pieces of the puzzle together. Needless to say, boxing is something we now bond over along with other things we have found that we have in common.

"Are you guys having a party without me?" Dedra questions with her hands on her hips as she approaches our table. She's dressed in a dark pink sequin dress that hugs every curve of her body. Erica, Jullian, and the three of us are celebrating. I figured Dedra would pop in to say hello.

"Of course not. We'd never dream of such a thing." I reply as Violetta hands her the last champagne flute that

I fill for her. We always save a spot for Dedra because she is usually around and she loves to pop in to say hello.

"Good," Dedra smiles as she slides into the booth. "Congratulations are in order." She cheerfully says.

"Yes, there is much to celebrate from gaining a new family to new friends, and even starting a new business adventure. I'm so happy to get back into scrubs and help people all thanks to my two men, my Kings. I'm happy you two dragged me back and showed me where my true home is." Viloetta declares, raising her glass. We all clank our glasses together.

I love watching Violetta beam her happiness as we toast and drink to new adventures. I'm so proud of the woman she has become. I'm proud of her for spreading her wings and embracing her life with me and Anthony. I love watching her blossom into the fierce woman she is becoming. I've always known this side of Violetta existed, but she buried it away for reasons I honestly haven't figured out. Whatever the reasons were, they are her own, and honestly I'm not sure it even matters now because she is here with us. She's happy, and that's really all I wanted for her.

"So, you two are a thing?" Dedra questions, pointing a perfectly pink manicure finger between Erica and Jullian.

"Yes, we are officially together." Erica glows as she places a hand on Jullian's chest.

"Everyone is just finding a partner or two these days. I admire those of you who commit to a relationship, but your girl is single forever." Dedra replies, sipping her champagne.

"That's because there isn't a man who can handle you, Dedra." Villotta jests.

"Damn straight, Unicorn." Dedra replies and we all laugh.

"I'm never going to live down the nickname Unicorn, am I?" Violetta questions as she drinks some of her champagne.

"Nope. It's what everyone refers to you as now in both clubs." Dedra answers with a smirk.

"Of course they do. Eh, whatever, there are far worse nicknames to be called." Violetta contends with a shrug of her shoulders. I chuckle at her.

We spend some time chatting and eventually Erica and Jullian head out. We will be heading out soon too because of shitty adult responsibilities. Even in the underworld adulthood spoils fun. However, the three of us wanted to talk to Dedra about how to introduce anal sex into our sex routine. It's something we have talked about before and something the three of us are all interested in, but we didn't want to rush into it either. Especially because so much of this is a learning curve for all of us. So, once Erica and Jullian have left I decide it's a good time to broach the subject.

"Dedra, we need your wisdom once more," I declare, gaining Dedra's full attention as she raises an eyebrow at me in interest. "We are wanting to try to introduce some anal sex into our sex life. We wanted to know what you suggest for next steps and if you think some sessions with you will be helpful." I say, taking a sip of my drink.

"I was wondering when you three were going to venture into the anal sex world. I do suggest a session or two with me. We do need to stretch Violetta a bit so when you fuck her it's not uncomfortable. Anal is something I suggest we take baby steps with to ensure Violetta is truly comfortable with it. With that being said I do ask you to give it two to three sessions before you make up your mind if anal is something you enjoy or not." Dedra explains.

"I can agree to that. I figured the first couple of times might feel strange or weird. I'm all for exploring and playing to find the things the three of us enjoy and don't. I'm comfortable enough with the guys sexually to try this. You clearly know I have no experience with it." Violetta answers.

"Good, and yes I'm well aware of you, Unicorn. Now, you two. Any anal experience?" Dedra questions, pointing her pink pointer finger between Anthony and I.

"Honestly, no. I can't say I've ever fuck a girl in her ass." I answer honestly.

"I have a couple of times, but it's been awhile. I don't mind being the only one who fucks Violetta in the ass if you aren't into it, Nico." Anthony offers.

"Good to know. I want to try first to see how I like it. I've never had a chance to even try, and honestly, I want to try. However, if it turns out ot not be my thing it's good to know you wouldn't mind being the only one anal fucking while I fuck her pussy."

"Okay, we need to stop talking about this now." Violetta says as she shifts in her seat, trying to rub her thighs together.

"Oh, Unicorn, if us talking about it is turning you on then we might just be on the right track." Dedra jokes as Violetta groans, causing Anthony and I both to chuckle. "We will definitely get something on the books soon. You won't have to wait long, Unicorn." Dedra says with her own giggle shaking her head at Violetta.

We finish our drinks and say goodnight to Dedra before we head out for the night. Violetta has an early morning at the clinic, and Anthony has a meeting with the Irish to get updates on the Russian and Mexican war while I have things to handle at the casino. Casino is still a good business for us to run and something my family has personally worked hard to build, so I am determined to keep the business running. Anthony's family has their hands in the ports, which is certainly helpful. We are certainly competition to someone like the Russians. It's hard to know what their motives are and this isn't the regular world. We don't necessarily do things civilly because everyone is to be looked at as the enemy. Everyone is out to get you is the mindset one needs to have in the underworld, and with the way the Russians are picking off the smaller mafia families, it's good to be cautious.

THE MAFIA LOVE CODE

Once we are home the three of us unwind for bed. Violetta is doing her nightly routine of washing her face and moisturizing or whatever it is she actually does. All I know is it's part of her self care routine and helps her relax before bed. Like most of us in the underworld, we tend to be creatures of habit. Violetta's nightly routine is crucial for her to unwind for the night, so while she occupies the bathroom with her girly self care routine, Anthony and I wait patiently for Violetta. We have learned to do our stuff like brush our teeth before Violetta gets in the bathroom at night or we won't get a chance to get our stuff done. That's why in the house that's being built our bathrooms will be sort of split. Violetta will have her side with own toilet, sink, and storage. Anthony and I will have our own side similar to Violetta. Our own sides will have access to our walk in closets. Then the bathrooms will meet in the middle for a huge shower stall and one huge jacuzzi tub. The three of us are looking forward to our house being built. I also think we need to find a better place in the city. When I originally bought this condo I thought it was only going to be Violetta and I. Maybe a kid or two, but I always knew this place wasn't going to be long term. I guess we will be moving out sooner than I thought. Not that it's a problem. I'm more than happy to accommodate our family. While I might have not bought this condo with the three of us in mind, that doesn't mean we haven't adapted it to our needs. Still, a new place will be needed sooner rather than later. It will be something we all pick together because together is how we do just

Brit Leigh

about everything now, and I don't think any of us would have it any other way.

Chapter 35

Violetta

I'm unbelievably happy to be in scrubs again with a stethoscope around my neck. I still can't fully wrap my mind around the fact that Nico built this clinic for me. Yes, he found a way to do some illegal things with it, however, I actually agree with him on assisted suicide. Obviously, there's a process we have developed to screen patients and their families to ensure this is truly the patients choice, and that they are sound of mind. Just because we are doing illegal things doesn't mean that we don't need to have checks and balances in place. Especially with the morally grey area that assisted suicide falls in.

Besides the morally grey area of the Angel of Death Clinic, the legal side of things are also going well. I love that we are able to help a vast amount of people who might not have gotten care due to finances. That's one of the hardest things I had to process as a nurse was watching people not be able to afford medical care or medicine. I know I come from a privileged background. Even when I lived on my own and insisted on paying for everything on my own, I was still safe financially because I knew if for whatever reason I truly needed money for something I could go to Nico. It broke my heart the first time I lost a patient due to them not being able to have money for something that was dire to their health. In a way, the ER was nice because it made it harder to be attached to patients. However, despite this, I do like that bond that can be forged between patients and medical staff can be special. Sometimes, there's a patient or two that you will simply bond with and something special blooms. Still, giving bad news, whether you like the patient or not, is hard. It's even harder when you know they won't be able to afford the treatment. So having this clinic is huge, and I'm thrilled to be a part of it.

    Personal life is going well too. Sofia was just at the clinic for her own check up. One of the doctors on staff is an OBGYN so we can see pregnant patients for basic care and also offer women's health options. So, Sofia likes coming to the clinic now and it makes Anthony relax. He's so protective over her, and it's so sweet to witness. I have a feeling he will be the same way with our kids whenever that time comes. I might be having a little baby fever, but I'm also soaking up running the clinic and deciding what to do about furthering my education. I know I can be a mom and still go back to school even run the clinic at the same time if I'm ambitious enough. Plus, I have two men at my side who do anything to make me happy and support me. I simply need to decide what I want to do about furthering my education. On the kids front we are at if it happens, it happens. We aren't preventing it, but we aren't going to specifically try for pregnancy. It's less stressful that way for us as we do have other stuff going on, so to put pressure on getting pregnant doesn't seem wise.

My mind shifts to shutting down the clinic for the night. Anthony is handling some stuff with the Angel of Death Clinic. Anthony steps in and handles things for Nico when he is busy with the casino given its importance for income. Not to say that Angel Clinic isn't important, but it's easier for Anthony to handle the clinic right now because Jullian and Lorenzo have the docks under control. I secretly like when Anthony or Nico come to visit me at work. Even better when they both come, but today it's just Anthony. We are going to pick Nico up at the casino and go out to dinner for pizza and wine. Pizza is one food I will always be down to devour. Sometimes we take the food home and do a movie tonight, but tonight we are all craving some date like activity that doesn't involve the club. We love the burlesque and brothel. I never thought I would enjoy going to a brothel but it's also a slight sex club as well and that's the part I seem to enjoy. However, they do not consider themselves a dungeon. Connie is very serious about making sure the club is not labeled as a dungeon. Dedra explained the reasoning, but to be honest it went over my head.

Anthony finds me in the nursing station. "You almost ready, Little Violet?" He inquires.

"Yes, I just have to quickly change out of my scrubs. I'll meet you in the car." I answer as I shut down my computer for the night.

One of the doctors is still here in the office doing paperwork. I believe there are a couple other employees floating around in the Angel of Death clinic. That clinic runs on totally different hours than the legal clinic. I know soon guards will show up to keep an eye on the place. Plus, Nico has a very advanced security system in place that he uses for all his businesses. Nico takes security for his businesses very seriously because in the underworld not being prepared is a way for your enemies to make unwanted moves against you.

"You sure you don't need help changing? I hate to admit it, but you look sexy in black scrubs." Anthony says as I stand from my desk to grab my black duffle bag.

"If we did that, then we would be late to meet Nico." I remind him.

Anthony groans. "That's true, but maybe I'm okay with being a little late." His arms snake around my hips pulling me to him. I've barely got a grasp on the duffle bag and drop it as I try to steady myself in Anthony's arms. His lips fall on to mine and for several moments our lips are locked in a battle before Anthony's phone vibrating in his pants pocket interrupts us. Anthony groans in annoyance as he pulls his phone from his pocket. He looks at and chuckles before he shows me a text from Nico.

I'm on my way now, you two better not be late, or I'll know what you two were up to. We both agreed we fuck her in scrubs together, Tony.

I giggle. The guys agreed that they have a sexy little nurse fantasy they want to play out with me. I'm all for roleplay so I said yes. We have yet to have time to do live out this fantasy so the guys agreed they wouldn't fuck me in scrubs until the fantasy was fulfilled. However, they are both having trouble controlling themselves. I can't deny I'm enjoying the sexy attention.

"I guess I should go to the car before I break my pack with Nico. He only calls me Tony when he's in a cranky mood. I wonder if he had a stressful day with the casino. Go get ready. I love you, Violetta." Anthony declares with a kiss on my lips.

"I love you too, Anthony." I reply when we break our kiss.

Anthony releases me from his arms. I lean down to grab my duffle bag which invites Anthony to smack my ass. I yelp, but I'm so turned on by it. I hear Anthony chuckle as he leaves. I ignore his antics and head to the bathroom to quickly change. As comfortable as scrubs are, and I do enjoy wearing them, but they are not date clothes.

I quickly change into my dark wash skinny jeans and a black off the shoulder three quarter sleeve cashmere sweater to embrace the cooler temps. I pair my outfit with black ankle heeled boots with simple gold dangle earrings and a golden cuff bracelet. I quickly put on some dusty rose lipstick, light gold shimmer to my eyelids, and mascara. Nothing crazy. I don't wear makeup or even jewelry when I'm working. I just wear a simple black rubber band on my ring finger. With constantly washing my hands, slipping gloves on and off, and handling specimens, I rather not wear my nice jewelry. So I leave my wedding bands at home when I'm at work. I wish I was wearing them for dinner yet at the same time I don't have to worry about a potentially messy meal dirtying up my wedding bands. I'm anal about my wedding bands because one is a family heirloom I hope to pass to my daughter or daughter in law. The other is the first thing Anthony ever picked out for me and that makes it very special.

    I take my hair out of its ponytail and quickly run a brush through it. My hair is a bit bouncier from the ponytail, but I manage to make it work. Once I'm satisfied I toss my scrubs, sneakers, and makeup bag back in my duffle bag. I sling my duffle bag over my shoulder and head out to the car. I leave through the one side entrance that most of the staff comes in and out of. There's a small path that leads to the back alley where I know our town car is waiting for me. The second I walk out of the alleyway I turn right to head toward the town car, however someone grabs me from behind.

    I scream attempting to get Anthony and the drivers attention because I can see the black SUV. Something sharp pokes my right side as a strong arm attempts to hold me to their body with what I assume is a knife. A white cloth comes over my mouth and I start to feel nauseous as it burns my skin. My lungs begin to feel a bit irritated. I see Anthony lunge out of the SUV and pull his gun as he runs toward us. The man isn't paying attention as he's too busy trying to pull me away in the opposite directions. The man might not be focused on Anthony, but he never leaves my line of sight. Without hesitation, Anthony skillfully shoots my attacker in the head. The once strong arms fall limp as my attacker body falls to the ground with a thud. I feel unsteady from whatever he was trying to drug me with. Anthony rushes to my side and catches me before I hit the ground.

"Are you okay, Violetta?" His voice is laced with concern.

"I'm fine, I think." Trying to gather my bearings. Whatever was on the cloth made me feel sick and totally irritated my skin and breathing airways causing me to cough a bit. Anthony steadies me with his arms and a grasp onto him tightly feeling a little weak.

"Trevor, call Lorenzo and tell him we need clean up ASAP. Call Nico and tell him to get over here now! I'm taking Violetta inside to Dr. Frankfort to make sure she is okay." Anthony instructs. I turn to look at the dead body. The man has a mask on and the bullet hole in his head is bleeding some. I notice the cloth in his hand that was over my mouth.

"Anthony, that cloth had something on it that was making me feel sick." I inform him the best I can as I lean on him.

Trevor, my driver, immediately snatches the cloth, and hands it to Anthony who thanks him as Trevor has his cell to his ear. Anthony helps me back inside and calls for Dr. Frankfort who rushes to help. They get me to an exam room and up on a table. Dr. Frankfort looks me over and declares that some fresh air should help the symptoms from the chloroform that is most likely on the cloth. Luckily, I wasn't exposed very long to the chloroform. I'm honestly already feeling better, but I know some fresh will definitely be good.

Nico arrives shortly after Dr. Frankfort declares me okay. He rushes to my side. "Are you okay?" I can tell he's panicked.

"I'm fine. My nerves are a little shaky, but other than that I'm okay." I answer, leaning into his arms. "Anthony is the one that saved me. Thank you by the way."

"You don't have to thank me. It's my fucking job to protect you." He says before he kisses me softly on the lips.

"I'm glad you happened to be here." Nico adds.

"Me too. I think I need some self defense classes and a gun that I need to learn to shoot." I request.

"Absolutely, Butterfly. Whatever you want." Anthony gently kisses me on the forehead.

"You are a hell of a shot, Anthony. I saw the body before they hauled it away." Nico comments.

"I told you, I'm not a man to fuck with because I know how to kill in many ways, quickly, and without hesitation." Anthony answers, making me glad his dark soul is belongs to Nico and I.

"I never doubted you and never will," Nico declares as he pauses for a minute to gather his thoughts. "Do we think this is from the Russians or Mexicans? Are either of them finally making a move?" Nico ponders out loud.

"I don't know. I say we head home and get our pizza delivered. Lorenzo will try to see if he can ID the attacker. They will thoroughly check the body for any evidence. I'll send a text to Connor to let him know we need an immediate meeting with his father." Anthony suggests.

Nico and I agree so the three of us head out together after thanking Dr. Frankfort, who is also now heading home for the night. Nico is having the guards come early. I'm relieved when the three of us make it home. I let the guys do the stuff needed while I go take a warm shower to calm my nerves. I might even pop one of my anti-anxiety meds to help me relax and sleep. Tonight's events certainly call for it. After I'm done with my shower, the three of us eat before heading to bed to attempt some sleep because after tonight we definitely don't want to be caught off guard due to lack of sleep. I must confess, I feel better now that I'm sandwiched between the two men that I love and trust to protect me. Embracing the safe feeling I allow myself to drift to sleep.

Chapter 36

Nico

Two days ago, Violetta was attacked by an unknown attacker. We thought it might be the Russians finally making a move against the bigger mafia families, but there's no proof that is the case. We are also looking into the Mexicans as well, but the Russians seem more likely since they are bigger and have more to gain by taking our territory. We just ended our meeting with the Irish, and even they aren't sure what to make of the attack. The biggest and most worrisome question is, if it wasn't the Russians or the Mexicans, then who the fuck could it have been?

It's no secret that being in the underworld, you are bound to make enemies for one reason or another. Sometimes it's as simple as having what your enemy desires. We are certainly a target with our success in the casinos, the Angel Clinics, and control of most of the docks. With the Italian faction being completely united, and clearly we won't be divided, makes us a threat. The Russians are clearly seeking war with the Mexicans. It's not hard to assume they would want to come for other families. So the attack made us all jump to the assumptions that it was the Russians, but it might not be them which means it could be the Mexicans or another unknown enemy.

I'm worried about Violetta. She was doing so well embracing her life in the underworld, and then the attack happened leaving her edgy. Understandably, of course. Anthony and I have already shown her some self defense moves and have her scheduled with a top self defense instructor that we trust. Anthony immediately bought her a gun, which she carries with her in her purse or duffle bag. We gave her a rundown on how to use it but we both will be taking her to the shooting range to let her practice. I'm glad that she is taking initiative to protect herself because we all know it was lucky that Anthony happened to be with her when the attack happened. My guess is that her attacker didn't plan for Anthony or I to be with her because normally we aren't.

The reality is, this shit happens in the underworld. It's the shitty part of it. That's something we all have to accept in this life. I accepted it at a young age, and so did Anthony, but Violetta has fought her place in the underworld tooth and nail. I hate that when she is finally embracing it and thriving, she fucking gets attacked. It's frustrating and annoying because I don't want Violetta to go backwards, and while I understand her skittishness so soon after the attack, I don't want her to regress from the progress she has made. Violetta needs to make peace with this life like Anthony and I have. She is on the right path, but I hope that this bump in the road does not discourage her from moving forward. It's been a painstaking path for me to get Violetta to even embrace this life with me. I would hate for her to go backward.

Anthony seems to think Violetta will be just fine, but he's not the one that has had to fight tooth and nail with her for years about this. Anthony also told me I should give Violetta some of the benefit of the doubt because she has grown so much, especially since we built our union. Part of me knows he's right. Violetta is certainly not the girl she once was. She has found a fierce fire within her that she is using to light everyone on fire that dares cross her path. She truly is a butterfly, and I've enjoyed watching her spread her wings. Yet there is a part of me that fears if she regresses, if she begins to hate this life, she will come to resent me since I'm technically the one that dragged her back. I was always going to be the one to do it, and I've always been terrified that she would hate me for it.

Deep down, I know Violetta is happy with Anthony and I as well as the life we are working to build. Anthony pointed out I was letting my fear skew my view. I hate that he is right. It's not just her hating me, it's what if something bad happened to her. I don't know why, but I would feel responsible. It's not logical, but emotions often don't abide by logic.

Pushing the thoughts away, I focus on talking plans over with the architect we have hired to build our house. It's something positive to look forward to. The three of us are eager and excited for our house to be built. We can make it our own and our bedroom and bathroom are designed for our unique relationship. It's actually fun building a home that we can design together. We have a future to build, a family to have, and we aren't going to let anything get in our way. The three of us have embraced our roles as the leaders of the unified Italian mafia or the Italian Trinity as we like to call ourselves. The three of us will defend our kingdom. Even Violetta is willing to learn to fight and shoot a gun, yes it's for self defense, but it's more than that. I realize it's her way of fighting to protect what is ours. The realization washes whatever irrational fears I had with Violetta. She's our queen, and she's determined to help us keep what is ours. Whatever we might face, the three of us face it together.

Chapter 37

Violetta

It's been almost two weeks since my attack. We still don't know if the man who attacked me was associated with the Russians, Mexicans, or perhaps another enemy we aren't fully aware of yet. This is the downside to underworld life. It's one of things that made me want to run from this life. For so long, I fought against this life and the attack was a reminder of why I never wanted to come back to this life. It was a jolt to reality from whatever fantasy land I've been living in. Things were going so smoothly without much incident that I forgot about the dangers that can lurk in the shadows.

There would have been a time that the attack would have sent me running for the hills, changing my name, and hiding away in fear. I'd be lying if I said there wasn't a part of me that felt that way. I wanted to run far away from the underworld. It was my first instinct to be honest. However, leaving the underworld would mean leaving Anthony and Nico behind, and I can't fathom my life without them now. They are vital in my life. I love them more than I ever thought I could love someone. I'd rather slum it out in the underworld with them then live a safe life without them.

It's not just about not having my kings in my life, but it's more than that now. The three of us have done something that many thought would never happen. We unified the divided Italian mafia once more because it should have never been divided in the first place. We are stronger and fiercer together. There's also the fact that I have something I love and am proud to be a part of with the Clinics. Sure, I primarily work in the Angel Clinic, but that doesn't mean, as the Angel of Death Clinic begins to see patients, that I won't be down there. Our clinics are doing so much good for the community, and I don't want to give it up.

With my resolve to stay at my two kings sides and be their queen has me taking more precautions to be better prepared if I'm ever attacked again. I felt helpless mainly because I didn't know how to defend myself. I'm still so thankful that Anthony was there and that he's one hell of a shot. Erica and I have started self defense classes that we do twice a week for the foreseeable future. Erica decided to join me after she heard about my attack, and she doesn't want to be helpless in case she ever becomes a target for our enemies. I also have a gun that the guys taught me to use. I have to be honest, shooting a gun is exhilarating. I might get a bit high off the feeling, which is why the guys and I decided that the house we are building in the basement will be a gun range for us. I mean really could I call myself a mafia wife without carrying a gun on my person?

Embracing the underworld even with the bad, it's liberating in a way. I feel more confident and powerful than I ever have. I also have a sense of purpose. Running the Angel Clinics is what I always wanted. I didn't know I wanted it or needed it, but Nico did. Nico and Anthony have a part to play in my new sense of self, but a lot of it is finally embracing my role in the underworld. I'm starting to believe the reason I was so resistant in the beginning was due to my father. He painted his picture to me so that I would be seen and not heard. I would marry, have heirs, and fade away into the background. It made me feel so insignificant like what I wanted didn't matter. I was simply an object or a pawn to be used in a game I wasn't allowed to play.

I allowed my father's distorted picture of my future to consume me. It began to be something I had to fight against. That I was the only one fighting for what I wanted because it didn't seem like anyone would come to my side. I put all mafia men in a category with my father that I let distort my view of Nico. Even with a bond of friendship as we got older and he fully embraced being the next Don and for me to be his wife. The word wife meant a prison sentence to me that I was determined to never end up in. Nico being my warden back then was something I saw in a negative light. I felt controlled by everyone around me only solidifying my fear that I was nothing but a pawn even to the man I loved and cared about.

I unjustly transferred my father's distorted view to Nico. I hate that I did that. He didn't deserve it yet he took it anyway. He took my resistance and strong will to be free from the underworld like it didn't bother him, but I now know it did. He would never admit because he wouldn't want to make me feel guilty knowing my father is to blame for my attitude. Nico knew how my father operated. I never gave Nico credit where I should have. He's always been a support, a friend, and someone who loves me. I'm glad to no longer have a distorted lens where Nico is concerned and even the underworld because it's a whole different place when I can play the game. I'm not just playing the game now, I'm playing it as queen and not a pawn. That alone makes all the difference.

With all the new found confidence, I head to see my first patient for the day. I'm doing intakes, vitals, and some of the lab stuff until we can get a few more trustworthy nurses on staff. We weren't fully prepared for the patient traffic that we have. I've reached out to a few contacts I've met through my time in the legal medical field world. I know some nurses that might be okay hopping to the not so legal side of things. We also have some other feelers out from our doctors who have contacts that are okay with the not so legal side of things.

I open the door leading to the waiting area. "Helen." I see a middle aged woman stand and head toward me. "Good morning." I greet as I shut the door behind us and head to take her to the scale.

"Good morning." She greets back with a smile.

After I take her weight, we head to one of the patient rooms. Helen walks in and takes a seat at the chair near the little station where my computer is on as well as some other things like the BF cuff, pulse ox monitor, and other stuff we need for basic exams. I park my butt on my wheelie stool and begin to type in the password to the computer to open patient charts.

"Can I see your finger?" I ask, picking up the pulse ox monitor. She offers me her pointer finger and slips it on. It quickly reads what I need. "What brings you in today?" I question as I slip the pulse ox off her finger and open her chart on the computer to input the vitals I've taken.

"I'm here to speak with you Miss. Violetta. I come in peace and with a message from Misha Romanov." Helen informs me. My blood runs cold for a moment at her words before as I let them settle over me. Misha Romanov is the head of the Russian mafia. I think they call themselves Bratva. I don't know all the various terms tossed about as most in the underworld say mafia or mob and don't do the specific names.

"Oh, is that so?" I raise an eyebrow at her, keeping my calm composure.

"Yes. You can pat me down if it makes you feel better, but I promise I'm not here to try and hurt you. I'm just a trusted messenger." She replies calmly and confidently.

"Okay, what is the message from Misha Romanov?" I question because I can't deny that I'm not curious.

"He wants you to know the Russians were not behind your attack that recently happened. He has no intentions of harming the Italian faction. He wants to meet with you, Nico, and Anthony. You made an alliance with the Irish, and now the Russians would like an alliance with the Italians. Misha requests that you meet him at Lodge SteakHouse tomorrow night at seven." Helen relays her message.

"I will relay the message to Nico and Anthony. Tell Misha we will be there." I reply without hesitation.

With that I lead Helen out and she leaves the clinic. I immediately pull my cell out of my pocket before heading to the break room where I will have some privacy to break the news to Nico and Anthony that I just agreed to a meeting with the Russians. It's not like I had much of a choice. I can't say no that would certainly start a war. Not that I wanted to say no. The Russians are finally making a move, and it's not a move any of us saw coming. They want an alliance with us. Who would have thought us unifying the Italian faction and making an alliance with the Irish would lead to an alliance with the Russians who are the most difficult of us all. It just goes to prove that nothing is off limits and the unexpected certainly happens in the underworld.

Chapter 38

Nico

I've just arrived at the casino. Fuck, I swear sometimes I feel as if I live in this fucking place. There are seriously some moments where I would be fine if I never heard the sound of pinging slot machines ever again in my life. I enter my office and set my venti cappuccino on my desk debating if I'm about to make it an Irish coffee. Violetta has her anti-anxiety pills, Anthony has his killing and torturing, and I have alcohol as my stress reliever. When you live in the underworld you're bound to have a couple of bad habits.

    All of us are edgy since Violetta was attacked mainly because we don't know who it was. It's totally possible it was random, but nothing is ever truly random or coincidental in the underworld. My worry is whether it's the Russians or Mexicans. Shit, part of me almost hopes that it is one of them because it would almost make things easier. If it's not one of them then we might have bigger issues at hand. Not knowing shit in the underworld can get you killed. The most disturbing thing about this whole situation is that we might have an unknown enemy targeting us.

My phone vibrating in my pocket pulls me from my thoughts. I reach into my suit jacket pocket and pull my cell out. Violetta's face is lighting up my screen. It's barely after nine in the morning, she shouldn't be calling me for anything. "Violetta, what's wrong?" I answer the call.

"Well, aren't you just Mr. Jump to Conclusions." Her sassy tone relaxes me a bit.

"Yeah, well, I want to know why you are calling us." I hear Anthony chime in making me realize this is a three way call. Now, I'm back on a high alert.

"Do you want the good news or the bad news first?" Violetta probes.

"Bad news is always first, you know that." I remind her, trying to hide my slight irritation at her games. Normally, I find her games fun and they usually lead to something sexy, but I don't enjoy her games when it comes to business.

"The bad news is that the Russians weren't behind my attack. So, that means it might be the Mexicans. The good news, we are having dinner with Misha Romnov tomorrow at the Lodge SteakHouse because he wants an alliance with us as well." Violetta informs us.

"I have so many fucking questions." Is all I can manage out.

"Yeah, Butterfly, we are going to need more than that." Anthony reasonably adds.

"He sent a messenger. She was my first patient. She delivered her message, and I told her to tell Misha that we would see him tomorrow at dinner. I know you might be mad at me for making that call, but it seemed to be the only thing to do since the Russians were waving a white flag. Helen, the messenger, made it clear Misha wanted us to know it was not him." Violetta answers.

"Do you really think we would be upset at you for agreeing?" I ask in disbelief. Here I am trying subtly not to worry about Violetta regretting her choice to come back to the underworld instead she's embracing it. Anthony was right, I was letting my fear cloud my judgement.

"Well, I don't know. It's kind of a big deal isn't it?" She questions, almost unsure if she did the right thing.

"Violetta, you made the right call, and I'm damn proud of you for making it." I compliment

"It was the right call. We both would have made the same call, Butterfly. I'm proud of you as well, Butterfly," Anthony pauses, and I know him well enough now to know he is gathering his thoughts. "Alright, so the Russians want an alliance so we hear Misha out and see what he is offering. The other problem now, is who the fuck was behind the attack? I guess we have to consider the Mexicans at this point. I don't like that we haven't been able to figure this out. At least, we know it's not the Russians." Anthony adds.

"Anthony, you should let the Irish know what's going on. I'll fill Jullian and Lorenzo in on the new developments." I direct.

"Sounds good to me." Anthony agrees.

"Well, I should get back to the clinic. I'll let you know if any more developments happen. I'll see you two at home later. I love both, my Kings." Violetta's sweet voice says.

"We love you two, our Queen." Anthony and I say in unison as we all hang up.

The Russians wanting an alliance might not be a bad thing. They are proving they are certainly a strong force to reckon with. They aren't necessarily an enemy I want to fight. An alliance might be what we need to survive whatever unknown enemies we have lurking in the shadows. If the Mexcans are a problem then the more alliances the better. The alliance with the Irish is turning out to be beneficial, so an alliance with the Russians as well would give us even more security. There's always someone who is willing to make you their enemy and even start a war to try and take what you have. So the fact that the Russians and Irish want an alliance instead of war is almost a relief. However, that doesn't mean we don't have potential enemies who do want war. Someone had to have been behind the attack on Violetta. It wasn't a mugging or something that would make me believe it was a random low life. The attacker had a rag with fucking chloroform on it. He was trying to abduct Violetta. I doubt it was random. For now, we will meet with the Russians and see what they have to offer while trying to find the culprit behind Violetta's attack.

Chapter 39

Anthony

Violetta slides into the town car we are taking to meet the Russians. The woman is ready for battle with her makeup expertly done, by Erica I'm sure, a form fitting dark red wine wrap dress paired with a black leather crop jacket, and black heeled thigh high boots. Fuck, she looks sexy. I notice Nico soaking up our queen's sexiness as well. Usually, we would play a bit with her before we arrived at our destination, but we are all a little unsure what to expect with this meeting. Yes, we know they want a treaty, but that doesn't mean we will agree with their terms.

The Irish are curious as well as to what an alliance with the Russians would like. They certainly aren't a warm bunch, but then again are any of us? You have to be a bit cut throat and slightly morally compromised to live a life in the underworld. However, the Russians have a reputation for being less friendly than the rest of us, so for them to out of the blue to want an alliance, I'm not sure how I feel about it. I'm skeptical to say the least. I know Nico and the Irish are also skeptical.

THE MAFIA LOVE CODE

    We arrive at the restaurant, and are led to the table by the hostess to where Misha sits. He's a very hairy man, in my opinion. Misha is in his early forties, and the white peaking through his thick dark brown hair proves it. He's also a bit on the plumper side, like a slightly thinner Santa Claus. He has a thick, bushy short beard. He gives a wide tooth grin as our waitress immediately comes over while the hostess walks off.

    "The Italian Trinity has arrived," Misha exclaims. "Come, sit, let's get a bottle of wine. I assume you like wine?"

    "A Malbec, please." Violetta sweetly requests.

    "You heard the lovely lady," Misha says to the waitress who nods her head with a smile before walking off to fulfill our request. "Thank you for agreeing to this meeting. I know it may have caught you off guard. That was not my intention. I had planned to reach out to you when I had things more controlled with the filthy Mexicans, who I believe may have sent that man to attack you, Violetta. When I heard that you thought I could be me behind the attack, I knew it was time to officially set the record straight." Misha explains.

    "Well, we are certainly curious about what you have to say, Misha." I reply, eyeing him up in an attempt to gauge where this man is going.

    The waitress comes back and pops open the bottle of wine while another waiter holds wine glasses for her to pour the wine in. The waiter passes us each a glass of wine while the waitress puts the rest of the bottle in a silver bucket of ice. The waitress then proceeds to take our orders. At this rate, we have been here often enough to know what's on the menu. Also it's a steakhouse. They primarily serve a lot of steak in a variety of ways with splendid options of sides. Once the waitress has our orders, she heads off to the kitchen.

"I'm sure you are curious. You would be foolish not to be, and you three are clearly not foolish. You managed to unite the three Italian factions, something none of us thought would ever happen. The Italians have always had strong roots in this city, probably more so than anyone else. When the three families divided, it was a good thing for all your enemies. Then the Calla family lost their power to the DeLucas and Ronkas. It divided the power of the strongest mafia faction for decades until you three came along and changed the game once more. Only this time you turned it so you benefited, which is the wiser move. Now, I could be a greedy man and envy the power you have, but even I draw the line somewhere. I know it's in my best interest to have an alliance with you. If the Italians, Irish, and Russians, the three major families of this city are united we would be pretty damn impossible to fuck with. The reason this is important, the reason I've been picking off lesser families isn't because I'm greedy. It's because of the threat they pose. Now, you might ask what threat? Well, Japanese are primarily on the west coast because it's close to their country and mine, but unfortunately they are far too strong out there. The Mexicans have roots in every damn state that touches the fucking boarder or is near it. We have the damn east coast and that's about it. Sure, the Japanese and Mexicans have roots in our city because our city has been around for so much longer. Japanese are easy to put in line. The Mexicans are greedy fuckers, and they are bringing their shit heroin into the drug game which you know I have my roots in. I don't like having bad products on the streets. It makes me look bad, and well honestly, all of us when teenagers are easily ODing. Not only that but the Mexican fuckers are heavy into sex trafficking. I don't know about you, but I am someone who doesn't tolerate that type of shit. We all know sex trafficking exists in our city, but it's very small right now. Almost non existent because it's the one thing most of us in the underworld stay clear from. They want to bring sex trafficking to our city on a large scale. They want this to be their hunting ground, and it's also easy to get girls out of the country with ports nearby, which means they will start infringing on your territory of the ports that the Ronkas control. They are already breeching on my territory with the drugs, I can handle that part. I can't fight them with the sex trafficking as well. That's where our alliance would come in." Misha explains as the three of us drink our wine trying to process the shit load of information.

"Let me get this straight. The alliance would be between the Italians, Russians, and Irish. The ultimate goal is to put the Mexicans in their place so they know who rules this city essentially." Nico summarizes.

"Essentially, yes. Anthony's sister married Shamus's son to solidify your alliance with them. I propose something similar, but with my son, Maxim who is four, and your first born daughter. I'm aware you aren't pregnant yet and that you might not have a daughter, but I'm willing to adjust the treaty if need be. It's more or less to have something on paper." Misha explains.

"I don't know if we can agree to that." Nico uneasily replies, looking at Violetta.

This is a touchy subject for her. Technically, her and Nico were an arranged marriage; they just happened to be friends and have feelings for each other so it worked. With Sofia and Connor they had a relationship before she got pregnant and then they married. We just got lucky they wanted to marry, and with Sofia being pregnant, it made it easier. This arrangement, though, is not like either of those.

"We can. There will be some stipulations, of course, to protect our children and their best interests. I can not guarantee we will have a girl, although I'd like one of each ideally. If you are willing to adjust the treaty, providing we do not have a daughter and whatever other stipulations I might have as you must understand my need to protect my future daughter's interests. You know as well as I that women tend to be taken advantage of in the world in general, but especially in the underworld. I, for one, will not stand for sex trafficking in my city." Violetta boldly intervenes, shocking both Nico and I. Never did I imagine she would agree to such a thing after the hell she gave Nico. I guess our butterfly has spread wings in ways we are just beginning to see.

"You heard our queen, so what do you say?" Nico questions.

Misha chuckles. "Violetta is indeed a worthy queen. I agree, and I'm glad someone has our children's best interest at heart as well as the city. If you three would kindly set up a meeting with the Irish to make things official, I'd be grateful. You simply tell me where and when, and I'll be there," he smiles and waves his hand as if brushing off all his problems. "Now, business is out of the way. Let's spend time getting to know one another, afterall our families might be joined one day. Not only that, but I think we all have plans for the future of this city and that is always welcomed."

The rest of dinner is surprisingly nice. Misha is a jolly guy, something I did not see coming. Perhaps he's only jolly when he's getting his way. I have a feeling when things don't go his way the jolly of St. Nick leaves and the spirit of Krampus takes over. Overall, I'm impressed with Misha. He's far more open minded than I would have thought. He also has ideas about selling drugs in the casino, which isn't a bad idea. Alcohol and drugs make people do stupid shit like gamble massive amounts of money.

Misha offering this alliance with us and the Irish to make us a unified trinity of our own means we will be damn near unstoppable. We won't have to worry about two powerful mafia families being our enemy, and the same would go for them. On top of that, Misha has useful information about the Mexicans. They are known to be crafty in silently making their way into cities to do even worse deeds than those of us that live in the underworld.

I can't see the Irish having any issues with it. In fact, Shamus might be relieved. I'll inform them tomorrow, as well as set up the meetings. I like doing all the odds and end stuff. I'm a bit of a jack of all trades, and I enjoy putting it to use. Working with both the Irish and Russians is creating a type of utopia I can get behind.

Chapter 40

Violetta

The meeting with Misha went smoothly. I don't know what came over, but when he offered the alliance with the condition of marriage between our children, well, his son and our future daughter I wanted to refuse. I wanted to scream at him and ask him who he thought he was to ask something of a child not even born. I felt everything my father shoved down my throat came rushing back. All the hard work I've done to undo the shit colored lenses that he put over my eyes seemed to temporarily disappear. It was when I heard Nico say we couldn't agree to it that something in me snapped back to reality. The reality that I have control. That I'm not a fucking pawn and neither is my future daughter. I'm a damn queen now and I have a say in how the game is played. I can make my own demands now.

The truth is, we need this alliance with the Russians for a variety of reasons. We benefit greatly from it. I also don't want sex trafficking to become something that this city tolerates. We can't stop it all, but we can at least stop the main source. Making an unnecessary enemy of the

Russians is foolish. I can't let the false sense of unimportance I might feel from my father's mental trauma because I won't be the fool he was. I can make calculated decisions. I can put my own shit aside and think about the good of others. There are many who benefit from our alliance and I won't be the reason we stupidly go to war.

I had to intervene at that moment. I know Anthony and especially Nico wouldn't agree to it for my sake. They would stupidly go to war if it meant I was happy. I won't be that petty woman who makes her men go to an unnecessary war. What I can do is make sure the marriage arrangement is good for my daughter and Misha's son. Arranged marriage doesn't have to be the curse I perceived it to be. I can make sure my daughter's best interests are protected. I can do better than my dad did for me. Hell, if it wasn't for Nico and Anthony being rational and determined to break the tradition of what a mafia wife meant then I would still certainly be nothing but a pawn.

Thankfully, my kings do not think the way our fathers did. That also makes me feel secure in my choice to go along with the arranged marriage part of the treaty. I know they will also look out for our daughter and her best interests. An arranged marriage doesn't have to be the death sentence I thought it was. The three of us can do better than our parents. We already are in so many ways, and we will keep doing so.

"Butterfly, what the fuck was that tonight and where have been hiding that side of you?" Nico questions as the town car drives us to our condo.

"I don't know honestly. Lately, it feels like a switch has flipped inside of me. Plus, you two have no idea how to handle jolly men. I know you deal with cut throat assholes often, but you two don't know how to not to be defensive, domineering men. So, I thought the charm of a woman was needed." I explain.

"She has us there. I didn't know how to react Misha being so jolly like fucking Santa Claus. I was expecting him to be, well, like us and Shamus." Anthony adds.

"Yeah, I have to admit I was at a loss with that. Never have ever meet a fucking jolly mafia leader. It's possible he was like that to make it clear he wanted peace. Still, I wasn't sure how to respond. Thankfully, sweet Violetta was on it." Nico says as he places his hand on my inner thigh.

"She was and it was sexy to watch." Anthony adds before his hand lands on my shoulder brushing some of my hair away.

Tingles of anticipation course through me. I'm high off taking charge of the meeting. I hadn't intended it, but shit it felt good to put things on my terms for once. I don't feel like a damn pawn anymore. No, I feel like a fucking queen and I have my kings at my side. I want them. I want them so fucking badly. Their touch alone sets me on fire. I can't help but rub my legs together in anticipation earning me a chuckle from them.

"Eager, Butterfly?" Nico taunts.

"Of course she's eager, she's always eager for what we have to give her." Anthony adds.

"True, but the question is how to reward her for doing such a good job tonight." Nico ponders out loud as his hand on my thigh moves up slightly toward the place I desperately want his hands to go.

"Hmm, the better question is do we make her wait to play with her or tease the fuck out of during our ride home." Anthony ponders as his hand rubs my shoulder in a relaxing and teasing way.

"Okay, make a choice please," I beg. "You two are killing me with the suspense." They both chuckle at me.

"I say we tease her, but she isn't allowed to cum." Anthony declares.

Nico chuckles some more. "I like that idea." Nico agrees.

Fuckers. I have no one to blame but myself. I did ask them to make a choice, and they did. Of course, I'm not sure if it's one I will like. Oh, who am I kidding? These two know how to set my body on fire with just one touch or kiss. I'm putty in their hands and they fucking know it too.

Anthony and Nico take a moment to rearrange me to their desired position. My head rests on Anthony's legs well my legs are propped on Nico's legs. My ass is between them on the seat of the car. Nico spread my legs. I'm not wearing panties because I knew there would be no point. Also my kings have told me not to wear panties except when I'm on my period. I'm not on it so I'm commando. I never thought I would like going commando, but surprisingly I love it. It's freeing in a way I didn't expect.

Nico slides his hand right to where I want it to go as I eagerly widen my legs, giving him all the access he needs. Neither of them hesitate to put their hand on my body as Nico begins to rub my clit while Anthony slips his hand over my lace bra and starts lightly pinching my nipples. Before long Nico is inserting two fingers inside of me while his thumb slowly, teasingly works my clit as Anthony works in tandem playing with nipples. My eyes close, letting pleasure flood my body and over take me.

The slow build of pleasure almost feels torturous, and when they originally started edging me I hated it. I let my brat side out and totally fought against it because I was greedy. However, my warden and dom were determined to teach me that I would learn to love edging. Now, I love it when they edge me. It's the same with anal. I wasn't sure how I felt about it at first, but I was willing to try. The guys have been stretching me slowly with different sized butt plugs. I think tonight is the night I'm going to have them fuck me at the same time. They have been patiently waiting for me to decide when I am ready. I'm high off the success of the night and the pleasure these two men have throbbing through my body solidifies my choice to have them both inside me at the same time.

They are working my body in such a teasing manner that the build up to my orgasm is almost painfully slow, yet I know they aren't letting my cum until we are home. This is their game, they love to play with me. As much as I'd love to say I hate it, I secretly love it and they know it. To my delight the town car stops and I hope they let me cum, but they don't. They both quickly remove their hands from my body, making me shoot my eyes open. They are both looking at me like I'm prey and they are going to leave me sore tomorrow just the way I prefer it.

Nico gets out of the car before pulling me by my ankles to him then he picks me up, tossing me over his shoulders like a rag doll. Anthony gets out of the town car and leads the way up to the condo. The next thing I know I'm put on my feet before the guys expertly strip me from everything I have on even my jewelry. Of course, they are teasing as they strip me with kisses, bites, and pinches along the way. I'm so wet from their teasing and desperately wanting to cum and having them inside of me at the same time.

"Warden, Dom." I say gaining their attention once I'm finally striped.

"What is it, Butterfly?" Anthony questions as he softly kisses my shoulder.

"I want you both to fuck me at the same time tonight. I'm ready and tonight just feels right." I make my request known.

"We will happily oblige, Butterfly," Anthony responds eagerly.

"Yes, we will and if you decide in the moment you don't want to, you can tell us. We won't be mad." Nico adds.

THE MAFIA LOVE CODE

"I know. I trust you two for a reason." I reply sweetly with such honesty that I realize I trust them both more than anything or anyone. They have my whole heart and I know I have theirs.

"Good. Now, get on the bed and play with yourself while Nico and I get things ready." Anthony instructs.

I do exactly what I'm told. The guys are even more eager than before. I know they have been waiting for this and so have I. I get myself comfortable and slip my hand between my legs as I begin to touch myself enjoying the view of my kings striping themselves of their clothes. Once they are out of their clothes Anthony heads to their closet and retrieves a black nylon rope. Nico helps Anthony secure it to the beam between the bottom two posters of the bed causing anticipation to course through me. I have to be careful not to cum without their permission. The last time I did they punished me with ten orgasms. At first, I didn't think it was going to be that bad, but I learned after orgasm number five that orgasms can turn into painful pleasure. An amazing painful pleasure that I'm not eager to earn again anytime soon, so I do my best to hold off, but I am getting close. Too close.

"Alright, Butterfly you can cum." Anthony commands, and I let my orgasm flood my body with pulsating pleasure.

My body relaxes as my hand falls to my side. Nico hands Anthony a bottle of lube from the nearby dresser we keep our sexy fun time stuff in. Nico stands at the end of the bed and motions for me to come to him. I immediately jump at his silent command. Anthony is getting on the bed as I move toward Nico. Once I'm in front of Nico I feel the bed dip behind from Anthony. Anticipation and need courses through my body as Nico and Anthony secure the nylon rope around my wrists that are together. They make sure the rope isn't hurting me and that I'm comfortable.

"Are you ready, Butterfly?" Nico questions.

"Yes." I reply rather quickly, causing both men to chuckle lightly. They fucking love how eager I am for them. They get off on it, and so do I, if I'm honest.

"Good, now you are going to wrap your legs around me. We will help guide you." Nico instructs.

They help me and before I know Nico's dick is deep inside of me as I lock my ankles together to secure myself around Nico. Nico moves slowly in and out of me allowing me to adjust to the deepness of the position. I hear Anthony open the lube bottle and squirt some out. I'm used to the feeling of the lube since they have used it on the but plugs to help stretch me. It doesn't take long before I feel Anthony at my back entrance.

"Are you ready for me to take your ass, Butterfly?" Anthony's deep voice reverberates in my ear.

"Yes," I reply, breathless with anticipation at being taken by them both at the same time. We have all been waiting for this moment and it's finally here.

Anthony grabs my hips as Nico stills for a moment so Anthony can enter. I feel his tip go past my entrance as he slowly fills me. I feel incredibly full yet I love it. It's different, a good different. I know this is not something I would be able to do all the time but it certainly something to toss into the mix.

Nico and Anthony begin moving in and out of me before they find a rhythm. When one is pulling out the other is going in so I'm never without one of them. It feels amazing. Nico holds my hips as Anthony's hands come around to cup my breast before his fingers pinch and pull my nipples switching from soft to hard. I can't help but lean my head back onto Anthony's shoulder as pleasure floods me on all fronts. This is good, almost too good. It's unbelievable heaven that I didn't think could exist, but I should know that anything involving these two men will surely be pure bliss.

My moans and their grunts of pleasure fill the room. My eyes are closed, completely lost in the unending pleasure that the three of us are experiencing. I know we are all in the sweet nirvana we have created. This is our nirvana and I can't imagine life without Nico and Anthony. I love the life we continue to build together, the Italian Trinity. We are breaking the old way of thinking and improving the underworld. The way Nico's dick is rubbing my clit is just right and Anthony has never stopped playing with my nipples that they are beginning to feel deliciously sore. I'm also enjoying Anthony fucking my ass. I'll admit I had my hesitations, but I agreed to try it at least once. I'm glad I agreed to try it because I do enjoy it.

"Please." Is all I can manage out between my moans.

"Yes, cum, Butterfly." Anthony commands me from behind because Nico won't take his lips off mine or my neck that definitely has a couple of bruises.

Following my Dom's command, I cum so hard my body shakes and both my holes clench causing first Nico and then Anthony's own orgasms. We all take a brief moment to catch our breaths before Anthony slowly pulls out of me and begins to untie my hands from the nylon rope. Nico pulls out of me and catches me as Anthony lowers my arms.

"Do you want to shower now or tomorrow morning? We can go in late and have a nice brunch." Nico poses.

"Shower in the morning. I'm way too tired and the sheets need to be changed anyway. So I vote to sleep." I suggest.

"Works for me." Anthony agrees.

"Alrighty then, sleep it is." Nico hands me to Anthony who drags us both back into the bed while Nico comes around the right side of the bed. The three of us get positioned under the covers.

"So, how did you like anal?" Anthony questions as he drapes an arm over me.

"I enjoyed it, but I don't think I could do it all the time." I answer honestly.

"We can work with that. If you are in the mood for it, or one of us is, we will just toss it out there and go with the flow." Nico suggests.

"I can work with that," I agree. "Now can we get some sleep?" I ask with a small giggle.

THE MAFIA LOVE CODE

"Yes," They both agree at the same time.

"I love you both so much." I confess.

"We love you too." They both say to me. Anthony kisses me first and then Nico does. Then they both kiss me on either cheek.

The three of us settle into our positions with me on my back while they lay one their sides facing me with either their arms on me. I'm continent and happy. I feel like I've won the mafia wife lottery with these two men who have become my world. This life we are creating is amazing and I can't wait to add kids to the mix eventually. I'm deciding to let it happen naturally. I'm still on the young side, and I know it can take time to happen naturally. In the meantime, I will continue to build our empire with my kings.

Chapter 41

Nico

The next morning, things feel surreal as the last night's events replay in my mind. I'm beyond proud Violetta. She is emerging out of cocoon beautifully and in ways I didn't see coming. The fact that she agreed to an arranged marriage for our future daughter still shocks me especially how dead set against she was to marry me for years. Technically, we had an arranged marriage. It helped that we were friends because it softened the blow. With Anthony, Violetta was promised to him too, so technically, they too had a type of arranged marriage. It's just Violetta didn't know about it due to her father being a sneaky fucker.

I understand wholeheartedly why she agreed to the arranged marriage for our future daughter. In the underworld it's not uncommon for marriages to be arranged in some fashion. It's perhaps medieval thinking to secure alliances with marriage, but when the rules of the regular world don't necessarily apply to you there has to be a way to hold accountability. Arranged marriages are a way to hold that accountability. Having an alliance with the Russians and the Irish is gold, and I'm delighted that Violetta realizes that. I never knew how accepting she truly was going to be as a leader in the underworld with Anthony and I at her side.

Violetta stirs next to me before she pops her head to look at me with a content smile. "Morning, Warden." She says before she kisses me sweetly on the lips.

"Morning, Little Dove," I reply. "Wake up your Dom and I'll go get our shower started."

"As you wish." She replies as she goes to plant kisses all over Anthony to get him to wake up. That man is hard as hell to wake up.

I head to the bathroom and start the shower. It's a bit cramped when we all shower together, another reason I'm eager for our house to be built. The foundation is being laid out and I'm paying extra to have this done a bit sooner than later, so it better be done in the six months I was promised for the amount of money I have to shell out. Just because I have money to spend doesn't mean I spend it without thought. I am a businessman after all, I spend my money wisely.

It doesn't take long for Anthony and Violetta to join me in the bathroom. Anthony yawns as he covers his mouth. He is not a morning person. Violetta has always been a morning person. I only became a morning person in my early twenties when I started to really take on responsibilities in the family business. I also probably have more caffeine than one person should in a day.

The shower is warmed up so the three of us step into the shower. Violetta wastes no time getting to work on cleaning us up. When she washes our dicks, she plays with them. She's gotten damn good at giving us a hand job at the same time. She is also getting good at sucking one of us all while giving the other a hand job. She is certainly coming out of shell in the best ways possible.

Violetta kisses our bodies as she washes them taking turns to show us each loving attention. I never thought I'd enjoy sharing my woman, but I don't mind sharing Violetta with Anthony. We have a platonic love for one another that makes me enjoy sharing Violetta with him. Anthony has quickly become my best friend and someone I can't imagine not having in my life. He's a vital part of my life now, just as I am his. We balance one another, and Violetta balances the two of us. It's a pretty damn perfect Italian Trinity we have formed.

After Violetta washes us, we take our time cleaning her up. Anthony washes her hair while I take care of her body. Sometimes our intimate showers turn into sexy fun, but this morning we are back to business mode as there is plenty to address this morning. However, that doesn't stop any of us from a little teasing.

Once we are washed up, we get out and dry off. Then Anthony and I get dressed in our casual suits while Violetta gets dressed in her black scrubs. Damn, I'm so making her help me live out my sexy nurse fantasy. I know Anthony is on board as well. We have talked to our butterfly about it and she is also for it, it's a matter of finding the right moment which I know will come when it's time just like last night with Anthony and I fucking her at the same time.

After we are dressed we head to the town car and head to one of our favorite dinners in the city. While we are there we discuss what terms, boundaries, and other things should be set for the arranged marriage. Anthony and I also confirm that Violetta is still okay with her choice to agree to the arranged marriage which Violetta confirms she is confident with her choice. It's honestly a relief and I'm glad she can see the reason.

I didn't want to be the asshole to force something on her she didn't agree with but if it meant avoiding war with Russians I would have had no choice. Thankfully, she came to the conclusion on her own. I completely understand her hesitation and there is a part of me that also wants to say no so our daughter can have complete freedom in her life. Unfortunately, right now she is a pawn to help secure an alliance we need. I hate saying she is a pawn, but I have a feeling she will turn into a queen just like her mother has.

It's insane to be thinking about a child we don't even have yet and to be planning her future when she isn't even born yet. The truth is, I'm sure that we will be having a baby sooner rather than later. I see how Violetta is around Sofia, and I know as soon as the baby comes her baby fever will light ablaze. She's always talked about being a mom although it's been awhile until recently. I think the three of us are eager for our family to grow. We are working on it, and Violetta is strong in her belief that it will happen when it's supposed to.

After our little brunch date, the three of us go our separate ways. Violetta is off to the clinic, Anthony is off to inform the Irish on the latest development with the Rusisians, and I am off to the casino for some business before I meet Anthony and Violetta at the Burlesque club tonight. We try to go at least once a week, but some weeks are just too busy. It's been about a week since we last went and I think we are all craving a little public attention. Also I can imagine Violetta is excited to tell Dedra about us finally fucking her at the same time. Next time, I'm going to be in her ass and Anthony will get her pussy. Although, I bet Violetta has already texted Dedra to tell her the news. I think it's cute Violetta is proud of her sexual accomplishments and wants to share them with her mentor. Dedra has become a close confidant to all of us. It's nice to have people we can trust because the underworld isn't always a safe place.

Chapter 42

Anthony

Shamus looks at me, dumbfounded. Never in a million years did either of us think we would be having this conversation. To be honest, I thought I would be talking with Shamus on how to fight against the Russians. Instead, I'm talking to him about an alliance with the Ruissians. Shamus is silent letting my information soak in. While I wait for Shamus to get over his initial shock of the situation, I think about last night and how satisfying the whole evening ended up being.

Violetta's smooth talking Misha was great to witness. It made her even sexier which I didn't think was possible. Then finally fucking her at the same time was is a high I will always enjoy getting off on. All three of us enjoyed it, but I understand it's not something for the everyday sex play we tend to engage in.

The thought of kids has, of course, crossed my mind several times. I know the three of us are ready to introduce kids into the picture when the time is right. With all the sex we have, it's bound to happen. The three of us all tend to have a high sex drive so even when we aren't necessarily fucking, we are are always playing and teasing. It's been amazing exploring sex with Nico and Violetta. Nico and I have got our co dom smoothed out. So many things are falling into place in such a perfect way it always makes me afraid that something bad is going to happen. I'm a little paranoid. I'm a little psycho. What can I say?

"So, the Russians want an alliance, and the Mexicans are the real problem?" Shamus's question pulls me to the present moment.

"Yes, that about sums it up." I agree.

"Well, shit. Did you say yes to the alliance with them with the arranged marriage between your kids?" Shamus eagerly questions as if we might have fucked up and declared war.

"Yes, we agreed. We have some terms to set, but Misha is okay with that. He's honestly more flexible than I thought he would be. I take it you want a meeting set up?" I question.

"Yes. The sooner the better. I don't like the dirty Mexicans trying to be sneaky in our city. It's always one of the lesser families causing trouble." Shamus answers not hiding his displeasure at the Mexicans.

Not that I can blame him because none of us are thrilled with what the Mexicans are trying to do with sex trafficking and then impeding on established bigger families turf with drugs and ports is not okay. We might be the underworld, but we aren't total fucking savages. We do have rules and respect for one another. There hasn't been a turf war in decades mainly because everyone was sticking to their turf. The Mexicans threaten the basic peace that the underworld has worked hard to establish. They have a lot of nerve to do what they are doing.

"Consider it done. I'll have the details to Connor, and he will pass it along to you." I advise.

"Works for me. Whatever you are doing with my son to get him to turn into a man, thank you. You are doing what I could never manage to do with the knucklehead." Shamus says with a nod of thanks.

I'm shocked by his gratitude. I honestly haven't done much where Connor is concerned. I left him in the hands of Lorenzo and Jullain. I've done my best to get to know Connor, but the truth is I'm selective of who I enjoy around me. Violetta jokes and calls me a cat because I can be sociable when I want and completely content on my own for the rest of the time. Although, I don't crave totally alone time as much as I used to. I've grown accustomed to having Nico and Violetta around. They have become so vital in my life that I think I would be lost without them. I feel a little more on the sane side when I'm with them. Connor on the other hand is just too young for me to take under my wing. Plus, I can tell he doesn't want to do leadership on the front lines like I do. Connor likes being in the background much like Jullain and Lorenzo. That's also why I put him in their hands to mold him into an excellent member of the underworld. I guess they are doing a good job at it. I have to say I've seen the change too, but I honestly thought it was more to do with my sister and the fact that he's about to be a father.

"I can't take credit. Julain and Lorenzo are the ones he works with the most," I confess, honestly. "Plus, I'm sure Sofia has her ways of putting him in line." I add, causing Shamus to give a big belly laugh, making me laugh along with him.

"That might be true, but Connor strives to earn you respect and that has made him get his ass in shape." Shamus answers, throwing me a little off kilter.

I didn't think I was all that important to Connor. I always thought he saw me as his crazy brother in law who would chop him into pieces if he hurt Sofia. I didn't think he would value my respect or even approval. I figured if he did it was because I was his wife's brother and he wanted to be in my good graces. I didn't believe it was genuine respect that Connor was giving me. I guess I was wrong. It would seem Connor wants to have a respectful brother relationship. I should probably not be so distant with him now that I know his respect is not out of obligation but out of genuine heart. I really have to start giving that damn kid more credit than I do. He's stepped up to the plate with marrying Sofia and being a good husband, so far, to her. The red headed Irish boy makes my little sister happy. The least I can do is throw him a bone and attempt to forge a bond with him. I was able to do it with Nico when I was skeptical that I could. Now, Nico is one of the most important people in my life next to

THE MAFIA LOVE CODE

Violetta, Sofia, and Lorenzo. It can't hurt to add one person to that list.

I end my meeting with Shamus and get to work organizing the meeting with all three families along with Connor. I'm going to have him shadow me for a couple days a week. I realize I have knowledge I can pass along to him that I will also pass down to my children. I have to stop looking at Connor as some annoying kid and more like the adult he is. He's also my brother in law making him family. It would seem having my butterfly and Nico as my partners is making my cold heart soften where it needs to, allowing me to open myself up in ways I didn't know were possible.

Chapter 43

Nico

Last night we had the meeting with the Irish and Russians. Misha agreed to all the terms we set up for the arranged marriage between our kids. We had a contract drawn up that we all signed detailing the arranged marriage since our children aren't old enough to get married yet. Also, we don't have a daughter yet, but something in my bones tells me it won't be much longer. Violetta has been talking more and more about having kids especially since Sofia is close to popping in the next month give or take.

With the treaty signed we can start getting to work on putting up blocks and other things that will make it harder for the Mexicans to bring in their sex trafficking. We all don't want them to think they can do whatever they want in our city. Especially if they are encroaching on our territories and business. We have had an understanding for years in the underworld not to fuck with on anothers business . The Mexicans don't care about the unspoken rules that have been set in place. That's a problem, one that we plan to fix. We have ways of putting the Mexicans in their place.

Now with the treaty in place, I'm going to start working with Misha to incorporate drugs into the casino and perhaps the burlesque club. Connie isn't a fan of having drugs in the brothel, and I don't blame her for that so she decided to test the burlesque club first to see how it goes. The Irish are going to supply extra guns for our guards to carry. We don't trust that the Mexicans won't mess with our new business arrangement. We have extra body guards and bouncers around the club, casino, docks, and even the clinic. Especially the clinic since they were bold enough to attack Violetta at the clinic.

Violetta and Erica have been keeping up with their self defense classes and we take Violetta for weekly shooting sessions at the gun range so that she never feels rusty with shooting a gun. We also run scenarios of how someone could attack her and the best ways to get out of it. I'm glad she is taking her safety seriously and putting precautions in place. We will be able to do more once our house is built with our private shooting range, sex dungeons, and gym.

The three of us are eager for our house to be done. Violetta is already picking out color schemes, furniture, and more. We have a damn storage unit now of fucking shit that she has ordered for the house that is just starting to be built. I can't blame her, she's excited, and her shopping for our new home shows how happy she is with us. I love watching her blossom. Her nonna would be so proud Violetta. She always wanted her to be a strong female figure in the underworld that would give the men a run for their money. That's exactly what Violetta has become. I wish her father was here to see her success because she would enjoy rubbing it in his face. He ruined the underworld for her for most of her life and only now is she finally seeing she can make a difference.

The three of us are making a difference in the underworld and the legal world. Our Angel Clinic for the community has been praised highly. For the first time in a long time, those with bad insurance or no insurance can afford health care. I'm thinking we might need a second clinic at some point with how well it's doing. We are booked for months with appointments. The underworld side of the clinic is also doing well and smoothly. Violetta loves running the clinics. It's become her passion project, and I'm glad I was able to do this for her. I wanted her to have something that she enjoyed and could be just hers. I wanted her to be happy with me because I was afraid she would run off, and I would never be able to find her. I've known for years that I could not live without her in my life. Even when she was off at college getting her nursing degree it was hard to be away from her. The only thing I had to ease the pain of her absence was knowing I still knew where she was.

Violetta also led me to Anthony, the unexpected third wheel to our relationship that none of us knew we needed. What started off as a simple arrangement to share Violetta and unite all the Italian factions has turned into a loving poly relationship. The three of us are a unit now. The three of us love the strange yet beautiful relationship we have created. That is what gives me hope for our daughter and her arranged marriage to Maxim is that maybe they can find love like we did. Maybe they don't have to be doomed as our fears want us to believe. Perhaps they can have a happy marriage that blooms into love. It worked for Anthony, Violetta and I, so why not for our kids too? Not everything in the underworld has to be doom and gloom, there can also be goodness and happiness, even love.

Chapter 44

Violetta

Weeks have passed since a new treaty has been made between the Irish, Russians, and Italian families. I'm still confident in the choice we made, and I'm happy that Misha was so accommodating and understanding of my terms. Misha is really jolly and I kind of like him for it. He also throws the guys off, which I personally find funny. Misha is a breath of fresh air compared to the normal stuffy mafia guys. No offense to my kings, but they can be stuffy mafia men when they want to be.

Nico and Anthony might be stuffy mafia men on occasion but they are never stuffy with me. That's why I find it a little ironic as I look at my bloodwork confirming my recent suspicions. Pregnant. I'm not surprised with all the sex we have been having. It's not like we were exactly aiming for it but in many ways we were. I'm happy and I can't wait to tell my kings, but I'm going to hold off. I notice my levels are getting higher quicker. This is the third blood test I've done because I can't believe it. The urine test didn't feel real. I thought the blood test would make it feel more real and in some ways it does. I'm going to have an ultrasound soon from our OBGYN doctor. Dr. Mullens is very sweet, and we all love her. I want everything confirmed before I tell the guys anything.

The other reason I don't want to say anything is because Sofia is having her baby shower this weekend. I don't want to overshadow her moment, and boy is it her moment. Sofia is a little diva, but she's a fun diva. She is having a boy and so everything is blue and fancy. The theme is a cute woodsy theme with cute little woodland creatures. Sofia has every detail planned out, and she is in full blown nesting mode with setting up the nursery. Joy fills me at the thought of decorating my own nursery. For now, I'm glad our house is finally making some real headway. I've been enjoying decorating it and picking things out. Now, I have one more fun reason to look forward to our house being built

I hope I'm having a girl for the sake of the treaty and because I've always wanted to have a daughter. I also remind myself it's too early to get too far ahead, but it's hard to not be excited. I let my mind begin to play fun ideas on how to tell my kings the good news while helping Erica double check everything for Sofia's baby shower. We are also doing work for the clinics as well while we finish off details for the baby shower that is supposed to be a surprise but totally isn't. Only Sofia could manage to throw herself a surprise baby shower.

While I have hope for the future with my positive news, I do worry about the stability of that future. I'm hoping with the three major mafia families all on the same side we can push out our enemies and solidify our hold on the city. The Mexicans are starting to back off, but they are a bit more aggressive than I personally anticipated. I think the men all saw the push back coming from the Mexicans because they have more experience with this side of things. However, they all seem to appreciate a woman's touch where it's needed.

I suppose war is always a possibility, even in the regular world, there is always war being threatened among countries. War is always a threat even when it feels like there isn't one. However, avoiding war, I think, is usually the goal of most people. I know it is for us and those in the new alliance. The alliance that no one saw coming, not even those in it. However, it's an alliance that is needed to ensure peace in the underworld.

When Anthony, Nico, and I formed our Italian Trinity we honestly thought we would have more push back from other mafia families, maybe even from some in our faction. I think we thought for sure we were going to make an enemy out of someone just because of our alliance. We had no idea the changes that would come with our trinity. First, an alliance with the Irish, and then with the Russians. These are alliances that would never have happened with the old ways. Shamus and Misha are aware of that too. I hate to say it, but I think the stubborn Italians were the ones holding everyone back in old ways.

With new alliances and fresh new takes on the way things are run in the underworld things are changing for the better. There is a lot of power, money, and other perks to our alliance. The Mexicans are certainly not happy and while they might be starting to back off there's no guarantee they will back off all together or permanently. They are determined to have some territory in the city. We aren't against new mafia families coming into the underworld per say, but it has to be done in a non threatening manner which is the exact opposite of what the Mexicans are doing. After their attack on me, which has been confirmed, they aren't on anyone's good side. Plus, most of us draw the line at sex trafficking. I know it seems crazy to think the morally grey mobsters would draw the line with something illegal, but we do have our limits. We all have a line that we won't cross for one reason or another even Anthony with his secret sociopathic side has a line he won't cross.

    I don't understand the need for sex trafficking when there are plenty of legal and illegal brothels. I know not all brothels are run the same. I've learned a lot from Dedra and how the brothel works. The women's safety is the most important, and Connie runs everything so well, especially with her right hand woman, Dedra, who I've come to view as a close friend. While I know that legal and illegal brothels aren't all equal, that doesn't mean someone should resort to sex trafficking. There are better ways and while there might be some sex trafficking I can't stop, I will do my best to limit it. Drugs and guns are dangerous. They can certainly take lives yet somehow they seem less dirty compared to sex trafficking.

"Hey, girl!" Erica's voice breaks my focus from my lab work. "I need more caffeine if I'm going to survive the rest of the day." Erica declares.

"Late night?" I jest with a giggle.

"Of course," She winks at me. "I have to keep up with one man and his libido, you have two."

"I wouldn't have it any other way. I have a higher libido myself. I never realized it until I finally had sex." I reply, switching to a chart that isn't mine. I don't want anyone besides Dr. Mullens to know about me being pregnant because I honestly haven't fully processed it yet.

"Good for you, Unicorn." She jokes.

I shake my head. "I'm never living that nickname down am I?"

"Nope, not if Dedra and I have anything to say about it. I've got orders from the other staff, so do you want anything?" She replies and we both giggle.

"Yes, I'll have a tall hazelnut latte with extra hazelnut please." I request. I secretly had decaf coffee this morning, but I want my caffeine now because first trimester fatigue is real. It's oddly my only symptom so far besides the occasional nausea which I can quickly fix with some ginger ale. I'm sure I'll have more symptoms the further along I get.

"You got it, Unicorn." Erica says with a wink as she turns on her heels to head out.

I secretly like the nickname even if at first I found it embarrassing. Now it's cute and Dedra won't stop buying me unicorn shit. She even has Erica and the rest of the ladies in our orbit calling me unicorn now. It's almost like my stage name at the club, not that I would ever dare to dance or do anything sexually in public unless it involves my kings. I might be more comfortable with sex and even sexual displays in public, but that doesn't mean I'm ready to be a sex performer. I'm perfectly content doing things with my kings in private. Still, the nickname has totally grown on me, but I'll never admit it out loud.

I flip back to my chart and smile at the results. I take a deep breath and think about how far I've come in the last several months. I never thought I would accept the life I fought so hard against. I certainly didn't think I'd be happy, but I am happy. Anthony and Nico make me beyond happy in ways I never thought were possible. I'm a mafia wife to two powerful men who lovingly share their power with me. I have my own clinics that I can use to make a difference for those struggling with life and those ready to face the end due to a worser fate. I'm proud of myself and the strides I made. I'm glad I'll be a better example to my daughter of her role in the underworld. After all, she is destined to be a mafia wife, and just like me, she doesn't have to conform to what is expected of us. I broke the mold, and she will too, in her own ways. Providing I have a daughter, but my gut tells me I'll be having at least one daughter. The guys and I haven't talked about how many kids we will have. I think we are just going to play it by ear and let nature take its course for now.

It's almost relieving to know my daughter, or daughters, don't have to have to be pawns. Sure, our first born is a pawn, but just like me, I will help her go from pawn to queen. Our children will not be helpless but instead fearless like their fathers and strong like their mother. The future still has so many uncertainties floating around, but the best thing is I don't have to face it alone. I have my kings that I love, my friends that I adore, and a life that leaves me feeling fulfilled. I thought my happiness lay outside the underworld because I saw the underworld as a cage. However, the reality is my happiness lies inside the underworld and it's definitely not a cage, it a fucking kingdom that I rule side by side with my kings.

The End

Epilogue

Anthony

I'm holding my nephew, Trey. He's adorable, and it has me excited for my own. When Violetta told Nico and I she was pregnant, we all were so thrilled yet that wasn't the biggest surprise we found out. Violetta soon found out she was not only pregnant but pregnant with twins. We had paternity testing done. It didn't matter who the father was, but we need to know only to ensure both families carry on it, not just name but blood as well. Blood and names mean everything in the underworld. That's when we got an even more shocking surprise. One twin is mine and the other Nico's. It's an incredibly rare phenomenon called superfecundation, so Violetta is thrilled to be living a medical marvel.

We will do a paternity test when the twins are born to confirm that the blood test was correct. Normally, we wouldn't go that extreme but with how rare our circumstances are, it's best to confirm the so called medical marvel. Still, twins are crazy enough and as I bounce my nephew I wonder how the hell we are going to handle two babies at once. I guess it's a good thing that there are three of us. We will need all of us. We decided to not find out genders until later on. Sophia is already insisting she is in charge of a baby gender reveal.

Sophia is getting into event planning and wants to go to business school and eventually open her own event company. I think it's beyond wonderful she is finding something she has passion for. I also didn't want her to be stuck just being a mom and wife. I'm not saying women can't be satisfied with just those things, but it doesn't hurt to want more for my baby sister. I want her to have passion projects, a family, and a career if she wants it. I don't want her to feel limited in any way.

The same goes for my children. I want them to be more than just mafia leaders or partners. I want them to have more than this life. I think Nico and Violetta agree with that. The underworld life can be all consuming. It's easy to get lost in it like I have and even Nico to some degree. Violetta has her passion for being a nurse and caring for people. She's even talked to us about going back to school for midwifery or a nurse practitioner. We support her, of course, and anything she wants to do. The point is, she has a passion that she can take outside the underworld if need be where Nico and I can't.

Violetta has opened my eyes to so much. I realize I was fairly closed minded before Violetta and Nico officially entered my life. I was consumed by the darkness of the monster I had become. I need them to ground me and keep me sane so I don't snap. They have softened my heart and allowed me to have a better relationship with my sister and even her husband who is growing on me the more I work with him.

    At first, I didn't buy their relationship. It felt rushed and became something convenient for the treaty with the Irish. Over time, I've come to see that they do love each other and while it might have felt quick, they are happy. Not that I can talk much because everything with Nico, Violetta, and I were in a similar situation. Our poly union was needed to unite the three Italian families under one leadership. It happened fast too. One moment I was prepared to steal Violetta from Nico, and the next I'm in a poly relationship with them. It felt like zero to hundred in minutes. Fast, thrilling, and fueled by desire that has now turned to love. We wrote our own code of love because we are the Italian Trinity that no one saw coming, not even us. Now with our new code of love embedded in the underworld it's time for us to make our mark on this city that we call home.

The Mafia Love *Arrangement*

Book 2 of the Underworld Love Guide Series

Preview

Brit Leigh

Chapter 1

Maxim

Glancing down at my Rolex, I realize I have about five hours before my yearly date with my intended bride. Antonia and I have had an arranged marriage since I was four and she was nothing more than a fetus in her mom's belly. Arranged marriages are nothing new in the underworld especially when it comes to treaties. That was the case for me and Antonia or Toni as she prefers to be called. Our marriage solidifies the alliance with the Russians and Italian mafias, who also have an alliance with the Irish, which was a different arranged marriage long before Toni and I were arranged to be married. The alliance has been known to be called the Alliance Trinity.

I'm next in line to be the head of the Russian mob once I get married to Antonia in a month. The arrangement is that we will get married when she is twenty. Her and her twin brother, Leonardo, who goes by Leo and will be the next leader of the Italian mafia, turned twenty about two weeks ago. Trey, their cousin who will take over for the Irish because his uncle, the current leader, has no kids. Leo, Trey, and I are all good friends and we work well together. I'll be the first to take over because my father is the oldest out of all the current mafia leaders that are a part of the alliance trinity as our parents so lovely decided to call the alliance. My dad wants to retire and live a life somewhere cold so he can ice fish whenever he wants with endless top shelf vodka. My dad waited until he was in his forties to have me with a woman who was looking to get paid and didn't care about signing her rights away. I've never met my mom, and I'm strangely at peace with it.

Our wedding has been in the works for years so most of it has already been planned by Toni, her mom, and her Aunt Sofia who happens to own an event planning and catering business. To my delight our wedding is a month away and I have to control myself tonight when I see Toni because I know she will look hot as hell as she always does. While we are engaged so to speak, I've never even kissed Toni because in the underworld old fashion values still run deep. Out of respect for Toni's two fathers and her brother who I am friends with, I haven't touched her. I want to so badly that it's given me blue balls over the years making me seek sex with other women. Natalia Green, who is half Russian and has been my go to fuck toy for years now.

I didn't intentionally mean to keep the same woman around for two years. The plan was fuck them once and never touch them again. That was the plan the first time I fucked Nat, which is what Natalia prefers to be called. I've been fucking since I was fourteen. There was no way I was waiting until marriage. Then there is the fact that being a male virgin in the underworld past sixteen will get you called a weak ass pussy because if you can't fuck than you aren't a man. Nat and I started consistently fucking was something that happened out of convenience and because I don't mind having her around. I know I can't be attached to her and I'm not, but I can't deny the slow friendship that has built between us. Yet it changes nothing. I don't love Nat. We are just fuck buddies, we are both Russian, and we both spend a fair amount at the Casino that the Italians own. Nat works there as a waitress and sometimes runs the roulette tables. I'm there because that's where the Alliance Trinity headquarters are. We both have been well aware of the fact that when I marry Toni the sex between us stops. I'm not sure if we can remain friends as I don't know if Toni will be comfortable with that. If she isn't, I'm prepared to end everything between me and Nat including our friendship. I won't be the stereotypical mob husband who cheats on his wife and has five mistresses on the side. I also won't force her to have to deal with my friendship with Nat. Ultimately Toni is all that matters. She's everything I want in a wife.

    On top of being sexy as hell with some meat on her bones and I personally enjoy thicker women. I'm a sucker for thick thighs and an ass, which Toni checks the boxes on. Toni also has an outstanding personality. She's kind and caring yet a total fucking badass mafia princess who is not afraid to stand her ground. I've seen that woman tell grown men who would scare a normal person where they can go because she is taken. Toni has no idea how in love with her I am. Finally, the time is coming to make my mafia princess all fucking mine.

Chapter 2

Antonia

Baking and cooking are what make me happy. Starting a donut and bakery shop that also has an attached coffee shop with my best friend, Lucy, is a dream come true. I'm in the kitchen of our bakery now, shaking my hips to some pop song while mixing a huge bowl of donut batter to have for the morning. Lucy and I come in at five am to start making donuts, adding icing and fillings, and whatever other touches that are needed. Our baristas are about thirty minutes after us for a six am opening. We do have pastry chefs and assistant bakers who know our recipes by heart. They tend to get the pleasure of making their own hours as long as there is someone here to make sure the goodies get baked, decorated, and sold.

    I have about three hours before I have to leave for the day and head home to get ready for my date with my future husband. Maxim Romanov is a sexy ass devil with his black hair cut so short it's almost a buzz cut. His deep, dark green eyes combined with his light scruff but never clean shave and never a beard. His ivory skin is covered in tattoos. He has tattoos covering his arms, chest and back from what I've seen. I think he has some on his thigh. I've tried not to look at them for too long so that Max wouldn't catch me admiring his ink. Let's not forget that angular jaw adding to his sexy, domineering look. He's a sexy devil and I know he's nothing but sin.

The only problem with my future husband is I'm not the one he wants. I'm nothing but Max's obligation. His true desire and love seems to be fucking Natalia. I never thought I could loath a person so much, but that bitch is intruding on my territory and distracting my man from me. However, as much as I want to throat punch that bitch, I can't. I can't stop Max from fucking other women or even having a mistress, which I assume Natalia will end up becoming once we are married.

It hurts, but I stuff all down because I know my duty. I've never fought against my fate and maybe there is a part of me that wants to, but there is no point. I know even in a loveless marriage, I can be happy. I have LT Donut, Bakery, and Coffee shop that I own with my best friend. I also get the amazing privilege of working with my cool Aunt Sofia, helping her create award-winning dishes for her catering and party planning business. I have hobbies and other things that make me happy. Eventually, I'll have kids because Max and I will have to procreate.

I have to admit, I'm curious what sex with him will be like. I hope it's good, but he might just want to get it over with until we have a couple of kids and then I'm sure

Natalia will be where he spends most nights. While I have adamantly remained untouched by men because I'm expected to be a virgin while Max can fuck other women, that doesn't mean I haven't had sexual experiences. Around fifteen, Lucy and I decided to experiment with kissing and touching. It's how Lucy figured out she was full on lesbian and now is in a loving relationship with Roxy, a dancer at the burlesque club my family owns. I figured out I was bisexual with our experiments. Maybe once I'm married and do my duty of having kids, I can have my own side piece. Not that I want that. I want to have a happy and loving marriage like my parents do. Hell, they are in a damn poly relationship. My fathers were enemies, and they came together to share my mom. In the end, they found a happy, loving, nurturing marriage. I wish my marriage had a happy ending, but I don't know how that can happen when my future husband prefers the company of someone else.

    I'm not stupid; I knew Max would fuck around before we got married. I assumed he would sleep around with random women as one-night stands. I never imagined that he would end up with a permanent other woman at his side. For the last two years, I've watched him with Natalia. For events we sometimes go together as a couple while other times he's there with Natalia on his arm. Those moments are the most painful. I hate seeing him with her and that bitch always has a smug look on her face as if she has won. Maybe she has on some level, but at the end of the day, I will be taking his last name for better or worse.

I hate how much I desire Max. I hate pushing down my feelings, but I have to protect my heart. It sucks that I have to protect my heart from the one person I want to give it to, but what's a girl to do when the man she wants doesn't want her? I have to do my duty because I will not ruin the alliance our parents have fought so hard to forge. I can't even be mad at my parents because they didn't make the decision lightly. Not only that, but they have made sure I am my own person. That I have something outside of the underworld that I can call my own. That's why when I told them Lucy and I wanted to open our donut shop, which has only expanded further into a bakery and coffee shop, my parents gave us the money to do it. My dad, Nico, who is super business and real estate savvy, helped us find the right location that would fit our needs while also bringing us the most customers. My parents have always supported my dreams. They even paid for me to take classes from top chefs and pastry chefs. My parents have done everything they can to ensure I'm comfortable with the arranged marriage. It's not their fault that Max is a manwhore.

A tap on my shoulder has me stopping my dance and mixing to turn around to find Lucy. Her short golden blonde hair is in a cute bob above her shoulders. Her blue eyes pop thanks to the makeup she has on and the tight blue short halter dress paired with her sparkly silver heels.

"I know you aren't planning on baking like that." I comment while pausing my music.

"Of course not. Roxy and I are heading to an elite party on some river cruise thing. I don't know all the details. All I know is that Roxy was invited by one of the regulars at the burlesque club. He basically wants pretty girls around to flirt with his high-profile guests. Roxy and I are going as dancers and it pays two grand for each of us. Extra money for me to buy my Michael Kors bag and maybe a new pair of shoes or two." Lucy informs me.

Roxy and Lucy sometimes do events for rich regulars from the burlesque club and other wealthy clients. It started off as a way for them to get the apartment I temporarily live in with them until I'm married next month. Now, they do it for extra spending money. I've already started packing my things because I'm expected to move into Max's house after we are married. I do wonder if we will share a room or not. I doubt it. I'm sure we will have separate rooms, but I will make some ground rules. He is not allowed to have his little mistress in our house. I am a mafia princess and while I've never killed anyone, I will kill Natalia if she enters the house I live in to fuck my husband.

"I forgot you guys had that gig tonight. I take it we have closers?"

"Of course, girl. Did you think that I forgot about your annual date with your future hubby?" She taunts.

"No. I'm just flustered. You know how I get before I have to see Max." I say, turning back around to finish mixing the dough.

"I know you get flustered because you love that man, yet you completely loathe him at the same time." Lucy accurately points out.

"That is not the point," I defend. "It's the fact that I have to sit there and pretend to be a woman that is okay with him being in love with someone else."

"Girl, you don't actually know he loves Natalia. Even Leo and Trey have said Natalia is just a fuck toy and nothing more." Lucy reminds me as if I can ever forget that my brother and cousin are totally on Max's side. I don't know if it's because they are men and they don't see the issue or because they rather keep the peace with Max because they have to work together for the alliance's sake. Either way, I find it irritating.

"They are his good friends and they will all run the alliance together soon enough. They have to side with him for the sake of keeping the peace. Plus, they are men too and they tend to hide each other's dirty deeds." I effectively point out as if I haven't had these bullets in the chamber ready to fire.

"True, but I think you need to give Max a chance to explain himself. You've never actually confronted him about Natalia and who she is to him. I know it's because you are terrified that you are right. You are protecting your heart. I understand that. I just don't want you to be miserable in your marriage if you don't have to be. Don't go into with the prenotion that Natalia is the love of Max's life because you only have assumptions and fears. You have no proof and you have never heard Max say he loves Natalia. Be smart and not a stubborn ass Italian woman is my point." Lucy advises, and I know she is right. Of course she is. She's been my best friend since we were twelve. She knows me better than I probably know myself. I know it's possible my green-eyed monster is skewing things where Max is concerned. I'm also aware that my pride and natural stubborn nature could also be skewing my view where Max is concerned. I suppose I should heed my friend's advice, and find out the damn truth before we get married.

"Fine, I'll make you a deal. Tonight, at dinner, I will ask Max what his intentions are with Natalia once we are married. Will that do?" I turn around to face her and raise my eyebrow while putting my free hand on my hip.

"Yes, that will do. Roxy and I will be home around eleven, so text me if we need wine and ice cream because you were right or if we need to stop by the burlesque club and raid the jelly shot stash with cheesecake sample platter from our secret frozen stash of goodies." Lucy agrees.

"Sounds like a plan to me. Dinner with Max usually goes to nine or a bit later with the fancy full course meal he orders at whatever fancy restaurant he picks. That should give me time to get home, text you, and decompress with a hot shower and some self care before you two bitches get home," I agree. Lucy gives a huge belly laugh and I can't help but join her. "Now, go before I decide to flick some batter on you." I threaten raising my spoon.

"Alright, bitch. Love you. See you later." She says as she blows a kiss before turning to leave the kitchen.

I go back to mixing my dough. Normally, I used the giant ass electric mixer, but I need to do something soothing before meeting with Max. So, I'm doing it by hand while I shake my big ass. I finish up what I'm doing at the shop before making sure our staff is okay before I leave. We have a bunch of sweet women who work for us from single moms, to teens working their first job, to college girls looking to make some money while they get their education. The girls working say they are good, and wish me a good time on my date with Max. They all are invited to the wedding; we are closing the shop on the day off. I will, of course, be making my own damn wedding cake with Lucy as well as the bakery providing donuts and other goodies. My aunt's business is in charge of catering and the venue. I am actually looking forward to our wedding day because if anything I get my dream wedding. Now if only the mafia princess could get her Czar, that's my secret name for Max that only those in my trusted circle know I call him. I guess tonight I'll find out if I get my dream wedding and my Czar or if I'm doomed to be in a loveless marriage. That's providing I have the balls to confront my Czar about the elephant in the room because sometimes fear is stronger than our will to learn the truth.

Pushing my thoughts away I finish my task and then head out to get ready for my date. I focus on making sure I look hot as hell because I am dressing to impress. I want Max to desire me. I slip into a deep red off the shoulder silk cocktail dress that hugs my curves and ass perfectly while my very expensive supportive sexy lace bra perks my DD boobs perfectly. The dress ruches in the tummy area hiding my small muffin top. I like to eat, sue me. I keep myself healthy and fit with daily dancing or walking. I even sometimes box with my dads and brother. My parents made sure I knew how to throw a decent punch, shoot a gun, and learn basic self defense in case our enemies dare to try to abduct me. I've paired my dress with black lace Jimmy Choos, a simple black lace choker that has a small oval onyx stone dangling from it, and black lace fingerless gloves. What can I say, I'm a combination of a gothic diva. I like what I like.

 I currently have my dark mocha hair styled in a wavy lob, which is just a bob that is a little longer because the length goes slightly past my shoulders. My hair is naturally wavy, granted they are very light waves, but when I style them they are bouncy, adding volume to my overall hairstyle. I put on some light makeup. Despite having a girly side, makeup is not where it clicks for me. I'm more into clothes, shoes, and other accessories. Satisfied with my look, I head down to meet my driver, who is picking me up to take me to my date. I don't drive. I don't even have my drivers license. I do know how to drive a car if I actually had to, but living in the city and being able to afford personal drivers there is no point for me to go through the hassle of getting my drivers license.

On the drive over to the restaurant, I focus on my stubborn nature, but not in a bad way. I'm being stubborn in the sense that I'm not leaving this date without answers on who Natalia is to Max. Tonight, I'm getting answers even if they are answers I don't want to hear. I have to play this smart. I need to know exactly what I'm walking into with this marriage. My determination out weighs whatever fears I might have at the moment as the driver pulls into the drop off line for the restaurant. I catch a glimpse of Max who is patiently waiting for my car to get to the front of the line. My focus now is on Max and getting the answers to the questions that burn in my anxious brain.

Other Books by Brit Leigh

Through the Flames of Desire

Visit Brit Leigh's website to locate her other books, updates, and merch!
bandbromancebooks

Books by Birdy Rivers

The Coven Series

The Coven of the Crow and Shadows: Legacy book 1 of the coven series

The Coven of the Crow and Shadows: Ghost Opera book 2 of the coven series

The Coven of the Crow and Shadows: Mayhem and Death book 3 of the coven series

The Coven of the Crow and Shadows: New Era book 4 of the coven series

Retellings

The Children of the Empire: World on Fire (Snow White, Beauty and the Beast, Cinderella, Sleeping Beauty, and Rapunzel)

The Children of the Empire: Reflected Mirrors

A Thousand and One Wishes: Book 1 of the Wishes Duet (Aladdin)

Hunting My Wolf (Little Red Riding Hood)

Superhero Series

Heroes & Villains: Destiny Calls: Book 1

Heroes & Villains: Destiny Awaits: Book 2

Heroes & Villians: Destiny Unknown: Book 3

Follow Birdy's social media pages and website to find out where to locate her other books, updates, and merch!

Facebook Page
Birdy River's Readers Group: Birdys Magical World

Instagram-@birdyriversauthor

bandbromancebooks

Made in the USA
Columbia, SC
09 June 2025